SWEET LIES

"Good night, Palladin."

He leaned down and kissed her forehead then brushed her lips with his. Her face tilted upward and his kiss became deeper before Jesslyn pulled away.

"Good night, Jesslyn." He turned and pressed for the elevator.

She turned, opened her door and forced herself not to look at him. She put her coat in the foyer closet. Her mind jumbled with thoughts of the rights and wrongs of getting involved with this man. Not since breaking her engagement had she even considered having a real relationship. She liked safe men—the ones who didn't interfere with her life. She knew in her heart that there was nothing safe about Palladin Rush. So what was she getting herself into? And why couldn't she stop it?

ENJOY THESE ARABESQUE FAVORITES!

FOREVER AFTER (0-7860-0211-5, $4.99)
by Bette Ford

BODY AND SOUL (0-7860-0160-7, $4.99)
by Felicia Mason

BETWEEN THE LINES (0-7860-0267-0, $4.99)
by Angela Benson

SWEET LIES

Viveca Carlysle

Pinnacle Books
Kensington Publishing Corp.
http://www.pinnaclebooks.com

PINNACLE BOOKS are published by

Kensington Publishing Corp.
850 Third Avenue
New York, NY 10022

First Printing: August, 1997
10 9 8 7 6 5 4 3 2 1

Printed in the United States of America

To my family who said of course you can write a book
To Rochelle Alers who said Do It Now!
& To Vivian Stephens who showed me how.

One

THURSDAY, JANUARY 25

"If you're not out of my office within the next thirty seconds, I'll have Security handle this." Jesslyn Owens stood up and pulled her body to its full five-foot two inches as she glared at the six-foot plus man sitting across from her.

"Ms. Owens, I don't think you want the police involved," he said. "Your reputation couldn't stand another negative attack."

"That may be true," she bluffed. "But how much negative impact can your career stand? The Senator may not appreciate the publicity this could bring."

Hank Reynolds rose slowly from the chair and started for the door. "This isn't finished, you know."

Jesslyn rested her hands on her hips. "It is for me."

"Maybe you should design a gift basket for people in mourning, something your family might like." He never looked back as he opened the door and left her office.

Her breath caught in her throat at the veiled threat.

A month and a half ago, the first time she'd met Hank Reynolds, he reminded her of an old-fashioned minister, with his soft-spoken ways and his slightly stooped posture. Of course, that all changed when he unleashed a string of epithets over the phone about a missing diskette. Now he'd actually threatened her. She was trying to decide whether or not she should call Security when her sister came in.

"What did he want?" Lena asked.

"What else? The diskette."

"How many times do we have to tell him—we don't have it?"

"I know if I find it I'm going to throw it in his face."

"Aren't we going to find out what's on it?"

"One, that's unethical, and two, I don't *want* to know." She shook off the urge to talk about the threat.

Jesslyn knew that Lena would assume her older sister-protector role if she mentioned the threat, so she changed the subject. Lena, older by eight years and taller by six inches, had always tried to fight her battles, especially when Jesslyn insisted on fighting her own.

"Carolann is not working out as a partner and don't say I told you so."

"You think you have to hook up with her just because Egyptian Enchantment gave both of you a raw deal," Lena said. "Hello! She's looking for a free ride to the top. And isn't she the one who brought us the client-from-hell, Hank Reynolds."

"True. But she also brought us three corporate clients," Jesslyn said. "I just meant she needs to spend more time here and less time scouting."

Lena shrugged. "So tell her."

"Right. Well, Carolann and I are having lunch, and I hope we can get around to discussing her pulling her weight or selling her share back to me."

The partnership, less than a year old, had been terrific at the beginning, but now problems kept cropping up, most of them with Lena and Carolann. Jesslyn maintained they were so much alike they were bound to set off sparks sooner or later. Each liked her share of good times with only occasional hard work. Each accused the other of not putting more time in the business, and Jesslyn had to admit Lena was doing a lot more duty in the shop than Carolann.

"What if she doesn't want to sell them or tries to make you pay a lot more to get rid of her?"

"Then I'll just have to find a way to make her so miserable she begs me to buy her out." Jesslyn grabbed her navy peacoat from the closet. "See you later." She hurried through the World Trade Center Mall to the subway.

Jesslyn decided to buy the suit in the Saks Fifth Avenue window because it had saved her life. For fifteen minutes while waiting for her partner on the corner of Fifth Avenue and 49th Street, she scrutinized the outfit the whole time to keep her mind off the cold. She preferred a conservative look, usually described by her friends as "old-fashioned." This blue raw silk number with a tight skirt, however, would probably leave four inches between its hem and her knees. Although she hated to shop, the suit held her attention and it drew her to the window again and again. The outfit certainly had no place in her Victorian style wardrobe. Yet it was just the thing to startle all her colleagues at the dinner-dance on Saturday.

Jesslyn decided that while her two pair of stockings, stirrup pants and navy peacoat kept her warm enough, she needed to go indoors for a few minutes. It was either Saks or the bookstore.

She opted for the Barnes and Noble bookstore a block away. She stepped off the curb, since the light was about to change for her to cross, then decided to take one more look at the suit. As she stepped back onto the sidewalk, a red Jeep whizzed past her close enough to brush her shoulder bag. The driver took advantage of the slight break in traffic and sped off.

"Are you all right, Miss?"

Jesslyn turned and nodded to the man. The camera in his hand and his pale face alerted her that he was a tourist. New Yorkers were generally unsympathetic toward someone who stepped off a curb on a busy street without paying attention to traffic.

"I'm fine," she told him. "New York drivers hate to miss lights."

The man nodded, unconvinced, and turned to walk in the direction of St. Patrick's Cathedral. Probably going to pray that he makes it back home, Jesslyn mused. Praying wasn't a bad idea for her, either. Not only had she been lucky the Jeep hadn't hit her, but prayer might help with her concerns over her business. Word had gotten to her that, everyone was buzzing about her successful comeback one week, and the next that something serious was wrong.

Five years ago, her world at Egyptian Enchantment Cosmetics had caved in. After brooding for a couple of months, she decided to fight back and now owned a small business rather than work as a big business executive. It gave her the one thing she needed: control.

She'd made it back to the top and, while her profits went back into the business, unlike the bonuses she'd once received, the sense of satisfaction was beyond measure. Sometimes, she thought the messenger service, Federal Express and Airborne were really her silent partners. Most of the carriers were on a first name basis with her. That was another thing she liked about the little shop at the World Trade Center—the sense of community among the employees.

It had taken so much out of her when she need partners to handle the expansion. Lena, in her usual big sister bulldozing manner, had insisted on using part of her divorce settlement for 30 percent of the company. Carolann had seemed pleased originally with her 19 percent but lately had been griping about wanting more. Still, business was in the black and orders continued coming in. They'd even snared a few executive accounts. Things were great and still she felt lousy.

The near accident made her decide to be daring. Forget the nagging feelings of pending disaster, she told herself. Buy the suit and go to 44's for lunch. You'll feel better.

She walked through the store, ignoring the offers of perfumed cards touting a designer's newest perfume and the cosmetic makeovers. Her clear, medium brown skin responded best to products of Naomi Sims Salon just a few blocks away. The former model had been the first ebony-skinned model to grace the covers of *Vogue* years before and she had built a thriving skin care business for people of color. She'd have to call for an appointment and change her look if she didn't chicken out of wearing this suit to the dinner.

Twenty minutes later, she exited the store carrying a white shopping bag with Saks Fifth Avenue printed across it in black and a more than expected deflation in her bank account. "But worth every cent," she said aloud.

Her timing was perfect. She spotted Carolann getting out of a dark green car, putting on her mink and talking to the driver. Jesslyn couldn't see the man behind the wheel, and he drove away just as Jesslyn reached the car. Her partner kept bragging about this mystery man who had made her forget her ex-husband.

Carolann turned, her face paled under her pecan-colored skin and took a backward step as she saw her partner standing there.

"What's wrong?"

"N . . . Nothing." She said. "I didn't expect to see you with a Saks bag in your hand. You hate to shop. What did you buy?"

"That!" She turned and pointed to the suit.

"I don't believe you." Carolann screamed. "All your dresses and skirts come down to your ankles. You planning to spring a new fella on us at the dance?"

"Well, after the suit saved my life, I had to get it."

With that remark, Jesslyn turned and walked toward the corner but it only took her partner a few long strides to catch up.

"I want to hear that story from the beginning," Carolann said. "Let's get something to eat."

"I'll tell you over a burger at 44's."

The two women waited for the light. And Jesslyn had to ask, "Was that your mystery man?"

"I beg your pardon?"

"Come on, you know, the one who makes your voice drop to a whisper when he calls and then you get this really dreamy look on your face."

"That sounds more like your sister's way of describing something."

"You're right. But how about it?"

"I'll tell you right after you tell me about the suit."

Jesslyn checked each corner of the two one-way streets before going across. She would not tempt fate again. They were silent as they walked over to 44th Street then toward Sixth Avenue to the Royalton Hotel. Jesslyn always felt like a dwarf with Carolann. She barely cleared five feet, and her partner was a former runway model. As they passed the Harvard Club, Carolann spoke and pointed to the building. "This reminds me, I asked my ex to come to the dinner."

"That's right. He went to Harvard, didn't he?"

"Yeah. Turned out to be a pretty good businessman before he did the Secret Service bit. I hope to show him I've done okay without him or his advice."

"Did you get his advice when I offered you a part of the business."

"No, and when I told him, he wasn't too thrilled about it. Said I should have let him check it out first. But he gave me the money. After all, it was his idea to tie my money up so I could have a healthy retirement fund. I don't want money later. I want it right now. That's why I invited him."

"Is he your date?"

"No . . . Uh . . . he's just my guest. I want him to find a way to get my money. But I'm not even counting on him to show up."

"I get it. You want to show him who took his place. Is that smart?"

"What do you mean?"

"You said he was tough and had some sort of nickname . . . something to do with ice . . ."

"Glacier," Carolann supplied. "He's that cold and that hard."

For months, Carolann had said that she was involved with someone, but they couldn't be seen in public yet. Was her ex-husband still pining for her?

"If he shows up, does that mean he wants you back?"

"No way. The man can turn off his feelings at the snap of his fingers. Except guilt. If he feels guilty about anything, he'll try to make it right. It's definitely over. Any woman is welcome to him. He'll show up to check on me. I want him to find a way to untangle my money. He set it up and he'll want to know why I want it."

"Maybe he's changed his mind and wants you back. What are you going to do?"

Carolann stopped and looked at Jesslyn. "He *never* changes his mind, and I don't care."

"Does that mean I'm going to finally meet your mystery man in your life?"

"Uh . . . maybe." She blushed and flashed a dimpled grin. "If he can get away from work."

Jesslyn didn't press the issue any further. Carolann had been saying this guy was everything she wanted and now she was shying away from showing him off.

The restaurant 44's was a big hangout for the fashion publishing crowd, and despite the Fashion Café's lure, it still had a loyal following. They got a table and made themselves comfortable. This was where Carolann and Jesslyn learned the art of ordering a hamburger off-menu from a *Vogue* editor for whom Carolann had done some modeling.

They acknowledged a few people among the crowd of diners, ordered and hardly had time to catch up on the day's projects before the food appeared. The chopped sirloin was served on an English Muffin with little dishes of ketchup, mustard and hollandaise.

As soon as the food arrived, Carolann pounced. "How did a suit save your life?"

Jesslyn relayed the circumstances without stretching the truth in any way. When she finished, Carolann's stern face gave her pause. "Maybe you should be as upset as that man was?"

"Come on. If you live in New York and haven't been brushed by a car you're living on borrowed time." Jesslyn ignored the strained look on Carolann's face and signaled the waiter so they could order drinks. New York was a tough town, but Jesslyn loved the heartbeat of the city.

"Enough about me. Was that the new guy or not?"

"Yes, but I'm still not sure we're ready to go public. It would upset a lot of people, including Palladin Rush."

After she'd left the cosmetic firm, she'd never run into Carolann until eight months ago, when she'd decided that building baskets was a lonely business and she'd like some partners. A mutual friend, Frank Mason, had hooked them up and it had seemed to be right at the time.

"I'm glad we're partners, even though I'm not a full one," Carolann said.

"I'm not ready to turn over any more of it, yet. In fact, I may have turned over too much."

"We've known each other since you were an executive at Egyptian Enchantment. This gift basket thing turned into a gold mine. I can't believe how fast our accounts are growing."

"That's true. And that's why you, Lena and I need to sit down with a new schedule. You've missed a few turns working in the store."

"I thought we needed more accounts," Carolann's face slipped into a pout. "We can hire someone to run the store."

Jesslyn ignored Carolann's fudging of the truth. Actually, they had a nodding acquaintance at the cosmetic firm and never saw each other socially. It was only when she found she could get a space at the World Financial Center that her friend Frank Mason had suggested she get partners, rather than try to take on the astronomical rents. He'd suggested Carolann.

"We're a long way from hiring a manager."

"Why do you say that?"

"I feel this is the calm before the storm."

Carolann frowned. "Our bottom line looks great. What kind of trouble could we be in?"

"I don't know, but I'd like to leave things status quo until I find out. I've heard rumblings . . . and then there was that call from Hank whatshisname?"

"I told you. I took care of that, and if he has any more questions, he's to see me. He won't bother you again."

"Well, he paid me another visit today. Next time, I'll just call Security."

"No. Don't. I promise I'll take care of it. I don't want to fight with you about selling my share. We can work things out."

Knowing when to back off was something both women understood, and even though Jesslyn wasn't too sure things were as settled as Carolann insisted, it was time to change the subject.

"Is Lena bringing Jeff?" Carolann leaned forward and asked.

"Unfortunately, yes."

Jesslyn's sister had the knack for finding men who were good looking but as lazy as old cats. Jeff had been around longer than most but he wasn't one of Jesslyn's favorites.

"Shame on you. What have you got against him?"

"I don't know. He's annoying. He thinks he's flirting, but it rubs me the wrong way."

"He just likes to act Big Time."

"He's still a jerk. I guess I just don't want my sister to get hurt again."

They sipped their drinks and were silent for a few minutes.

"Why don't you join the Breakfast Club?" Jesslyn suggested.

"I thought power breakfasts were passé?"

Jesslyn laughed. On one hand, Carolann wanted to be a "major player" in the business world and on the other she didn't want to work too hard for it. Of course, if she mentioned that the women in the group wore designer suits and tried to look business-like and sexy, Carolann would have jumped right in. Clothes and competition made her day. Since Jesslyn's tastes were usually on the nondescript side, they'd never gone head to head in a fashion sense. Now that she planned to wear the sexy suit, she wondered if Carolann would wear something so stunning that other women would pale by comparison.

"But are you going to ignore all that for Lena?"

"Of course. She's always going to go after men who are wrong for her. I tried to talk to her, but she just flips into her 'baby sister go away' attitude."

"You can't stop people from making mistakes. Especially those you love."

"Like your ex? You seem to disagree with his new lifestyle."

"Yeah. Who would want to live on a mountain, for God's sake? Can you imagine the winters?"

"You never said why he quit."

"Remember, a few years ago, some fast food place wouldn't serve these black men?"

"Oh, that! The Secret Service men?"

"Yeah. He flipped. He just walked away. Others stayed and the restaurant got into real trouble, but Palladin just walked."

"Just *one* incident made him quit?"

"Uh . . . he said something about it being the last straw."

"Burnout?"

"I guess . . ."

Jesslyn wondered what would have happened if she walked away from the business world and lived on a mountain. How tough could this man be, if he couldn't handle the pressures of everyday life? She couldn't imagine not being in touch with the things that were happening all over the city. The one thing that she was going to try next would be the Internet. She'd avoided it because she knew that if she went on line someone somewhere would bring up her past and she still couldn't explain how she was innocent and looked so guilty.

"Maybe he's just a guy who loses his cool a little faster than others, or he'd had enough?"

"Are you kidding? *Glacier* is a well-earned nickname. That's why I didn't understand this running away."

"So that's why you broke up?"

"In a way . . ." She looked pensive for a moment then said, "I promise I'll stick with a schedule for the store. If Lena can, I can."

It wasn't the first time Jesslyn had heard that promise. She didn't want to get caught between her sister and her friend. She could only hope that Carolann was telling the truth about wanting to be part of the team. Jesslyn had fought too hard to get back to where she felt good about herself. No one was going to take that away again.

Two

FRIDAY, JANUARY 26

Palladin Rush rolled up the sleeves of his black shirt and added a belt to his black jeans. His hair still seemed fresh from his trip to his hairstylist in New York the day before. After nearly five years, his dreadlocks hung just below his chin. This time he'd allowed Jalisa to give him the Silky Locs she'd been trying to get him to try for months.

If Mac had known he'd been in New York and not called, he'd have been upset. Palladin wondered if he'd deliberately not called him. He sensed bad news was coming and avoided talking to him, as if that would prevent hearing someone was in trouble and Mac wanted him to bail the person out. He went to the kitchen and prepared a tray of fruit, crackers and a pot of coffee and took it to the screened-in wraparound deck at the rear of the house. He strolled back to the kitchen, grabbed his café latte and went back to the deck to wait. He'd picked up the habit of having café latte as a breakfast drink during his sabbatical in Italy just after he quit the Secret Service and his marriage fell apart. He kept in contact with his ex-wife, or rather, she kept in contact with him—every time she needed money, at least. And he always gave it to her, despite his friends' disapproval. She'd carry on about needing the retirement money, but he knew that she'd spend it all. No matter what she said, she'd need it more later than she did now. Carolann didn't have any family and he still felt he owed her. When he wanted to check out her partners and the company she was buying into, she'd asked him not to do any investigation and he'd complied only after Mac said he'd keep his eye out for any little problems.

He sat in the rocker and stretched his long legs out in front of him while he waited for the past to intrude on the present. He'd picked the chair up at a garage sale because it seemed to fit the house. As he rocked back and forth, he breathed in the mountain air that invigorated him. He'd already heard the weather report. Snow was on the way—again. Soon, the mountain would be covered with a white blanket, and he'd hibernate for a few weeks. Recharge was the operative word. The log cabin he called home had been a good decision. After seeing his friend's place in Wyoming, he knew he had to have more than just an apartment to call home. He wasn't into the environmentally-correct living Kaliq insisted upon for his house, but it suited him.

Sometimes, he couldn't believe that when he'd found this place it was a 16 x 30 foot cabin but now it spanned 7,600 square feet of kiln-dried Norway red pine logs and the original room had become his study. He'd acted as general contractor and helped build every addition. The people who loved him knew he used the manual labor to keep from thinking about his resignation and his divorce. Some friends were afraid that after everything was finished he'd have to find a new project to keep his sanity. Others thought that he'd return to the Service or get married again. He'd laughed when they articulated these fears. Six years after his marriage ended and three years after the house had been completed, he hadn't done any of those things.

He wasn't quite a hermit. There were women who passed through his life, but none were in for the long haul. And there were his "kids," the little hockey team he chaperoned when they had to travel, since their coach rarely left Pennsylvania. He was solitary, not lonely. Well, not often, he admitted to himself.

Although the green BMW was not designed for the narrow road, Palladin thought Mac's vehicle climbed the mountain better than the four-wheel vehicles he owned. He'd turned off the security system to the house the minute Mac called and said he was on his way. Usually Palladin did his early morning run and left it on until noon. The land surrounding him had been fenced in and had a double gate at the foot of the mountain. Designed by another friend from the Secret Service, the house was protected against intruders, whether on two feet or four. Few people came this way without an invitation. Foes came in all shapes and sizes and the political arena was fraught with men looking to make their mark by getting to the man who went behind enemy lines alone and rescued a friend. Still, there were others in his own country who hadn't liked Palladin's decision to leave the Service, those who thought the president's demands for a public apology were quite enough. When Palladin quit, there were some who organized demonstrations and the fast food restaurant had never recovered because any time it made the news for something, reports reminded people of its previous practices. He'd let people think that was the reason why he left. It made more sense to have some cause distract him from the personal pain he was going through when he returned with Kaliq.

Shortly after his marriage, he had to rescue a friend and former college roommate, journalist Kaliq Faulkner, prisoner in Central America. Palladin felt that the people handling the negotiations were dragging their feet. The rescue mission had been simple to put together. Calling in favors from old friends who were now Navy Seals as well as some mercenaries, Palladin had gone in and brought his friend home.

It wasn't the only reason he left. There were times when he blocked out the other reasons—a failing marriage, and Carolann's miscarriage, among others. Neither he nor Carolann ever discussed these things with anyone, not even Mac.

This had brought his deteriorating marriage to its final resting place. Carolann had returned to the cosmetic firm, and he'd started looking at plans for the house. He had deliberately cut himself off from the outside world.

Working with Kaliq was another distraction from the disintegration of his marriage. His legs had been damaged beyond repair. He would need a wheelchair to get around for the rest of his life.

Palladin was always in control. The idea of burnout was foreign to him until it happened. He needed some time to himself. Before he realized it, days turned into weeks and weeks into years.

His first step back into the normal world was to take Kaliq's advice: get involved with kids. He'd loved sports and skated most of his life. So when he learned that the area was looking for a hockey coach, he stepped forward. It kept the kids busy and he taught them about team work.

Palladin waited until the car pulled into the carport and went out to greet his guests.

"Mac," he enveloped the man in a bear hug. "Good to see you."

"These old bones can't make this trip too often, you know. You've added something since I last saw you." Mac pointed to the neatly shaved mustache and beard.

"I call it 'getting in the spirit.' "

"I call it 'getting too lazy to shave.' " The older man had never liked to leave the house without shaving. His designer suits and hand-painted ties were his trademark.

"I'll have you know it takes more effort to keep this neatly trimmed than it takes to be clean-shaven."

At six feet even and one hundred and eighty pounds, Mac was four inches shorter and forty pounds lighter than his protégé. His ruddy skin a contrast to his shock of wavy, white hair and cornflower blue eyes. The "old bones" was a joke between the two men. Mac was as fit today as most men twenty years younger, which was the exact number of years that separated them.

Mac's blond driver got out and stood by the car. Palladin acknowledged him with a curt nod, which the man returned. Skip Logan and Palladin tolerated each other for Mac's benefit alone. Skip, the son of a former FBI man, couldn't handle playing second to Palladin Rush. It wasn't a question of race as much as it was a question of the healthy dose of ego and good leadership skills that were destined to clash. The men shared an alma mater and Skip, a year younger, found himself competing with

Palladin academically, physically and socially before they'd even met. He competed but never quite matched Palladin, and that became a bone of contention between Skip and his father at first. The pattern repeated between Skip and Mac, as his shortcomings followed him as he tried to stand out from the rest of the men in the Secret Service. He'd then joined Mac in the business sector and felt good in his position as the heir to the throne.

"Come on in." Palladin motioned to the men.

They followed him and settled at the round picnic table at the far end of the deck. His guests helped themselves to coffee while Palladin decided he'd had enough caffeine.

Palladin was the perfect host, and the men chatted about the security business Mac owned, with Skip as his chief administrator.

Finally Mac got to the point. "I think Carolann's in trouble."

"What kind of trouble?" Palladin asked. The mention of his ex-wife's name brought only a tiny flicker to his eyes.

"She's a partner in a gift basket business with a Jesslyn Owens and her sister Lena Owens Carter." Skip answered.

"Gift baskets? She didn't tell me what the business was."

Mac frowned. "You talked to her about the company?"

"Only when she wanted the money to buy in."

"So you actually kept your word about not checking it out."

Palladin looked out at the leaf-bare trees. "We have an agreement. I'm not allowed to asked questions. She thinks I'm too cautious about some things. What about these gift baskets?"

"Sounds innocuous enough, but from what I hear, they've added a new twist," Mac explained. "Industrial espionage."

Palladin laughed. "You're kidding, right?"

"It's not a joke to the two companies whose ad campaigns landed on their competitors' desk," Skip said.

"Three women are using a gift basket business to steal company secrets? Are they from companies where you manage security?"

"No way," Skip howled.

"Calm down," Mac ordered then turned to Palladin. "One of my companies was on the receiving end. They think it's great. I've been keeping in touch with Carolann, as you asked, and I think it's going to lead to more problems."

"And she doesn't need another failed career move," Palladin said.

The marriage was over, but he knew his ex-wife craved success so badly she might make a grab at the brass ring any way she could. "Why do you think Carolann is involved?"

"She delivered the basket with the prototype of the ad campaign. Besides, the Owens woman was suspected of this a few years ago."

"Any real proof on the first time this happened?"

"No. That's why they asked her to resign. They didn't dare try to fire her."

"What about proof for this new outbreak of industrial espionage." He said it without cracking a smile, but inside, Palladin wanted to roar with laughter. Just when you thought all the tricks had been used, someone comes along with a twist. He found himself feeling a sort of bizarre admiration for Jesslyn Owens.

"Not yet, but a good source told me they're ready to go public."

"My ex-wife is a beautiful woman but smart enough for this? No way."

"Jesslyn Owens was asked to resign when a top cosmetic product was leaked before the testing was completed. They never proved that, either, but her reputation was in shreds after the incident."

"How good was she?"

"Fast track. Top black female executive forced to resign from a $160,000 plus job."

"I'm usually up to date on my brothers and sisters in the business world. How did I miss this story?"

"You were busy with this," Skip said as he waved his hand around the cabin.

"Oh, then." Palladin remembered. "But why should I get into this? Carolann listens to you more than me."

Palladin knew that Carolann always ran to Mac whenever she had gotten in over her head and needed someone to bail her out. Nothing she'd done before had ever come under the category illegal.

Mac drained his cup and poured another one. "She can't just walk away. The Owens woman is one smart lady. If anything goes down, we think she can make it look like Carolann was the spy."

"Was the company she resigned from Egyptian Enchantment?"

Mac yelled, "Yes! You tied them together."

"Terrific," Skip said in a low, dejected voice. "Probably knows everyone in the company. I hear you had to keep a pretty tight reign on your wife."

"How would you know?"

Time had not erased the need to bait Palladin. Skip's thin lips formed a smile. He leaned back and took a sip of coffee.

"You'd be surprised at what I know about your wife."

"Ex-wife. And no one keeps a reign on the lady. No one can or would want to."

"The right man could do it." Skip rose and turned as if looking at the scenic view.

"I've seen her around Mac's office. And, one day, I'll tell you how I know."

Palladin's jaw twitched and he stood up. "We both know that can't be you. Carolann prefers men who are stronger than women, Lucky."

Mac stepped between the two men before words escalated into something more. He'd had to do this while the men were on his team, especially after one of the female recruits had executed a perfect hip toss on the veteran agent. Skip had never quite lived it down. His nickname, Lucky Logan, had taken on a new meaning—one that hinted he was lucky he was already in the Service or that would have washed him out. Mac had recruited both men. Skip wanted it, but Palladin had to be dragged kicking and screaming into the Service. But, once there, he had set an example men were still trying to follow. Even his fights with Skip had never gotten too physical. Only the respect they both held for Mac and the Secret Service had prevented them from crossing the line to a real fight.

"I told him the same story and he didn't see it. Still doesn't."

"Educate me, Mr. Rush."

"Carolann modeled for Egyptian Enchantment as a

prize for the beauty contest she won when we first met. She told me about a year ago that one of the women got fired for trading secrets, and she thought it was a trumped-up charge. She didn't give me a name and I didn't ask. Now she's in business with the woman.

"The worst part is that she's been making noises about not having a bigger share of the business," Mac added.

"So what do you really think, Mac," Palladin asked. "If she gets what she wants, she could be crawling out on a very weak tree limb. Or maybe she knows more about the true operations of this little business than either of us cares to admit."

"Did she ever tell you why she and the Owens woman hooked up?"

"No. She made the same protests when she worked for Egyptian Enchantment. She wanted shares of the company as part of her modeling contract. Maybe it ties back to what went on there?"

"Insisting on stock? Not a good move."

"Which brings me to my problem with the partnership? Why, if Jesslyn Owens was such a hotshot before, would she want a loose cannon like Carolann?"

"So far, she's the only one who's had a meeting with the victims in this case and the recipients."

"So," Skip added. "It could look as if she was the culprit in both cases."

"How do you want to work it?" Palladin asked Mac.

"Get the goods on the Owens woman. Fix it so she has to take a heavy fall or let Carolann out of this mess. I'll convince your ex to invite you to the dinner dance she's attending."

"She already has. The invitation was here when I got back from the Bahamas. I hadn't decided to go." Palladin paused and then added, "If I do this, I'll need you to back off and let me do things my way."

"Deal. Although I did take the liberty of booking you a nice suite at the Peninsula Hotel."

"That sure of yourself, huh? Well I hope it's a two bedroom suite because I plan to bring a friend."

"This is supposed to be a job, Rush," Skip growled. "The company isn't going to pick up any tabs for you and one of your women . . ."

Another bone of contention between Skip and Palladin had been the women. While guarding the president, Palladin blended in with the crowd, but in the social scene, he stood out and attracted women as if he was a magnet and they were paper clips. Even if he stopped dating a woman they remained friends. Skip married first, and even at his wedding, Palladin had arrived with Carolann. The two made a stunning couple, and without trying or meaning to, they stole a little of the bride and groom's thunder.

Palladin knew Skip was remembering the playboy days of D.C. He wanted him clear on who called the shots then and now.

"The company will pay for anything I need, Logan." Palladin deliberately took on the tone of his adversary. "But, to ease your puny little mind, I'm expecting Kaliq Faulkner any minute now. He was scheduled to come up for a vacation, but I think I can use his help."

Palladin didn't have to look at Mac to know that he was frowning over this news. Mac and Kaliq were an oil and water combination. No tangible reason for their dislike of each other existed, but they didn't even try to tolerate each other.

"He's not bringing that stupid bird, is he?" Mac asked.

"No. The falcon is staying where he'll be safe from man."

"Well . . . I don't like it, but I agreed to let you do things your way," Mac grudgingly accepted.

"It's better this way. You know how Carolann is. If she feels she's lost control of the situation, she'll cut and run."

"We don't want that," Mac said. "She'd look guilty, and the Owens woman would simply cover her tracks faster than a lottery winner makes new friends."

"Exactly. So give me room to work."

Palladin and Mac shook hands and he stood on the steps. Skip pulled the car around and he and Mac were off. A good day had turned into a bad one. Despite all his efforts to stay away from trouble, he was being pulled back in. This time not kicking or screaming, but interested.

He perused the packet Mac had left. Pictures of the partners. Lena Owens, formerly Carter, had dropped the married name along with the husband and her divorce settlement gave her a healthy bank account. Carolann, as beautiful now as she was at twenty when he married her. His assessment of her skill remained. She was a follower. Only Jesslyn Owens had enough business sense and knowledge to create and run the business. Her dark hair was cut in a short style. However, if Jesslyn was the mastermind of the little scenario, she would do well before a jury. Her soft, dark eyes in her diamond-shaped face were as innocent as those of a cloistered nun. He hated the idea of another trip to New York. He hated the idea of Carolann being in trouble and Mac expecting him to get her out. He hated the idea of leaving his retreat.

"Jesslyn Owens, you're going to pay big time for dragging me off my mountain."

Three

SATURDAY, JANUARY 27

Still shivering the few short steps from the cab after entering the hotel and taking a quick trip in the elevator, Jesslyn stood outside the ballroom and, for a moment, let all her fears dance through her head. She slipped out of her mink jacket and draped it over her arm. She pulled the long chain of her blue and silver evening bag over her shoulder as she prepared to make her entrance.

She laughed at herself as she remembered the cabbie's puzzled look as she nibbled on dry crackers. Ever since she could remember, she got carsick, but when she took driver's ed in high school, she found that when she was behind the wheel she didn't have the same waves of nausea as she did when she was a passenger. Manhattan, however, was a tough place to keep a car, which was why she usually chose public transportation. The subway system didn't give her motion sickness so she used it most of the time. Tonight was an exception. The night temperature dipped to the teens and the wind picked up. She was grateful her doorman whistled down a cab so quickly.

Usually, she didn't care for banquets and award dinners. She'd had to do enough schmoozing at them in the corporate world, but tonight was special. She felt special. The award the company was getting would certainly bring the reporters out. Whatever made the papers or news broadcasts would be accompanied by a little reminder of the accusations leveled at her by Egyptian Enchantment, that she gave away information that set the company's research back ten years. Oh, they wouldn't ask her anything outright and give her a chance to tell her side of the story. It would be added as a side comment. They always chronicled her failure in corporate America. She felt that, even if she became a scientist and discovered a cure for cancer, the mention of the industrial espionage incident would creep in. That was the time when she'd lost her career, her friends and her man. She'd never let anyone make her that vulnerable again. Jesslyn hated to play hardball, but when she chose to do it, she was among the best in the business. Although Carolann had agreed to spend more time in the store, Jesslyn had decided that it wouldn't work out for them if she didn't. She would then demand Carolann sell her shares. Jesslyn would have her company family-owned by the end of the year.

Her short black hair peeked from under the silver tam, and the dangling silver earrings and silver high-heeled pumps had been added to complete the outfit. She felt like a mysterious, sexy woman.

As she pulled the heavy door her fingers slipped off and she stepped back slightly off-balance. About to laugh at herself for thinking she could ever be mysterious or sexy, she found herself firmly pressed against a man's body and locked in his strong arms as his deep baritone voice said, "I've got you."

Jesslyn turned to apologize and found herself staring

at the buttons on the man's tuxedo shirt. She followed the buttons upward with her head and found her brown eyes staring into hard black ones. The man had to be at least six-foot four inches and well over 200 pounds. His beard and mustache and the black tuxedo duster made her think of the Three Musketeers. His long hair hung around his shoulders in twists. He exuded power and made wearing dreadlocks part of that power. For a moment, she was caught by his mesmerizing stare.

"My . . . hand . . . slipped . . . I'm so sorry." She cursed herself for letting the stranger affect her.

"Don't be sorry. I thought we were getting romantic."

Jesslyn tried, but failed, to hide her smile. She held her breath as the man gave a sexy laugh then released her. He leaned past her and caught the door handle. "Allow me."

She turned and stepped inside, expecting him to follow her, but as she glanced over her shoulder, the door was closing and he hadn't followed her.

Her flowery perfume lingered in the air for a few seconds as Palladin waited until Mac joined him. He heard the strains of a band playing dance music filtering through the door. Judging from where her head hit his chest, he knew they would not make great dance partners. The women in his life were usually tall and willowy, not petite and curvy. Mac's voice brought him back to the present.

"What do you think?"

"She doesn't look the type, but I guess people said that about Lizzie Borden."

"Got a game plan?"

"I'd like to get to know the lady a little better before deciding."

Mac's brows knitted into a frown, and he ran his fingers through his thick white hair. "Don't get too close and lose your perspective. A lot of her friends still believe she was set up and unjustly fired."

"Despite the evidence?"

"Most of it was supplied by the man she was involved with."

"You know I prefer to make my own judgments, right Skip."

The man behind Palladin snorted. "Still think you're smarter than the rest of us, Rush."

"With you, it doesn't take much."

Skip took another step toward Palladin, but a warning stare from Mac made him retreat.

"What did you find out?" Mac asked.

Skip's eyes never left Palladin's. "There's no reason that Carolann was needed other than to spread the company liabilities around. So, it looks like the Owens woman is taking out a little insurance that she didn't have the last time."

"Why?"

"Don't know, Rush. You find out. They didn't need Carolann."

Palladin scanned the area. "Damn! I don't like this, Mac."

"What do you see that a mere mortal like me missed," Skip demanded.

"If you got caught in something like industrial espionage and wanted to make a splashy come back what would you do?"

"Make it look like someone else did it and framed . . . me." A red blush spread over Skip's face. "It'll look like Carolann was guilty both times."

"Think you could convince her to just back out."

"No way. I insisted on setting up her retirement, so there is no way she can touch it. I'm not going to have her reach fifty-five and have nothing left. She's determined to prove she doesn't need my help to be a success, and besides, the Owens woman might find another sucker. I want to put a stop to her."

"What else do you need?" Mac asked.

"To use your cell phone."

Mac gave it to him and he walked away, made a call, then returned.

"Thanks," he said handing the phone back. "Get me some info on the ex-boyfriend."

"I'm already working on that," Skip said smugly. "Okay, *Glacier,* do your thing." He saluted and started to leave only to find his way blocked by Palladin.

"Mac, who else in your organization can you trust?"

"I don't know. A couple of people."

"Good. Find one I can work with and reassign Logan."

Skip turned to Mac, "You can't do that. I . . . I'm the one who brought the Owens woman to your attention."

"Palladin?" Mac didn't have to spell it out. He was asking for a reprieve for Skip.

"Get me someone I can trust, or I'll just go inside and spend a few minutes with my ex-wife and her new partners and be on the road home tonight."

"Wait," Skip's voice faltered. "I started this whole thing. We can work together. I know we can."

"Fine. Bring the information to my hotel tomorrow," Palladin told him. Now that the lines of command had been fully drawn and Skip understood he was a soldier not an officer, working with him wouldn't be a problem.

Skip nodded his head and left before Palladin changed his mind about letting him stay in the loop.

The use of his old code name hadn't bothered Palladin as much as Skip's animosity. He never liked loose cannons, and right now, his old nemesis was beginning to fit that category. You never knew when a man who hated you would let you down or get you killed. He'd put the ball in Skip's court. Obey the rules or take a walk. Palladin was sure his back would be well guarded hereafter.

"Still having trouble with your fair-haired boy."

"He's still trying to live up to you."

"Rule number one."

Mac laughed then said, "Palladin's Rules of Life Lecture. The guys loved to hear you. All except Skip. Rule number one: Don't try to copy—be original. Rule number two: Fear can make a person do what he should have done in the first place. Rule number three . . ."

"I don't think I have time to hear my old lecture from the man who taught it to me."

"Yeah. Get in there and sweep Ms. Owens off her feet." As Palladin passed him, Mac caught his arm. "Remember one of those rules you talk about says that when the chips are down there are no rules. Be careful."

"I'll keep you posted."

As soon as she entered the ballroom, Jesslyn tried to find her sister and knowing her partner would not have yet arrived. Lena was always early, Carolann always late and Jesslyn right on time. In the short run, they'd been together as a team; that was the way they worked. The thrill of being back on top gave Jesslyn butterflies that seemed to multiply by the seconds. Vindication. Others might not see being a small business owner after riding the executive fast track with a cosmetic firm as vindication, but for Jesslyn the word described her mood. She'd proved all the skeptics wrong about her business demise. She'd found a way to make lemonade from the proverbial lemon. And yet she couldn't shake her feelings that something was wrong.

The pink and gold room was peppered with small round tables that would seat no more than six. The tables were draped in white linen table cloths with yellow, silk jonquils as a centerpiece. Spotting Lena at a table near the left of the stage, she made her way through the small crowd, stopping only to chat with another refugee from the world of downsizing big business. Frank Mason was one of the few people who said he'd keep in touch and had actually meant it.

"Jesslyn. Wow! Don't you look sexy tonight." The redheaded man threw his arm around her and pulled her to the side.

"I see you've been spending time in Florida again. You better watch that sun."

"I can't help it I'm just a snowbird at heart. Is everything going all right for you?"

"Couldn't be better, why?"

"I heard some rumblings that your company's being investigated."

"For what?"

"I don't know. Look, it may just be some reporter snooping around in your life, but be careful."

"I will and thanks for the warning."

The butterflies started dancing again and Jesslyn forced herself to smile and walked over to her sister. She draped her jacket on the back of her chair.

"Thank you," Jesslyn said as she sat down and noticed the glass of white wine in front of her.

"You're welcome," Lena replied as she raised her glass in a mock toast.

"Have I missed anything?"

"No, but have I? You look marvelous. So you really decided to wear that suit," Lena clucked.

"I spent too much money not to wear it." Jesslyn ran her fingers down the shimmery suit that hugged her curvaceous figure. The slim skirt's hemline fell four inches above her knees as she'd predicted. "I figure that if a suit saves your life you should buy it." She took off the fringed scarf that hung from the shoulder and draped it on the back of her chair with her jacket. "Lucky for me, the cabs pull under this building and it's only a couple of steps inside or I would have frozen."

Lena's brows knitted in concern. "I don't think that's funny. I wish you'd quit treating it as a joke. You almost get hit by a car and you buy a stupid suit."

"I beg your pardon."

"Okay, the suit isn't stupid. It's beautiful and you look great. And I take full credit." Lena pushed out her chest. Tonight she wore a strapless purple dress that draped her slender form.

"Really?" Jesslyn grinned. She'd always admired how her sister dressed. Lena's rich, ebony skin could handle strong, rich colors but the undertones in Jesslyn's skin called for more pastels. That may have been the reason she was drawn to the suit. It was the first pastel that made her feel sexy.

"Who's been after you to show off your body and get out of the Victorian era."

"I like the Victorian era."

The eight years that separated them had rarely been a problem. They often said that if they weren't sisters they'd have been best friends. Lena, at thirty-six, still bounced around from one interest to another. While Jesslyn, at twenty-eight, had already established herself as a focused career woman. Not even the fiasco at the cosmetic firm had slowed her down. She simply refused to be vanquished.

"You should have brought a date. They said we could for the opening party and the ball at the end of the week." Lena's eyes searched the room.

"Jeff's late again," Jesslyn said. "I don't know how you two got together."

"He was a lot more persistent than he is now. Think that's a problem?"

"I never comment on the men in your life."

"You need to get someone . . ."

Jesslyn interrupted. "Don't start on how I should be over Paul and throw myself back into the swing of things."

"Well, you need someone to bring you to events like this."

Jesslyn knew her sister wanted her to get on with her social life as she had with her business life. But she couldn't. "All the men in my life are business acquaintances, and I'm not sure I want one of them getting the idea I want to mix pleasure with business."

"The solitary life isn't one I want, and I know you need at least a 'significant other,' if not a husband. Wouldn't you like something like that?"

"I may have waited too long. Got too set in my ways." Then she thought about the man she'd literally bumped into. "Actually I just had a near romantic encounter in the hallway."

"You did *what?"*

Jesslyn stuck her tongue out at her sister. "Anything can happen in New York." Quickly, she explained.

"And a smart New York girl like you didn't get his phone number?"

Not wanting to admit how tongue-tied she'd become with the man in the hall, she tossed it off. "I have too many business things to think about."

"This business-first attitude has to stop. You say he had dreads?"

"More like tiny Senegalese Twists."

"And he was cute."

"Gorgeous."

"And you let him get away. Are you sure you're my sister?"

Lena had never been shy and would probably have the man sitting at their table right now if she'd had the same chance Jesslyn had.

"Did you remember to invite Jeff?" Jesslyn asked as she changed the subject. "Maybe he's not here because you forgot to tell him where to meet us."

"Of course I told him. Whether he'll make it or not is another story, so don't start."

Lena knew that Jesslyn wasn't sure this relationship was best for her sister. She didn't like the fact that he'd show up, make a play for every woman in the room and write it off as "just kidding."

Once, he'd suggested he was with the wrong sister. Jeff and Jesslyn sounded so right, he'd said. When she'd given him a withering look, he'd gone into his "just kidding" mode. He got the message, however, and knew not to say it again.

"I almost got a glimpse of Carolann's mystery man, yesterday."

"And?"

"He pulled off before I could get a good look at him."

"Darn! Maybe we should go to one of those stores that sell those cameras, you know, surveillance equipment?"

"I think he falls under the we-don't-need-to-know-until-formerly-introduced category. But if she doesn't do it soon, I may pay half of the camera price."

"Hate to bring this up," Lena began. "How are you coming with getting Carolann to admit that this partnership isn't working?"

"She started with how much she loves the business. I decided that if I ask her to go, she'll stay forever. So I'm going to find a way to let it be her decision to leave."

"I think she's a pretty good actress. Maybe she should move to California and try to break into movies."

Jesslyn wrinkled up her nose. "Why would you say that?"

"Just the way she convinced us that she'd make the perfect partner."

"I was looking for someone and why not another victim of Egyptian Enchantment Cosmetics?"

Lena tossed her head and curls from her dark brown hair played around her face. "She played us. And now, she's like a chameleon."

"Don't worry. I'll find a way to ease her out. I can't cause a flap because Frank says I'm being investigated, at least GiftBaskets, Inc. is being investigated."

"Why?"

"Probably one of those reporters doing a 'where is she now' follow-up." Jesslyn took a sip of wine. "I'll have to watch what I say and so should you and Carolann."

"Wow!" Lena's sigh snapped Jesslyn's mind away from Carolann. She turned in the direction of her sister's stare and echoed a whispery. "Wow!"

"The guy from the hall."

"How'd you guess?"

"There aren't that many brothers in the room with twists." Lena nodded her approval. But Jesslyn knew that Lena would approve any man. She'd even liked Paul at first, and that turned into the worst mistake Jesslyn had ever made. The man had helped find the information Egyptian Enchantment needed to ask for her resignation.

"He's looking for you."

"Don't be silly. He's probably looking for his wife," Jesslyn countered.

Still, they didn't take their eyes off him as he seemed to be asking Frank something and Frank pointed to their table.

"See. He is looking for you."

"I . . . maybe."

"My little sister's snared a good one. You didn't mention how tall he is."

Jesslyn glanced around at the tables near her, and no one seated at them appeared to be waiting for him. As he stopped a foot away from her, she smiled and then frowned as he announced: "I'm looking for Carolann Rush."

Four

Lena recovered first. "She's late. I'm Lena Owens and this is my sister Jesslyn. And where has Carolann been hiding you?"

"May I?" He indicated the chair next to Jesslyn.

"Of course," she hoped her voice didn't sound like a croak to him as it did to her. Mentally, she berated herself for assuming the man deliberately sought her out.

He sat down and Jesslyn noticed two things. One, he never answered Lena's question and two, he was more handsome than her original appraisal. His sienna skin seemed to show signs of a tan. His smile revealed strong, white, even teeth. His size had encroached on her space, but she knew if she moved it would show his effect on her.

"Judging from the looks on your faces, I'm a surprise."

"Not exactly. Carolann said that if you could you'd be here, but she wasn't sure . . ." Realizing she was babbling, Jesslyn stopped abruptly.

"I guess not too many women invite their ex-husbands . . ."

"Ex-husband?" Jesslyn and Lena chorused.

He laughed then leaned over to Jesslyn. "Let's try this

again. I'm Palladin Rush, Carolann's ex-husband. Who were you expecting?"

Rather than mention the mystery man who'd been occupying Carolann's time for most of the month, Lena found a way to avoid answering his question with the truth.

"You don't exactly fit her description," Lena said. "I thought you were the new guy in her life."

Their partner had given the impression that her ex-husband was sort of bland. That he was part of the team that guarded the president because he melted into a crowd. She tried to picture him with short hair and an off-the-rack suit, but somehow she felt he'd still stand out in a crowd. He was probably the one that made it easier for the others to do their job while drawing the focus to him. Jesslyn always assumed that was the reason Carolann hadn't show them his picture.

Had she been able to speak, Jesslyn might have agreed with her sister. Still, she remembered that, lately, Carolann had been experiencing regrets over her divorce and maybe he shared those feelings. Why else would he be here?

"I have to admit you ladies don't fit the description I got, either."

"Is that good or bad, Mr. Rush?" Jesslyn finally found her voice.

"Let's just say different." He smiled. "How long were you in business before Carolann joined you?"

"A couple of years." Lena supplied. "At least Jesslyn was in business that long."

"And you needed a partner?"

"I wanted a partner," Jesslyn answered. She didn't like his tone. She hadn't been away from the corporate world so long that she didn't recognize a question from a trap. "I don't *need* anything."

She wouldn't admit in public, and especially to Carolann's ex-husband, that the partnership wasn't working out as she'd hoped. She'd considered her another escapee from Egyptian Enchantment and thought they could be a team. Although the accounts Carolann brought in were pretty big, Jesslyn wasn't willing to let go of controlling interest. Carolann was insisting on a larger share, and now her ex-husband appeared asking questions. Was he the one who wanted Carolann to try for more?

"Can I get you something from the bar?" Palladin asked.

"I'd like another glass of red wine," Lena said.

"I'm a little nervous," Jesslyn admitted. "I don't think liquor would be a good idea." She'd already begun to feel the few sips of white wine.

With cat-like grace, he rose from the table and walked across to the bar set up on the other side of the room. Two pair of eyes followed him. One pair in awe the other pair filled with suspicion.

"He likes you! You go, girl!"

"Come-on Lena, stop."

"I don't care what you think. The man was looking at you and didn't even know I was at the table. I mean it."

"He's Carolann's husband!"

"Ex-husband. One woman's throwaway, another woman's treasure."

"I think she invited him to rekindle their relationship. Even though she swears there's someone else, we've never met him."

"Hey, he don't look like the type to let anything he really

wants get away. If he wanted her, she'd be living on that mountain you told me about. Besides she stole Kenny."

Kenny Weston was one of her suppliers, and they'd gone out a few times but nothing serious occurred. Then when Carolann came on board, he switched on the charm, and before anyone knew it, they were an item.

Since she really wasn't interested in Kenny, it hadn't bothered Jesslyn that the fire died quickly. Of course, when Kenny tried to lure Jesslyn back, she simply refused. The next thing she heard was that he'd taken a job in California. The men she dated were safe. And that's what she wanted. One look at Palladin Rush, and the words dark and dangerous took on new meaning.

"She didn't steal him. He wanted her and there's nothing you can do about that. I don't think the Owens women have much luck with men."

"Well *I'm* still in the ball game."

Jesslyn turned and watched Palladin at the bar for a few seconds then turned to her sister. "He wants something and it's not me."

"Stop looking a gift horse in the mouth. Go for the gold."

"Stop with all those slogans. They don't work."

"If you don't give it a chance, you could regret it."

Jesslyn didn't want to say anything else. Her sister believed that if one man didn't work another would. She'd only brooded about her failed marriage for as long as it took to get the final papers. This man's code name was Glacier, and he seemed to be as big and unmovable as one. If he fell on your heart you'd probably never recover.

"He lives on a mountain, for goodness sakes!"

"So what?"

Jesslyn smiled as Palladin returned to the table. He placed a glass of red wine in front of Lena and a champagne glass in front of Jesslyn.

"Ginger ale, to settle your nervous stomach."

She thanked him and spent the next few minutes watching for another trick question. But none came. He seemed to be genuinely interested in her now, not the business. Jesslyn would give him one word answers and Lena would supply paragraphs.

"So how long will your parents be on this cruise?"

"Months," Jesslyn said.

"They won't be back until Christmas." Lena added.

"You two share an apartment?"

"No way. I like my space," said Lena.

"I like my privacy," Jesslyn answered.

She wanted him to know that she didn't trust him. It was a subtle message and not lost on him. He arched an eyebrow and smiled.

"Not changing the subject, but what's wrong with Frank?" Lena nudged her sister.

"Nothing. Why?" Jesslyn turned her head slightly so she could see Frank. His back was to her but then he turned, then quickly looked away.

"Usually, he's all over you. Trying to get you to go out with him."

"I think he's a little worried about me."

"Maybe it's me," Palladin offered.

He leaned over and took Jesslyn's hand. She fought the urge to pull away. She wasn't even sure she could since his grip was deceptively firm.

"Maybe he thinks I'm your date. If his attentions are unwanted, I'd be glad to pretend we're . . . friends."

Their eyes met for a long beat that was only interrupted when Lena said, "Hi partner."

Jesslyn looked up and found Carolann glaring at her. Then she glanced around the room and saw that most of the men were checking out her partner while the women were not happy with her arrival. The silver dress she wore was more like an ace bandage and split to the thigh. Only someone with her figure could get away with it. She looked fabulous. She'd planned a very dramatic entrance no doubt for Palladin's sake, and Jesslyn somehow had ruined it.

Palladin stood up and placed a brotherly kiss on her cheek. Then stepped to the side and held a chair for her. She sidestepped him and eased into the seat he'd vacated forcing him to take the seat he held for her, next to Lena. Then she swiveled in the chair so she was facing him and her back to Jesslyn.

"I'm so glad you could make it." She told him.

"I'm glad you invited me. Your partners are very lovely women."

"Aren't they, just."

Jesslyn stifled a giggle as she watched Carolann try to figure out if they had been flirting with Palladin.

Carolann's eyes narrowed on Jesslyn's outfit. "That's so different from your normal outfits. The skirt's so short."

Palladin smiled and said, "I think she hit on the description of what a skirt should be."

"What's that?"

He winked at Jesslyn, "Short enough to be interesting. Long enough to show she's a lady."

Under the table, Lena tapped her toe against Jesslyn's leg as if to say I told you that he was interested in you.

"Hey, there's Jeff." Lena stood up and waved to him.

Jesslyn watched him ambling over to them. Everything about him was medium. His height, weight, everything.

As he reached the table, he stopped, backed up and said, "Mmm, Miss Carolann don't you look sweet. Too bad I'm taken or I'd definitely be after you tonight." Jeff's eyes roamed over her slender frame and long legs.

"This is Palladin Rush, Carolann's husband." Lena chimed in.

Jesslyn flashed a questioning look at her sister since, she'd been emphasizing the "ex" part all night. If Lena was that interested in Jeff, there might be wedding bells ahead and the thought of him as part of their family made her shiver slightly.

"Are you cold?" Palladin asked.

For a moment, she didn't know what he was talking about then rubbed her arms and shook her head and avoided looking into his eyes.

Palladin turned his attention to Jeff and stood up to shake hands and Jeff paled under his medium brown skin.

"Hey, man. Don't take it too seriously. I was just kidding. Lena's my woman. Carolann knows that. Everybody knows that."

"No problem and to keep the record straight I'm her ex-husband."

He chose that moment to offer his seat to Jeff, who was still so surprised by Palladin's dimensions he quietly took the seat and dropped a perfunctory kiss on Lena's mouth.

As if they'd just played musical chairs, Palladin was now seated on the other side of Jesslyn. No one else moved as the president of the group tapped his fork against his water glass demanding attention.

The speeches started and most were boring. The audience tried to be enthusiastic about some of the more tearful acceptances. When GiftBaskets, Inc. stepped to the stage to accept the award for their fast-rising business, most of the attention was on Carolann and her sexy dress. Jesslyn noticed several women give the men they were with an elbow to pull their attention away from Carolann. She also noticed that she got her own share of long looks.

The food was typical banquet fare, not bad enough to gag, but not good enough to want more than the tiny servings.

As the business of the evening ended and the dance floor began filling up, Jesslyn noticed that no one from their table seemed to want to move. She, Lena and Jeff wanted to learn more about Palladin.

"How'd you get such an interesting name," Lena asked.

"It's Native American for 'fighter.' "

"What kind of business you in, man. I might be able to help." Jeff always wanted to be the one who had all the contacts.

"Thanks, Jeff, but I'm retired."

"From what?"

"Government service."

Carolann had been quiet since her own tearful acceptance speech, filled with tears that didn't even last until she was back at her table. "He used to be Secret Service, but now he'd rather live in a log cabin in the mountains."

"What?" Jeff laughed loudly. "Like a black Abe Lincoln?" Then when Lena sent him a shriveling look, added, "I was just kidding."

Palladin's slow smile was a promise of something lethal happening if Jeff continued. The man who was never at a loss for words was suddenly silent. Jesslyn was amazed at how easily Palladin got people to do what he wanted. As if his black eyes carried the hypnotic power supposedly possessed by Rasputin, power to make you do things his way. She found herself drifting to slightly erotic thoughts and forced herself to listen to the remarks at the table and stop thinking about a man she just met. The man spelled trouble with big flashing pink neon letters.

"Maybe you need a place like that, Jesslyn," Carol-ann's voice dripped with sarcasm. "Keep you out of paths of red Jeeps."

"What does that mean?" Palladin asked. When he didn't receive an answer he turned, "What does she mean?" Palladin looked directly at Jesslyn and waited for an answer.

Jesslyn explained, trying to tone down the truth of the narrow miss. "Some dumb driver, that's all."

"Did anyone get a plate number?"

"In New York? Please." She hoped he would drop the subject, but he continued to press for information.

"Jesslyn, this isn't a joke. Drivers like that need their licenses pulled." Palladin knew the reason for reacting so strongly was the fact that he owned a red Jeep and understood their power. "If they have one," Jesslyn and the others laughed. Palladin didn't.

"Hey, it wasn't a big deal. Honest." She tried to convince him, but the determined look in his eyes and the set of his jaw told her that he wasn't satisfied with her answer. Somehow, she found his concern for her well-being pleasant, yet he seemed to be looking through her with his piercing black eyes. She couldn't turn away from his fixed look.

He'd been away from the city too long. He'd become accustomed to drivers who knew the rules of the road and lived by them.

They didn't see Frank approaching the table until he squeaked out a request to dance with Jesslyn. She jumped at the chance to get away from Palladin's intense stare.

They wrestled through a slow number, with Frank trying to hold her closer and Jesslyn trying to keep as much space between them as possible. She liked him as a friend but didn't want him thinking they could be more. While she wasn't the kind of woman men saw across a room and begged someone to introduce them, she knew she was attractive. Not beautiful like Carolann, but not plain, either.

Palladin had not taken his eyes off the couple since they'd first walked on the dance floor. This was the first chance he'd been able to study Jesslyn. Most of the time he preferred women who wore short skirts to long. Their legs seemed to go on forever. But Jesslyn's short frame didn't allow for that, and yet, he couldn't stop looking at how sexy she looked in a tight skirt, high heels and most of her legs showing. He wondered if his fingers would touch if he slipped his hands around her tiny waist. He was surprised at the thought but not upset by it. Jesslyn Owens was one of those women who could not be called beautiful by the usual standards. She seemed to rewrite the book on what was attractive without even trying. She'd been a strong woman to pick herself up after the cosmetics company fiasco. Palladin admired and respected strength. He'd just never seen it in such a neatly wrapped package of curves and curls.

His admiration didn't extend to Frank Mason. The man tried to pull Jesslyn closer as they danced, and so far, she had avoided him. Palladin wondered if he should cut in. He looked at his hands and saw they were clinched into fists as if he wanted to punch Mason in the face. Palladin opened his hands, grabbed a water pitcher and topped off the almost full glass of water in front of him. He lifted it, sipped slowly and let his eyes scan the room for anything that would take his mind off Jesslyn in Frank's arms. It isn't jealously, he thought to himself. I hardly know the woman, so why would I be upset at her dancing with an old friend. But as illogical as it may have been, that's exactly what he was: jealous.

"What's wrong, Frank?"

"Don't get too cozy with that FBI man. He might be part of the group that's checking out your company." As Jesslyn started to turn toward Palladin, Frank held her firmly so she couldn't do it. "Don't look. He's watching us."

"Do you know him?" Jesslyn stopped and stared up at him.

Frank shook his head. Pulled her back in his arms and they started dancing. "I just know what Carolann told me about him. That's he's very controlling. That's why they broke up."

"But he's not FBI anymore."

"Do you think those guys ever really quit?"

A couple of times, she glanced over Frank's shoulder at Palladin. He wasn't looking her way. In fact, he seemed bored by the whole situation. She wished she could dance close with him, but she'd only end up staring at the buttons on his shirt. Probably just above his waistband, she thought, and then giggled.

Frank took it to mean that she found whatever he'd said to her amusing. "I think you should really find out what's happening in your little company that the government is interested in. It could be big trouble."

"Thanks, I will."

"Why don't we have dinner, say tomorrow? Maybe I could help?"

"I don't think so. I'm going to be working in the shop."

"I could drop by and . . ."

"No. I'll call you if I need anything. Thanks for the offer."

Frank had come by the store a couple of times before he introduced Jesslyn to Carolann. He'd been the only one from the cosmetic company who had risked his job seeing her. Before Lena moved to New York, Frank had been Jesslyn's confidante. He'd answered her questions about expanding the business and a few legal matters with Egyptian Enchantment. While the company couldn't push the issue any further than they had, she knew that there were still executives who weren't satisfied with just her resignation. Some wanted blood. Others wanted the truth. Frank had been discreet as he helped her regroup, but Jesslyn instinctively knew not to talk about the cosmetic firm with him.

When the music ended and Frank led her back to the table, she was shocked as Palladin stood up, caught her hand and led her over to a deserted table for two.

Palladin had not taken his eyes off the couple since

they'd started back to the table. He stood up and took Jesslyn's hand, forcefully pulling her to the next table, ignoring Frank, who promptly scrambled back to his table.

"Sit," he commanded and added "please" when her stubborn streak kicked in and she didn't move. When she did, he dropped down in the chair in front of her, his size blocking most of the people from her table.

The dance floor wasn't as crowded and she saw several couples leaving the usual party litter. She glanced at her watch. In an hour, they would all have to leave, but she was starting to feel tired. When she got tired, she let her guard down. She instinctively knew that she didn't want Palladin getting too close too soon.

"I want to know more about this red Jeep that almost hit you. When?"

"A couple of days ago. Thursday. There is no more to tell."

"Any other strange things happening to you?"

She thought for a moment about a confrontation with a client over a computer disk he said was missing from his basket. But Carolann had promised to take care of that.

He mistook her silence for anger. "I'm not trying to upset you, but old habits die hard, and I'm used to questioning everything."

"I know. Your life depended on it."

"The president's life depended on it."

"Think you'll go back?" She was trying to change the subject They both knew it and he allowed it.

"No. I took a long, hard look at my life. I want something different now. I'm working with some kids who love hockey as much as I do."

"You went to live on a mountain."

"I'd like you to see it. Maybe spend a weekend?" It slipped from his thoughts into actual words and he fought to hide his embarrassment. He wanted to get her alone, but the request coming hours after their meeting was not his usual style.

"I don't think my partner would like that."

"She has nothing to do with us."

Jesslyn looked at Carolann and said, "I don't think it would be a good thing right now." It would give Carolann a good reason for wanting out of the company. She couldn't use him, however, simply because she wouldn't want anyone to use her in that manner.

"The invitation stands." He handed her a card. It was a specialty business card black with his name written across it in silver script and a phone number. Jesslyn arched an eyebrow as she noticed he had his own 1-800 number.

"No fax?"

He shook his head. "I tend not to like too much of the computerized world encroaching on mine."

"We'd better join our friends." She yawned. "I guess I'm a little tired. I want to go home."

"Fine," he stood up, pulled her to her feet and let his hand slide down her arm until he locked his fingers with hers. "Home sounds like a nice destination."

Five

"I hate to be a party pooper, but I've got to get home." Jesslyn announced.

"It's too early. We plan to close the place down and find another one," Jeff announced.

She waved to Carolann, who left her dance partner on the floor and sauntered over to the table. She didn't try to hide her smile when Jesslyn said she was leaving.

"See you Monday." Carolann smiled. "We haven't had our dance," she told Palladin.

"Another time. I'm taking Jesslyn home."

Carolann's smile changed to a pout. "She doesn't need a bodyguard. The cab stand is right under the building."

"I know, and she has a doorman, but I'm still taking her home. Good night. Thanks for inviting me."

Carolann's blank stare made him realize his mistake. He hoped Jesslyn hadn't picked up on it. His skills were more rusty than he'd thought. If he wasn't careful, he'd be worthless to Mac.

As Palladin held her coat, Jesslyn wondered again if dating him a few times would make Carolann more conducive to giving up her share of the company. But she reminded herself that sounded like she was using him and that wasn't her style. He didn't appear to be carrying a torch for his ex-wife anyway. She slipped her arms into her coat.

Just as he stepped away to allow Jesslyn to walk in front of him, Carolann caught his arm. Jesslyn saw his icy stare and understood why her partner withdrew her hand quickly.

"Just a minute," he told Jesslyn. He and Carolann stepped out of hearing range and he turned his back so she couldn't even read his lips. In only seconds, he was back at her side and her partner was decidedly pale with what could only be fear. What had he said to her?

He caught Jesslyn's hand and tugged until she fell into step as they headed for the door. She put her hand to her throat and remembered she'd been wearing a scarf.

"Walt," she said. "I forgot something."

He looked down at her and the cold look when he was talking to Carolann had vanished. How could he turn his emotions off so quickly? Was this the kind of man she wanted to even take her home much less continue seeing?

"I'll wait outside the door."

As she was about to tell Carolann that Palladin's taking her home meant nothing, her partner lashed out.

"Don't think you can hold his attention too long," Carolann whispered. "You're a city girl, and he's never gonna come off that mountain. But have a good time, okay."

"Then there's nothing to worry about, is there?" Jesslyn answered.

"You know there's another man in my life, anyway. And Palladin Rush is going to just die when he finds out who it is. I had a momentary jealous twinge, I admit it. No problem. But don't fall in love with him, honey. He's cold and he's ruthless, and he'll walk away from you and never look back—just like the way he did with me."

"I thought the decision was mutual?" Jesslyn stared at her partner.

"Yeah. I left because he could turn his feelings on and off like a faucet. But go on. Have fun. But you'll never get him to come off that mountain."

"The women said goodnight."

Lena watched from the dance floor, and when it seemed as though Jesslyn was in trouble, she left Jeff and came to stand by her sister.

"Problem?"

"No. See you Monday," she said and walked away but she did hear the final exchange between Lena and Carol-ann.

"He'll use her and dump her."

Lena's reply was simply, "Meow, Meow."

Palladin was waiting just outside the ballroom. They smiled at each other as he opened the door for her.

The elevators were slow due to another convention going on, and people scrambling from floor to floor to arrange the next day's excursions. Even in winter, tourists loved New York. It was easier to get on an elevator going up and ride back down than wait for one going down.

Five years ago, she'd been part of that kind of a group. She'd had those same conversations with people, and one week after the event, they pretended they didn't know her. That was when the rumors started, and at the first sign of trouble, corporate executives began putting distance between themselves and Jesslyn. When she learned that Paul, the man she was planning to spend her life with, had twisted a half-truth to save his career, she was devastated.

The loud voices snapped her back to the present and told Jesslyn that the group had done a little bar-hopping. A man with liquor on his breath leaned forward and stage whispered.

"Hey, honey. We're gonna have a party. Wanna come?"

She felt a frisson of current run down her spine. Ignoring a drunk could create more of a scene than answering. She shook her head.

As the elevator stopped and the man pushed to the front he added, "If you change your mind later we're in room 2306 and . . ."

Palladin's cold black eyes stopped him in mid-sentence. "Hey no harm . . . I was . . ."

"Yeah, just kidding." Palladin finished for him. He and Jesslyn laughed until the elevator reached the ground floor and they got out.

Two warring factions bounced through Jesslyn's mind. She wanted to see the man because she found him attractive and because his concern about her near-miss accident seemed sincere. But there seemed to be a dangerous edge to the man. If Frank was right, there was a business matter that needed her attention. She didn't need another complication in her life.

"Is there a chance that Jeff will be your brother-in-law?" Palladin asked.

"I hope not. I tell Lena she just got a divorce and give herself some time. She tells me the only way to succeed is to keep getting back on the horse until you learn to ride."

Jesslyn had decided that she wouldn't allow Palladin

to take her all the way home. She'd just let him get her a cab at the stand that was right outside the entrance. She'd just slip in the back and close the door.

As if he'd read her mind when they got to the door, he caught her hand and the only way for him not to get in the cab would be for her to make a scene.

"Most places a guy would get a ticket driving around like that," he said.

She followed his gaze to a slightly battered white car with only one headlight working. The man behind the wheel hid his face when she looked, but she noticed the beret that didn't quite cover his bald head.

Shrugging it off as another New York driver she got into the cab. The distraction of the white car gave him time to slide in beside her. So much for not letting him in the cab.

He could stay in the cab and there'd be no need for him to come inside. After all, she had a doorman and a concierge. She wouldn't let him take her to her apartment door. That's all. She was so busy figuring out how to keep him out of her apartment she forgot that he didn't know where she lived. In the back of her mind, something nagged at Jesslyn. She couldn't remember what Palladin had said to make her edgy.

"Give the man your address. Unless you'd rather go some place else."

She gave the uptown address softly then leaned back against the seat and wondered why it was so difficult to tell this man she didn't want him to take her home. Jesslyn admitted that was a lie as soon as the thought ran through her head. She did want him to take her home. She did want him to call her. She did want to take a chance to walk on the wild side. She just didn't know why. The sudden rise of nausea swept over her minutes after the cab started uptown. Trying to eat a cracker and not explain was impossible, so she quickly ran down the oddity of getting carsick unless she was driving. Palladin simply said he'd heard about that but admitted that he thought it had more to do with the mind than with the body.

She closed her eyes to avoid further conversation, but drifted off to sleep.

"Jesslyn, wake up honey, we're home."

She struggled to open her eyes. A spicy aroma was so close and she leaned forward to get closer to its rich smell. "Umm. Smells good."

She heard a low, male chuckle. He looked at her full red lips and wanted to kiss her. She was so innocent and vulnerable, but he preferred a willing participant in a kiss—not someone who was half-asleep. He put his arms around her and shook her gently.

"Wake up, sweetheart."

Realizing she was home, Jesslyn began pushing his arms away from her as she struggled to pull herself together.

"Why don't you keep the cab. You don't have to come in."

He didn't say anything, just got out of the cab and held out his hand. She took it and let him help her to the curb. He closed the door, leaned down, gave the cabbie a single bill and told him to keep the change. It must have been a good tip because the man yelled to them to have a good night.

She'd given up hope that he wouldn't see her to her door, but she didn't have to let him in. She was still safe. She didn't have to let him inside her apartment.

"I'm glad you're being reasonable tonight. I thought I was going to have to do something like throw you over my shoulder just to see that you got home safely."

"I'm being reasonable because I figured you'd do something like that."

She noticed the battered white car double parked across the street and flinched. She was sure it was the same car she saw outside the hotel. Palladin didn't seem to notice the car, only her reluctance to go inside the building. He walked over and took her hand.

She closed her fingers against the slightly calloused hand. Warmth seeped into her body. Jesslyn knew she wanted to see him again. It was like an enjoyable first date, with hopes there would be many more. Yet something made her pull back. Something he said. Something that was covered in fog in the back of her brain. She looked up and smiled at him and they started walking toward the building.

"Were you looking for someone?" He asked.

Not wanting to sound silly about an old car, she shook her head.

Palladin followed her gaze. "You have some jealous old boyfriends who drive cars like that."

"The men in my life wouldn't be caught dead in a car like that. I'd only be followed by Beemers and Jags."

"Well, I guess we're safe. I haven't seen one of those following us."

Cliff was still helping the tenant with his luggage when they walked by. Jesslyn nodded and the man nodded back. The recent addition of the doorman to help the concierge with late night callers made the owners feel a little safer. Someone would always be in the lobby to screen guests.

"Not very friendly."

"Sometimes it's better that way." She didn't tell him that the man was married and had once made a pass at her.

"May I use your phone? I'm staying with a friend and I need to tell him I'm on my way."

Jesslyn smiled and nodded. The nagging image became crystal clear. She knew what had made her more wary of the man.

"Good evening, Mr. Williams," Jesslyn said to the man seated behind the large mahogany desk.

"Good evening, Ms. Owens."

"My friend needs to make a phone call."

Palladin noticed a puzzled flash in the man's eyes as he looked at Jesslyn. Then, recovering quickly, the man turned the phone on his desk around to make it easy for Palladin to dial. He had no choice but to make the call from the lobby.

After he'd slipped the receiver back in place. "I'll be staying at the Peninsula Hotel while I'm here. I'll call you," he said to Jesslyn.

"You do that, Mr. Rush," Jesslyn said as she turned and headed for the bank of elevators. *Palladin.*

She knew he was watching her, even though she never looked back. The elevator doors closed and began its rise.

Palladin smiled as he watched the gentle sway of her hips. Just when he thought she'd be willing to invite him in for a drink . . . That she would treat him as she would a business associate who had been courteous enough to see her home.

The doorman nodded as Palladin strolled down the walkway and crossed the street to the battered white car parked there. The man behind the wheel wore a beret that tilted to the side showing his shaved head. The car was specially equipped for Kaliq Faulkner, a driver without the use of his legs.

"Was I ominous enough for the lady? I thought you'd get to spend the night."

"Yes, you scared her."

"So, what's next?"

Palladin shook his head. "I don't know. I've got a feeling about the lady."

"Uh oh. What kind of a 'feeling'?"

"That the lady is a lot smarter than we gave her credit for. She was fine in the cab, then she turned on a switch and became as cold as ice."

Kaliq laughed. "Sounds like what most people say about you."

"I made a mistake and the lady picked up on it."

"What did you do?"

"I mentioned her doorman as we were leaving the dance."

"And?"

"How would I know about her doorman? He's only been there a couple of weeks. I thought she missed it, but once she got inside the building she was a different person." Palladin took a deep breath. "I've lost my edge. I'm making errors a rookie wouldn't."

"Time to regroup," Kaliq said, as he maneuvered the car through the dwindling traffic. "Mac is so sure, but while the report says she's tough, nothing gives me the impression she's crooked."

"So are you going to see her again?"

"Absolutely. She might be a very worthy opponent. Someone to hone my old skills on."

Palladin thought about the way she looked as she walked to the elevator.

"And he's going to wonder if you're thinking with your brain or another part of your anatomy."

"You know me better than that."

"Right. But tell me the truth," Kaliq turned and stared at Palladin. "That was a pretty sexy outfit she was wearing. Did you try to stay?"

Palladin laughed and said, "Ever known me not to get what I really wanted?" Even as he said it, he thought about the ease with which Jesslyn avoided continuing the evening.

"Uh huh. About ten minutes ago."

Jesslyn thought about the close call with Palladin. She'd almost done something that any woman living alone should never do. She'd almost invited a complete stranger to her apartment. It didn't matter that she knew his ex-wife. The fact was, she didn't know *him*. What could she have been thinking? If she hadn't remembered his little comment about the doorman . . . it was something even Carolann didn't know.

Mr. Rush, you've been away from the cloak and dagger for awhile, Jesslyn thought The one slip he'd made was when Carolann mentioned her doorman and Palladin had said, "I know."

He'd been checking up on her. She wasn't going to make it easy. She knew he'd call her. Even if she saw him for a few evenings, a few very expensive evenings, she decided. There was no way she would let her guard down and trust this man totally. Whatever he wanted wasn't beneficial, Jesslyn's instinct told her.

She fumbled through her handbag for her keys. Jesslyn's apartment was her haven. She'd filled it with items that made her feel good, the authentic African masks, Toby mugs, and a small wine collection from her travels. Other things had been ordered from magazines to give her place a natural Victorian look. She flipped the light switch by the door and all the lights in the apartment came on.

She hung her coat in the foyer closet and continued past the long, narrow cherry wood table that served as a bar when she entertained. She tossed her keys in a little tray on the end of it, next to the wine rack. Jesslyn selected a bottle of red wine and opened it, letting it breathe while she prepared for her nightly cleansing routine.

"It's twelve o'clock a.m." announced a staccato voice in Spanish.

The talking clock could also be set to announce the time in English, but Jesslyn preferred Spanish, since it reminded her of the shopping spree in Puerto Rico where she'd found it.

Her stomach growled. Banquet dinners never filled her up. She'd fix herself a late night snack that was sure to add to her hips and then spend a couple of evenings in the building's swimming pool to work it off.

She continued down the narrow hall past the living room and entered her bedroom suite. This section, if nothing else, was the reason she purchased the unit. She went into the bathroom and started running water into the Jacuzzi-styled tub. She added a handful of crystallized lavender bath salts. The last thing she did was light the large purple candle on the stand next to the tub. Soon a fragrant lavender scent would fill the room. She returned to the bedroom and began undressing. The queen-sized sleigh bed was made of the same dark cherry wood as the hall table. It was covered with lace and satin pillows from other trips. The only item Jesslyn had added to the room was the closet. She'd hired a cabinetmaker to install a wall-to-wall set of cabinets that had drawers at the bottom. The widest cabinet held her work wardrobe in thirty individual see-through garment bags. She could easily go for a full month without wondering what she was going to wear.

She tapped her foot against one of the drawers at the base of the cabinet and it sprang open. She slipped off her shoes, pulled the drawer out a little more and dropped the silver sandals inside, then closed the drawer. She took off her suit and hung it in the cabinet above the drawer that held the sandals.

In her bare feet, she walked back to the hallway, retrieved the wine, stopped by the kitchen for a glass and returned to the bathroom. She stripped off her pale blue satin underwear, she dropped them in the clothes hamper hidden under the facebowl. She turned off the water, climbed into the tub and settled in for a long soak while she sipped her wine. She did her best thinking in the bath. She was now wide awake and her mind replayed the evening. The one thing she knew was that Palladin Rush was after something. Curiosity bedeviled her. Did she really want to find out the secret behind those dark eyes. She whispered a soft "yes" and relaxed. She'd take a very mild walk on the wild side.

Six

On Sundays, the shop was closed, and Jesslyn usually spent the time after church just lounging around and going through every section of the *New York Times.* But since she opted for the dinner on Saturday, she hadn't had time to catch up on her accounting, so she showered and dressed casually in brown leggings, a yellow sweater, and her navy peacoat. The weatherman had said light flurries, but New Yorkers had been fooled enough with the forecasts so she'd added tall brown leather boots and carried an umbrella.

She loved to walk, and not just for the exercise. The city seemed more alive when you were surrounded by people rather than cars. The buses were better than the subways. She hated being underground, but it was usually the most economical way of getting around. Since the snow hadn't started, she decided to walk over to Eighth Avenue and catch the A train to the World Trade Center. Jesslyn used the walk to think about Palladin Rush.

Nothing about the man said that he was pining away for Carolann, or that he wanted to use Jesslyn to make her jealous. He hadn't even danced with his ex-wife. And that bothered her a little. Why would he have accepted the invitation, unless he just wanted to make sure she was back on her feet. Did he check Jesslyn out so thoroughly he knew about a new doorman because he was trying to protect Carolann? Would he always feel responsible for her? At Egyptian Enchantment, Carolann tended to be possessive. Jesslyn got the impression she'd had to share a lot when growing up and resented it.

Only after her marriage broke up and she came back as a temporary spokesperson, did she open up with Jesslyn. While they didn't see each other socially, they enjoyed a good working relationship. So much, that whenever they had changes they thought would upset Carolann and make her revert to her old temper-tantrum ways, they asked Jesslyn to be the messenger.

Still, she didn't need any personal trouble. Jesslyn knew that Palladin wanted to see her again, and she certainly wanted to see him. So why not? Carolann didn't consider Jesslyn competition and probably felt that, if she really wanted Palladin back, she'd have no trouble getting him.

In the short time they'd been partners, the subject had come up. A supplier's representative had dated Jesslyn a few times but nothing serious had come of it. Then Carolann came to her and said the man had asked her out and she wanted to know if it was all right. Remembering made Jesslyn laugh. After she'd said she didn't mind, she learned that Carolann had been seeing the man every night for two weeks before mentioning the conflict of interest. It also annoyed Jesslyn that Carolann had used their partnership to end the relationship when that wasn't the case at all. That was about the time she'd started talking about this terrific new man in her life.

Jesslyn knew if she did see Palladin while he was in town it couldn't lead to any long-term involvement. He would return to his Pennsylvania mountain and she would stay in New York. By the time she got to the subway, she decided that he probably wouldn't call and all this worry was for nothing. Not walking on the wild side had its advantages.

The Trade Center was quiet on Sunday, as most of the businesses in the vicinity were closed. One or two might be open for those people with weekend shifts or those who preferred to shop on Sundays, but it was a far cry from the people-jammed walkways during the week.

Jesslyn let herself into the store and walked to the back to turn on the lights. She didn't change the "Closed" signed but knew that she would have to keep out of sight or someone would insist she was open and they wanted to buy. That had happened twice. She was amazed that people assumed if you were in sight you were open for business. One man had tapped on the window with his keys until she decided she'd better talk to him before he broke the glass.

Jesslyn's size didn't pose a threat to anyone, so she took her mother's advice and said a lot of words she'd read on the bathroom walls over the years. The man acted as if he was the offended party.

"Jeez lady, all you had to say was that you were closed," the man protested as he stormed off.

But that was business in New York and she loved it.

She was just starting on her books when she heard the front door open. It was Carolann.

"Thought I'd find you here," she said. "We have to talk about last night."

"Look, I don't want to fight. But if he calls . . ."

"No! You don't understand. I finally realized that it is over between us and I want you to feel free to go out with him."

Jesslyn was taken aback. This was the woman who at Egyptian Enchantment threatened to scar another model for using her dressing table during a fashion shoot. She was terrific as long as she didn't consider you competition. If she did, the claws came out and it wasn't a pretty sight.

It was almost as if Carolann had decided not to give Jesslyn any reason for pushing her out of the business, that all things were negotiable. Just as they had done at Egyptian Enchantment, Carolann and Jesslyn always found a common ground on which they could agree.

"I'll he honest. If you want to feel good by giving us your blessing, fine. Go for it. But the truth is that we like each other and we'll continue to see each other for whatever. But I don't think we're each other's type. So don't get bent out of shape, unless we send you a wedding invitation."

Carolann smiled as if she knew a secret. "We may be history, but I don't think you're his type and don't get your hopes up. Nothing gets him off that mountain."

"What are you really saying?"

Carolann leaned down and placed her hand on her hip. "I'm really saying don't come crying to me when he breaks your heart."

"I won't."

"Good, I've got to go. I'm meeting someone. I'm not going to get upset about you seeing my ex. And I plan to set up some real time schedules with Lena. Who knows—we may all become one big happy family."

Jesslyn relaxed. "The idea of having Jeff as a brother-in-law makes me want to join Palladin on his mountain."

"If you say 'just kidding' I'm going to punch you." Carolann said and laughed.

Curious about Carolann's mood swings, she asked, "If neither of you is carrying a torch, then why did you invite him and why did he come down?"

"Guilt."

"Why?"

"Don't worry about it. Use it. Guilt works every time."

Jesslyn put the ledger down and stared straight into her partner's eyes. "You know, Carolann, a few years ago the owner of a football team divorced his wife. He gave her the house, a couple of cars and even lifelong seats on the fifty yard line." She smiled then continued. "Some people said he did it out of guilt. Some said he was still in love with her. But you know what he said?"

Her partner leaned forward for the punch line.

"He said he was so sick and tired of her he'd do anything to keep her away from him. So maybe someone might leave his mountain to make sure you didn't come to him."

"You know what I do with people who upset me? I have a little diary. I write down the person's name and the worst thing I wish could happen to them."

"Are you still doing that? I thought the little notebook was just for models who were competing for your job."

"I've expanded on a few things. For you, I'll wish that you fall in love with my ex-husband. That's the worst thing that could happen to any woman. See you later." Carolann smiled and left.

Jesslyn continued working on the books, but she kept thinking about what Frank had said. Someone wanted to know more about her business. Someone thought something else was going on. Even at the cosmetic firm, Frank had contacts who told him certain things. But what could a little gift basket business in a large mall do to get in trouble.

Hank Reynolds had said that the diskette contained the names of all the people involved with Senator Gary's re-election campaign. But Jesslyn knew that it was a lie. She couldn't prove it without the diskette, and she really didn't know where it was.

Just as she was putting the finishing touches on her inventory report, she heard someone tapping on the glass door. She tried to ignore it but finally gave in and came out to give the person a piece of her mind.

The words from the bathroom walls were on the tip of her tongue until she recognized the large figure doing the tapping. It was Palladin. He seemed different from the night before. He'd traded his formal attire for construction-style boots, straight leg jeans and a navy peacoat. His dreads were pulled back under a brimmed-hat.

"What are you doing here?" She asked as she let him in.

"I called your house and got your machine. I figured that perhaps you were down here, so I took a chance." He lied smoothly. Mac called and told him exactly where she was and hoped she was meeting a contact. Someone to tie her into the thefts. Palladin had just hoped she wasn't meeting another man and had no answer for the jealousy he felt at that thought. He waited until Carolann left before knocking on the door.

"You took the train from your hotel?"

"I've been to the big city before. I know how to ride the subway and the Peninsula Hotel isn't that far."

"That's near Godiva Chocolates on 55th Street, isn't it?"

"That's the one." Palladin laughed. "You're showing your priorities."

He knew most women would have used the other stores as a landmark—Christian Dior on one side and Bijan on the other—although a pound of the candy might cost nearly as much as an ounce of perfume from either. It created another doubt in his mind. She didn't live above her means or crave jewelry. He couldn't think of a single reason that Jesslyn would do anything illegal, unless it was for revenge or for kicks, and neither of those reasons fit the profile he was gathering from being around her.

"How about an early dinner?" he asked.

It was nearing five, and Jesslyn hadn't had anything but a bagel with cream cheese and some tea. The mention of dinner made her realize that her stomach had been asking for food for a couple of hours, while she had ignored the rumblings and continued working.

"Great. Where?"

"It's your city—you tell me."

"There's a great place in the Village, if you like jazz."

"Fine with me."

Greenwich Village's reputation was for the offbeat, and outlandish, although it wasn't as wild as people thought. There was still the chance of seeing, however, the man they called "Rollerina," in his tutu and carrying his magic wand as he skated down the street.

They took the R train only a few steps from Jesslyn's store and rode it to Eighth Street. They walked two blocks to the Knickerbocker Bar and Grill on University Place. Tonight a pianist who's name neither Jesslyn nor Palladin recognized was featured. The music had a good beat and was unobtrusive to the diners.

They were shown to a booth immediately, as it was still a little early. They tossed their matching jackets on the bench between them.

As soon as they were seated the waiter brought them menus and gave them time to select before returning to tell them what desserts were available that day.

"Yes!" Jesslyn said gleefully as soon as he mentioned Mississippi Mudpie.

"I guess we've found the lady's weak point," Palladin told the waiter. He placed their order, agreeing to try this concoction that thrilled Jesslyn so.

Over dinner, he got her to talk about her experience with Egyptian Enchantment. He searched for something that would convince him of her guilt or innocence. He'd only heard about the company from the model's point of view and found it interesting that all the work Jesslyn was describing resulted in one photograph or advertising spot.

"Would you believe I was a black woman with a $160,000 a year job and they thought that I would jeopardize it for selling an ad campaign."

"So, they never found out who did it?"

"Never. That's why when something good happens to me I pray that it doesn't get in the papers."

"I thought there was no such thing as 'bad' publicity."

"There is if you had to read every time, 'Jesslyn Owens, who left Egyptian Enchantment under a cloud of suspicion,' before finding out whatever the story is really about."

"Do you ever think about who might have done it?"

"At first. I thought if they found the person right away I could get my job back. Later I didn't *want* my job back. Now," she paused and looked around. "I can live without high-paying, high pressure jobs. I'm happy. I also learned who my friends were."

"Would Frank Mason be one of them?"

She couldn't hide her surprise. "Yes. He said he'd keep in touch and he's done just that."

"I noticed last night that the two of you seemed close." Palladin said. He'd almost demanded a response. He looked into her clear brown eyes. So much innocence, and yet, he knew that the eyes weren't always the window to the soul. He'd seen enough men and women with soulful eyes who'd masterminded thefts, kidnappings and even murder.

He wanted to know more about Jesslyn and Frank. "You looked a little strained after you danced with him. Problem?"

"Business situation. Nothing to worry about."

He could see she was starting to close down. That there was still part of her life she wouldn't let a stranger know about. He didn't pursue it, but made a mental note to ask Mac to check the man out.

The waiter cleared the table and brought the dessert. Palladin had to agree that if you were a chocolate lover you'd be in heaven with this dish. Chocolate cake filled with nuts, raisins, triple chocolate icing and who-knows-what-else.

He took a bite and also had to agree it was delicious.

"What about you Palladin, do you miss the Secret Service?" she said, as she savored the rich tasting dessert.

"Sometimes. I'll see a presidential motorcade on television and wonder if I'd still be on that detail. But I don't miss it enough to try it again."

"So what do you do?"

"Dabble in the market. Act as a venture capitalist."

She let a cryptic smile cross her face.

"Had problems with venture capitalists?"

"Sorry, but the ones I ran into were willing to put up the money and let me do all the work while they wanted half the profits. I thought that was a bit steep."

It was one of the reasons she was so happy Carolann wanted to become a partner. The only other offer had been from a venture capitalist who wanted more of the business than she could ever part with.

"But, remember, if I'm putting up money I'm entitled to something."

"Sure. Just not my first born."

Jesslyn saw the grin leave his face replaced by a solemn frown and then it faded into a smile. That didn't reach his eyes. Somewhere, she remembered reading that a fake smile could be spotted if the left corner of a person's mouth didn't turn up. Since Palladin's didn't, she wondered why he had to fake the smile. Carolann had never mentioned children. Had that been another problem in their marriage? But even though she told herself this relationship had no chance of turning into a long-term one, she wondered about having children. When would she feel comfortable enough to settle down *and* have a family.

"I coach a junior hockey team," he said pulling her back into a subject that wouldn't lead to such introspective thoughts for either of them.

"Hockey?"

"Now you aren't going to go there about blacks and hockey are you?"

"No. I just got this picture of you slipping around the ice, dreads flying in the wind." She broke into giggles.

"I observe the rules, so my little soldiers can do the same. We wear helmets."

"How's your standing in the league?"

"We're next to last, but we had a few emergencies."

"Mmm?"

"Hey, it's tough when your star player's father has a change of assignment and has to move to California."

"So they're out of the playoffs."

He smiled, acknowledging that she knew enough about the game to hold a conversation about the game. Most women knew something about it. Her statement indicated she even knew the format of play.

"That doesn't matter. We're going to practice until summer."

"Oh, did I just hear the proverbial 'wait until next year' whimper?"

"Want to make a little bet about next year?"

"Business is pretty good. I think I could go for . . . ten dollars."

"Not good enough."

"Twenty?"

"How about a week?"

"I beg your pardon?"

He sat back and stroked his closely-cropped beard. "If we make the playoffs next year, you'll come spend a week on my mountain."

His bet indicated that he thought she wouldn't like the idea of being away from the city for even a week. But more importantly to Jesslyn, he was saying he believed they'd still be seeing each other in a year.

"And if you don't make the playoffs?"

"I'll spend, say, a month in New York with you."

Jesslyn held out her hand so they could shake on the

bet. And she found herself wanting to be around to win or lose this one.

Palladin decided that, while Jesslyn enjoyed the subway probably because it didn't make her carsick, he'd had enough of it and insisted on getting a cab to take her home. As they got in, he removed a plastic wrapped package from his pocket. Crackers. The kind you get with soup in most restaurants or maybe at a hotel's dining room. He remembered.

Seven

Cliff was on duty again and nodded to them. At that moment, one of the other tenants came running out of the building, followed by a little boy.

"Ah, gee Mom," said Hunter Rothstein. "You don't understand about Henry."

Palladin looked down at the little boy, who was just about the same age as the boys on the team he coached. The child's blond hair was wet and with the chill in the evening air, Palladin was afraid he'd catch cold.

"Is there a problem in the building," Palladin asked the man who was coming out the door.

The man started to answer, but then burst into laughter. "My wife has a little problem with our son's pet."

The woman blinked several times and jumped, as if she hadn't realized they were outside the building. She grabbed her son's hand and pulled him back into the lobby. Slightly embarrassed as she turned to Jesslyn and shrugged.

"They're impossible." She said to Jesslyn then turned back to her husband and son. "I don't want to understand about Henry."

"Honey, if you just calm down . . ." Her husband began, but as he turned away from his wife, Palladin saw it was to hide a grin and stifle his laughter. Palladin joined him.

"See Jesslyn, they're just alike."

Jesslyn slid her arm around the woman. "Come on, Eva. Let's see if we can't talk about this."

"Be reasonable, honey . . ." The man said then burst into laughter again.

Palladin found himself enjoying the little hodgepodge of hysteria and family interaction. He glanced over at the concierge and they shared a conspiratorial grin.

"No! Henry goes or I do."

"If you hadn't gone in the bathroom without knocking . . ."

"I wanted to see if Hunter had a towel. That's all. I wanted to see if my child had a towel."

"Come on, Mom," Hunter said. "Ms. Owens, tell her Henry's not bad."

Jesslyn slid her arm around Hunter's neck. "Didn't you promise you'd tell your Mom if Henry was . . . checking out the apartment?"

"Yeah. But I forgot."

"Right," Eva added. "Twice this week."

"Then she opened the bathroom door without knocking."

All eyes turned to Eva Rothstein. She looked at each of them and stalked off.

"I'm staying at my sister's. Thank God we live in the same building."

"I know, Ms. Owens, breaking a promise is bad, but Henry just looked so lonely."

"Hunter, sometimes we have to sacrifice what we love for *who* we love." Jesslyn explained as she ruffled Hunter's hair and left the Rothsteins to solve the problem of what to do with Henry.

As they got on the elevator Jesslyn couldn't contain the laughter she'd been holding back. She punched the button for the seventh floor. As soon as the doors closed she turned to Palladin.

"They live on the fifth floor. A month ago, Hunter and his father talked Eva into letting Hunter get a pet."

"Henry, I take it is the pet."

"Yes. Henry is also a six foot baby boa. Sometimes Hunter takes him out of his cage, or whatever you call a snake's home, and forgets to put him back."

"When she went in the bathroom, Henry was there."

"Well, since Eva was fully dressed, it wasn't as bad as before. Last time he 'surprised' *her* in the shower."

"Tell me she didn't run out of the apartment then."

"Yep. Grabbed a bath sheet and knocked on a neighbor's door. Hunter was in school, so Ed, her husband, had to come home and put Henry in his container before she'd come back in the house."

"You and Hunter seem to have a little rapport going."

"He's a great kid. He just likes exotic pets."

"You'd make a terrific mother."

"More like Auntie Mame." She said alluding to the character from the Patrick Dennis novel—a slightly zany woman who lived for the moment and tried to raise her nephew the same way.

He didn't care how she described herself. He hadn't found a word to characterize the many-faceted woman named Jesslyn Owens. She didn't quit or run when her career fell apart. She simply carved out another one. But did her personality have another facet? Could she look so innocent and still be a thief?

Just as Jesslyn had turned her back on big business, he had turned his back on the political arena of Washington for something more tangible. They were more alike than different. But that difference was also important. She loved the city, and he loved the mountains. And he'd seen what could happen when neither could live in the other's world. So why didn't he just tell Mac that the lady was innocent and to look elsewhere? He couldn't. Something about the lady fascinated him. She was tempered steel with a velvet covering and he wanted to spend more time with her. He'd just tell Mac it was going to take a little longer than they originally planned. As the thought crossed his mind that he realized it was the truth. What he really wanted *was* going to take a little longer.

As they walked to her apartment, she pulled out her keys. Deftly, Palladin took them from her and opened the door. He returned the keys to her and waited until she invited him in.

She didn't.

"There's a fund-raiser dinner at the Plaza a week from Friday," he told her. "Would you go with me?"

"What kind of fund-raiser?"

"Political. Mac invited me to meet the man who took his place at the FBI."

"Umm, I don't know . . ."

"Are you a registered voter?"

The question caught her off guard. "Of course!"

"Then, don't you think it's your civic duty to find out how government really works."

Jesslyn laughed. "Are you saying that decisions for the country are made at fund-raisers?"

"More seeds of change are planted at these things than

most people realize. A few new power players will be there. And I want you to meet some of my friends."

Jesslyn looked into his eyes. She bit her lip as she played with the answer in her head. She hated public events, but she wanted to see Palladin. "Okay. I'd like to go."

His face broke into a wide smile that showed strong, white teeth. "I'll pick you up at eight. Here or at the shop?"

"Here."

"Till then."

"Good night, Palladin."

He leaned down and kissed her forehead then brushed her lips with his. Her face tilted upward and the kiss became deeper before Jesslyn pulled away.

"Good night, Jesslyn," he said as he turned and pressed for the elevator.

She turned, opened her door and forced herself not to look at him. She put her coat in the foyer closet. Her mind jumbled with thoughts of the rights and wrongs of getting involved with this man. Not since breaking her engagement had she even considered having a real relationship. She liked safe men—the ones who didn't interfere with her life. She knew in her heart that there was nothing safe about Palladin Rush. So what was she getting herself into? And why couldn't she stop it?

She performed her nightly cleansing ritual and climbed into bed. She drifted off to sleep still wondering if she was getting into more trouble.

Kaliq was still up when Palladin got back to the hotel. "So, how's it going? Found a way to save your ex's bacon?"

Palladin walked over and sat on the sofa. Kaliq turned his wheelchair so he could face him. The wheelchair was black, without armrests and had oversized tilted back wheels. Kaliq preferred to use his hands to operate it, rather than use a motorized wheelchair.

"I don't know what to think."

"Uh oh. Gavin Macklin is not going to like hearing that!"

Palladin ran his hand over his face. "What can I tell you? If you want to know if she's smart enough to pull this off, then the answer's yes."

Kaliq nodded. "But if I'm asking did she do it?"

"I just don't know. I don't think I want to know."

Kaliq and Palladin had been friends since college and never had he seen his friend unsure about anything. For Palladin things were black or white, right or wrong. He'd make a quick decision about something and, sure enough, they would find out his instincts were on the money.

"We know Carolann wouldn't have the brains," Kaliq held up his hands when Palladin's eyes narrowed. "Not for something like this."

Palladin nodded. "You're right. She isn't stupid, but she would never think of all of the little things she'd need to do to protect herself."

"Why did you rule out the sister?"

"Lena was a suburban housewife in Michigan when most of this happened."

"So, my friend, it keeps coming back to Jesslyn Owens."

"My gut feeling says she's innocent, but I don't know if I'm missing something."

Kaliq rolled the chair closer to the sofa. "Or what you're really saying is you're not sure if you're thinking with your brain or another part of your anatomy?"

"Maybe. But if she is guilty, I'll see that she pays the price. That has nothing to do with anatomy and everything to do with what's right."

Kaliq ran his hands over his recently shaven head. "I wouldn't want to be in your shoes, man. That's a tough call. Turning in the lady you're in love with for your country's sake."

"Who said anything about love?"

"Love or whatever. I'm going to get some sleep."

"I invited her to the fund-raiser."

"Because?"

"I want to see how she handles herself with the movers and shakers," Palladin said aloud. And I want to see her again he thought. "Got a date for this thing?"

"No. I want to play observer."

The two men retired for the night.

The shop was crowded on Mondays. People sending little thank you baskets. Next to the "Office Support," the "Thank you" basket was their biggest seller. But Valentine's day was only a couple of weeks off, and that's when things truly got hectic. Jesslyn had already hired a couple of college kids to work in the store and get used to things before the crowds came.

Lena arrived a quarter after nine. "Expecting someone?" she asked as she studied her sister's outfit. The long slender dark blue velvet skirt ended just above the navy, Victorian-style lace up boots and was topped off by a long-sleeved white eyelet blouse. Lena compared it to the black slacks and burnt orange blouse she wore. "Kinda fancy for a day of nothing but work."

"I . . . I just felt like something different today."

"Mmm huh. Sure you did."

Jesslyn felt the heat in her face rise. "Well, you never know what might happen?"

As she said that, the office door opened and they looked up. Shock spread over both their faces as they stared at Carolann.

"What's the big deal?" she said, knowing why they were staring. "I know I'm early, but you don't have to act as if I'm something from a horror movie."

"We . . . hello, Carolann. How are you this morning?" Jesslyn asked.

"I'm just fine. So what's on the agenda?" She hung her mink in the closet. She wore dark slacks and a beige and jade green sweater. Her hair was pulled into a ponytail and held to the nape of her neck with a pearl and diamond clip. Her high-heel shoes made clicking sounds on the maroon terrazzo tile floor.

The women sat at their respective desks in the small office. They went over the previous week's totals and some plans for later in the year. Jesslyn was surprised to see that Carolann was even taking notes. When she first joined them, she'd just say "Whatever you two decide is fine with me."

They scheduled the times when each would manage the store alone. Jesslyn cleared her throat and took a deep breath before she said, "I'd like to leave by five on Friday." The shop was open until seven.

"Oh," said Lena, "got a hot date." Then she looked at Carolann, "Or something," she added.

Carolann's smile vanished. "I guess this means Paladin is still in town."

"Uh . . . yes. He and I are going . . ."

"Spare me the details," Carolann interrupted. "I'll fill in for you."

Lena cast a raised eyebrow look at Jesslyn and shrugged. "I guess that's settled. We'd better go help our staff."

Jesslyn was glad to have a busy day, so she didn't think about the situation she found herself. It was weird, knowing that he'd probably dump her, but she wanted to see Palladin, anyway.

By one in the afternoon, the crowd had eased enough for Jesslyn and Lena to take a lunch break together. They crossed the mall to the Italian restaurant and waited in line for five or ten minutes before they were shown to a seat.

"So, the man still hasn't said anything about running back to his mountain?"

"No, and he wants me to meet his friends."

Jesslyn knew that Lena and her parents shared the same sentiments about Jesslyn forgetting Paul and starting a new relationship. When she'd told her father that the engagement was off, he was elated on one hand but added, "There was a time when that boy would've been horsewhipped for not defending you."

"Ummm." Lena replied.

"What does that mean?"

"When men don't have family, they introduce their girlfriends to their buddies."

"I guess that means we have to double date sometime."

"Funny you should say that, Jeff has been suggesting the same thing. He's actually been concerned about you."

"Why? Never mind. You told him about Paul."

"Yes. And he agreed with Dad."

"Jeff?"

"Well, he can be sensitive some of the time. You just watch Palladin. And if he starts to go bad, treat him like a rotten tomato and put him down the disposal 'cause that's what I plan for Jeff if he starts getting stupid."

By the end of the day, Jesslyn was both pleased and sad that Palladin hadn't dropped by or called. The weather had gone through its usual New York changes. This morning showed a glimpse of spring, then knocked everyone to their knees with a snowstorm. Jesslyn and Lena had closed the shop a half hour early.

The man watched Jesslyn and Lena leave the Trade Center for their respective Manhattan homes. He waited until Carolann emerged from one of the stores.

"Hi, honey," he said, as he blocked her way. "Let me help you with these."

He twisted the large box from her hand and stepped to the side and caught her arm, and led her to a deserted alcove so they could talk. "Don't even think of making a scene," he warned.

"What do you want? Besides the diskette."

"You're going to get us both killed?"

"Or make us both very rich."

"Are you crazy? These people don't have any qualms about picking up the phone and hiring someone to take care of both of us."

Carolann laughed. "Don't be so melodramatic. As long as they don't know where the diskette is, they won't take a chance."

"So what's your plan now?"

"I'll know exactly how to make the trade Saturday morning. Then I'll call you."

"This better work." He said and stalked away.

"It will."

Carolann watched him for a moment, then said, "And then, I'll be rid of you too, Frank."

When Jesslyn got home her answering machine had three messages. One from Jeff reminding her that he thought a double date was in order, which was surprising. The other two were from Frank, but none came from Palladin. She called Frank. He must have some more information about her company.

She got his machine and as she started to leave a message, he picked up the phone.

"Aha! Screening your calls now. Hiding from the Feds, the cops, or a woman?"

"What if I said all of the above?" he joked. "Can you believe this weather? It was so nice this morning then a little rain, now snow."

"Yeah. It's not that great for my business. And speaking of my business, is that why you called?"

Frank's pause confirmed her suspicions. "I guess this guy you're having trouble with has enough connections to cause you trouble. Carolann told me he's been making some threats."

"Do you know him?"

"No. But I was never much for the political thing."

"I wish I knew where that diskette was."

"Would you give it to him?"

"No. I'd give it to the police. Let them give it to him," she said. "I never want to see him again."

"Well, maybe if you found it, you could make some kind of deal with him."

Jesslyn was about to ask Frank why she'd need to make a deal, when the call waiting signal beeped. "Hold on."

"Hello."

"Hello yourself," Palladin's deep voice came through the phone.

"Hold on. I'm on another call." Before he could say anything Jesslyn had pressed the button so she could talk to Frank. "I'm sorry. But I have a really important call now. I'll call you back."

"Jess, don't play around. If you find the diskette just call and tell the man . . ."

"Bye now. Talk to you later." She pressed the button again. "I'm back."

"So how was your day?"

"Started great, ended not so great."

"I guess winter weather can play havoc with any business. Except selling shovels and salt."

"Right. I guess maybe I need to create a gift basket with those items."

"I thought we'd go out for dinner, but you don't sound like you want to brave this weather."

"I don't. But you could come over for dinner and I'll cook."

"You cook?"

"I'm not Martha Stewart or Julia Child, but I do okay in the kitchen."

His voice took on a sexier tone. "I bet you're good in every room in the house. Especially the . . ."

"Hey! Don't get out of hand, or I'll rescind the invitation and you can have room service."

His rich laugh made her smile. "Okay. Can I bring a friend?"

"Absolutely."

"We should be there about eight?"

"Eight's fine. I'll call downstairs and let the concierge know I'm expecting you."

"See you at eight."

As soon as she hung up, she shook her head. "What have I done?" she said aloud. She hurried into the kitchen, opened the cabinet and pulled out a large binder. It was one she hadn't used since she left the corporate world. One filled with quick menus that had been tested and proven successful when she'd had to entertain after a long day at the cosmetic firm. Jesslyn ran to the bedroom and took off her blouse, put on a sweatshirt and returned to the kitchen. She flipped through the pages trying to find something that would dazzle her guests' taste buds.

Eight

Frank's trembling fingers dialed the phone and waited.
"Yeah," came a gruff voice.

"She really doesn't have the disk, Mr. Reynolds. She would have told me."

"I thought you said she trusted you."

"She does. She would have told me if she knew anything."

"Maybe she's beginning to suspect that you had something to do with her early exit from her sweet previous job."

"She doesn't suspect anything. She would have told me that, also."

"Honest to a fault, huh? What about the other one?"

Frank didn't pretend not to know what Hank Reynolds was talking about. His palms grew sweaty.

"Carolann says she doesn't know."

Reynolds laughed. "Not as honest as Ms. Owens, I take it."

"She will always do what is best for her. If she had the disk she'd probably be at your place making a trade."

"We'll see. As soon as I can get that former fed to go back to his mountain, I'll take care of *both* ladies."

"That's not such a good idea . . . I mean . . ."

"Frankie, Frankie, anyone can have an accident these days. *Anyone.*"

The line went dead and Frank Mason sat on the edge of his bed. He looked around at the apartment. All the modern trappings of wealth and power surrounded him in his Trump Tower apartment. Plaques on the wall showing milestones in his career. He'd climbed to the top and now he was perched for a fall. His deal-making abilities had vanished, and in their place was the very real threat to lose it all. He had to find out who had the diskette.

At three minutes to eight the concierge called to tell Jesslyn her guests were on their way up. Jesslyn was putting the finishing touches on the appetizer tray. She whipped off the apron, ran to the bedroom and changed from the sweatshirt to her white blouse. Just as she was buttoning the last button, her bell rang.

"Perfect timing," she said. I just hope the meal is as perfect, she thought. She stopped in the kitchen to turn the stove down so it would keep the food warm.

She opened the door and found herself staring at the men. Both were dressed in jeans and heavy jackets. The man in the wheelchair wore a beret and looked slightly familiar.

"Hi. Come on in," she told them.

"Jesslyn, this is Kaliq Faulkner. Kaliq, Jesslyn Owens."

"An honor, I'm sure," Kaliq said as he took her hand and lightly touched it to his lips.

The men came in and she closed the door. She hoped she hadn't made Kaliq feel uncomfortable by her staring. It wasn't the wheelchair that surprised her—although she was going to kill Palladin for not warning her—but her feeling that she'd seen him before. She took their coats and directed them down the hall to the living room.

She put away their coats, then went in the kitchen and retrieved the appetizer tray. Palladin stood up and took it from her, and placed it on the oversized glass and metal coffee table in the living room.

As she walked back to the kitchen, Palladin couldn't help but notice the gentle sway of her hips under the long skirt. He'd thought she was sexy in the short blue suit she was wearing when they met, but this seemed to be more her style, more of the real person. More of the person he wanted to know better.

When she'd assembled the china cups, silverware and scones she'd warmed in the microwave, she joined them. She noticed that Palladin had moved one of the wicker chairs to the side so Kaliq could maneuver closer to the coffee table.

"You have a charming place, Ms. Owens," Kaliq said.

"Call me Jesslyn and thank you." She sat in the chair nearest the kitchen.

"Then you'll call me Kaliq and you're welcome."

"I'm sorry. You seem familiar. Have we met before?"

"No. Haven't had that pleasure."

Palladin and Kaliq exchanged looks. Could she have remembered him from the first night when he was trying to throw her off balance by frightening her?

"You probably saw him on television. He used to be a hot shot journalist, but now he's found a new mission in life."

"Maybe I did see you on TV. What's your new mission?"

"I run a summer camp for city kids."

She was amazed that both the men worked with children, although their backgrounds didn't seem to fit the image.

From time to time, as they talked, Jesslyn checked on the food. In the meantime, Kaliq made Jesslyn roar with laughter as he told her about sharing a college dorm with Palladin and his adventures as a foreign correspondent.

"I traveled to so many places where I couldn't get a haircut. One day, while I was shaving, it dawned on me that I could do the same to my head just as easily."

"Actually," Palladin added. "He found a bald spot one morning in college and rushed off to the barber and had his head shaved so no one would be able to tell he was going bald."

"Tell the truth about that."

"Hey, it's not my fault you had a little too much to drink and sorta fell asleep at the party."

"Oh, no," she turned to Palladin. "You didn't." The huge grin on his face said otherwise.

"Oh, yes he did. He shaved a little spot in my head and never said a word until three weeks later."

"By that time, I'd gotten so used to the bald look, I just kept it."

"Es la nueva de la noche," came a staccato voice from the bedroom.

The men looked at Jesslyn.

"My clock. You probably just missed it when you came in. It announces the time every hour. And that should tell us it's time to eat."

"Only in Spanish?" Kaliq asked.

"English or Spanish. I prefer Spanish." She directed the men to the dining area while she returned to the kitchen.

The cream-colored dining room was a warm, welcoming room. Palladin gravitated to the love seat positioned on one side of the table and facing the open shelves that housed the cream-colored china on one shelf and the paler shade of cream dishes on another and crystal glasses on still another shelf.

Palladin especially liked the Waterford crystal chandelier that hung over the table. The table was already set as if she was expecting guests any minute.

"Do you entertain a lot?"

"No, not really," Jesslyn said as she took the chair opposite him.

"You have dinner here every night alone," Kaliq asked.

"Of course not. I just don't understand the idea of having 'good china' for guests and eating from cheap dishes if you're alone."

"I agree."

"My Mom used to say that it was better we set the table correctly all the time than to wonder if we were giving a party or having dinner guests."

"So you ate like this, and yet, you didn't learn to cook."

"I never said I didn't learn. I simply chose not to cook anything too creative."

Palladin enjoyed experimenting with foreign recipes. He'd taken a couple of cooking courses the first year away from the Secret Service. He called it his sabbatical. So far, most of the women he dated shared Jesslyn's aversion for kitchen duty. With her sitting across the table, he really didn't care what she'd put in front of him.

For a brief moment, he wished Kaliq wasn't with him, but the thought vanished as quickly as it came. He didn't want to share Jesslyn. At the same time, he wanted his friend's approval. "How big is this place?" Palladin was nearer the window and Jesslyn had removed the chair at the head of the table for Kaliq.

"There are two apartments on each floor, and they run the length of the building. I picked the one with the view of the park."

Palladin had been enjoying the view of Central Park only minutes before. "Didn't I read somewhere that the view was going to cost more?"

"Imagine—just because I can see the park I have to pay a special tax for its upkeep."

While it was a great piece of property, Central Park didn't mean as much as the view he got and his was free of charge.

As he bit into the last of the cranberry scones he commented, "These condos are really designed for kids."

"It's great. Close to museums and one of the best private schools in the city."

"So, how does a single lady end up here."

"I thought I was getting married. Paul, my then fiancé, lived in a tiny apartment so when this one came on the market, we decided it would be perfect."

"You bought it?"

"We bought it. But after . . . he got as far away from me as possible, lest he be tainted by my troubles, I bought him out."

"This decorating scheme doesn't look like a place for couples."

"I gave away everything and started over. That's the best way to do things. Not one little reminder that he was even here," Jesslyn felt the bitterness creep into her voice.

Around the apartment were little porcelain knick-knacks depicting a scene from something Norman Rockwell would have drawn. It was delicate. There were actually little pots of herbs on a shelf, much like the kind he grew. He felt a little like the proverbial bull in a china shop, but he also felt the warmth the whole apartment generated.

Jesslyn let him roam freely around the apartment She loved her place and was sorry she couldn't entertain as much as she would like. She was also glad she'd made the bed and spruced up the apartment, or else she would not have allowed him to wander all over. She got the feeling that he was trying to learn more about her and she wasn't sure she liked that idea.

When he settled on the sofa again and was sipping the coffee she served, he asked, "Why only a two bedroom apartment?"

She understood. How did she plan to have a family if she had only one bedroom.

"In New York it's pretty hard to raise one child . . ."

"I could tell you like kids by the way Hunter talked to you. Seems like you'd want more than one."

"I do . . . But it's better to raise one right than have a bunch and not be able to devote the time they need to their upbringing." Jesslyn paused, then asked Kaliq, "Did Palladin tell you about Hunter?"

"That's the kid who thinks a snake is a pet."

"Look who's talking."

She'd tried to wave off Palladin's attempt to help, but it didn't work. Soon they were almost like a couple entertaining an old friend. "Do you have an exotic pet, too?" Jesslyn asked as she went into the kitchen and brought out a platter of chicken cacciatore.

"It's not a pet, more a member of the family. His name is Namid."

"Namid?"

"Kaliq's falcon," Palladin explained. "His name is Chippewa for Star Dancer."

"But he's not a pet. No, he's helping me teach city kids about endangered species."

Jesslyn had added a tossed salad to the table and a variety of salad dressings. She noticed Kaliq preferred Italian while Palladin stayed with oil and vinegar. Palladin selected a bottle of red wine from her tiny wine rack and opened it so it could breathe.

"Where do you live?"

"Wyoming."

"You live in Wyoming?"

"Don't act so shocked. It's one of the states where the falcon is protected."

"I guess it seems kind of strange for you to go from traveling all over the world to settling in Wyoming."

"Who's taking care of this falcon?"

"My son, Brett," he said, then added. "His mother died a couple of years ago."

They drank the wine, talked some more about Wyoming and the art of falconry.

"You must bring her to visit me, old buddy."

Palladin nodded. He knew that Kaliq was really saying he believed that Jesslyn was innocent as he invited very few people to his home.

They spent the rest of the meal getting to know each other and Jesslyn learned that Kaliq would be attending the fund-raiser with them. Shortly before midnight, the men left. Kaliq volunteered to ring for the elevator as Palladin lingered to say good night privately. What he really wanted was to say goodbye to his friend and spend what was left of the night making love to Jesslyn.

He couldn't believe how fast the time had gone. He'd watched Jesslyn be the perfect hostess. He'd even forgotten his mission for a while—just for a while. He still wanted to find out about the industrial espionage. His reason had changed. He wanted to put it behind him so he could see Jesslyn without any ulterior motives, at least not the kind that wanted to put her behind bars. Kaliq kissed her hand and was waiting by the elevator.

"He likes you."

"Are you surprised?"

"A little. He takes a while to open up most of the time."

"Well, didn't he like Carolann?"

"No. He didn't. He doesn't bite his tongue with me."

Jesslyn's eyes widened. She'd assumed that Kaliq would like anyone Palladin chose, and if he didn't, he wouldn't say anything. Jesslyn recalled that she and Carolann weren't friends until after Carolann was divorced.

She walked him to the door and turned her face up to accept a polite kiss. Instead, his mouth came down on her, and he held her tightly until she felt the heat rising from his body. Then he released her.

"Till Friday," she said. It was a way of telling him she'd be too busy to see him before then.

He wanted to put Kaliq in a cab and spend the night, but that wasn't going to happen. "You're quite a woman, Jesslyn Owens. I'm going to enjoy getting to know you even better. Now lock the door. Even buildings with guards need locks."

She closed the door and waited a moment

"I'm not leaving till I hear the lock."

She laughed softly and snapped the lock into place.

As she put the dishes in the dishwasher, she felt terrific and understood how much she'd missed entertaining. She decided to do it more often.

The next day Jesslyn and Lena managed to have dinner together after closing the shop. Jesslyn told her about having Palladin and Kaliq as guests for dinner.

"Go girl!" Lena encouraged.

"Kaliq's very nice . . ."

"Don't. No matchmaker things for me. I like Jeff."

"But he's not . . ."

"Husband material? Anyone can see that. I'm not looking for a husband."

Jesslyn was secretly glad Lena recognized Jeff's flaws that they talked about other things.

"Carolann is becoming a real asset." Lena announced.

"Umm. So what did she do for you?"

"Not fair. I can think good things about my partner."

Jesslyn raised one eyebrow and stared at her sister, who finally confessed.

"She says she'll work this weekend so Jeff and I can go to Atlantic City."

It was amazing. The World Trade Center could be the busiest place in New York one minute, and as the commuters scattered to New Jersey and the financial sections closed, it became a ghost town.

"Did you see the papers on that new Senator Gary's campaign?" Lena asked.

"Yeah. I might run into him at the fund-raiser?"

"Well, don't talk about the diskette unless he brings

it up, and then just be vague. Hank Reynolds is enough of a nightmare. I can't believe I'm suddenly the one who remembers what goes on with the business. Hello!"

"Oh, yes. I hope we don't get too many customers like Reynolds. He's so picky that he insisted on being here when we put the basket together then called to say a computer diskette was missing." She paused. "The jerk! I guess Carolann talked to him. I haven't heard another word."

"Can you believe the change in her?"

"No. I'm not sure it will last."

"Cynic. Well, I think it's great."

"That's only because she's doing something nice for you and Jeff. Come to think of it, I haven't seen him for a while."

"He's on assignment." Lena told her. "Taking pictures of a wedding."

"I thought he'd quit his job and was just enjoying life."

"He's doing it as a favor. But he'll be back."

"Speaking of favors, I can't wait to see what you have to do for Carolann. She told me once that she has a little notebook and when she wants something bad to happen to someone she writes it down. I bet she has another little notebook with a scorecard. You owe her now."

Lena groaned. "I never thought about that part."

Frank was not having a good day. He turned the envelope over and over, wishing he didn't have to go. He'd been told that he was expected to show up and lend his support to Senator Gary. The last thing he wanted to do was party with the rich and powerful while he hadn't found the diskette. But he had no choice. It wasn't an invitation, but a direct order. Even he'd started worrying about what was on the missing diskette. He needed a date. He picked up the phone and dialed. He was about to launch plan B.

Kaliq and Palladin were having a good day. They'd dropped Palladin's tux off at the cleaners and rented a tux for Kaliq. He'd sworn never to wear what he called a "penguin suit" again, but now said he didn't want to miss this night for anything. Kaliq and Palladin were getting out of the cab when Mac and Skip met them.

"Where have you been all day?" Mac asked. "We have to talk, now."

Once in the hotel suite, Kaliq insisted on joining the conversation.

"What have you found out about Jesslyn Owens?"

"That she's innocent, Mac," Kaliq said.

"Really?" Sarcasm dripped from the word.

"Really," said Palladin.

"Is that where you've been all day? Finding out she's innocent?"

"I know it's not what you wanted to hear," Palladin told him. "But the truth is the lady isn't part of whatever is going on."

"Great," Skip said. "Carolann is innocent, Jesslyn is innocent, we already ruled out the sister. So who is the guilty party?"

"I don't know . . ." Palladin began.

"Then how do you know everyone's innocent?" Skip demanded.

"Don't interrupt me again," Palladin turned from Skip and spoke only to Mac. "I don't know who's guilty yet.

But you can count on me. I'll find out. I'll give you irrefutable proof, and then I want you to leave me alone the next time you have a problem."

"How long will it take?"

"I'll know after the fund-raiser. I want to meet this Senator Gary, who seems to be in the middle of the mess. I got in late last night and I had to go out early this morning. I'm tired. I'm going to take a shower and get some sleep." Palladin started for the bedroom. "Oh, by the way, my date for Friday will be Jesslyn Owens. Be nice to her."

Before Mac or Skip could say anything, he had closed the bedroom door and neither of them dared to open it. Mac turned to Kaliq.

"What the hell is going on?"

"A phenomenon. In the middle of a New York winter, a glacier melted."

Nine

Palladin stepped under the stinging hot shower. He was shocked by his actions. He'd actually told Mac he was bringing Jesslyn. A woman he'd only shared a few kisses with had made him fight with his long-time friend and mentor. What was he thinking about? Dumb question. He was thinking about Jesslyn Owens. The way she laughed, her voluptuous figure on such a petite frame. He'd wanted to protect her almost from the time they'd met. It was one of the reasons he'd asked Kaliq to meet her. Was his desire to protect her simply that he found her attractive, fascinating and he wanted to go to bed with her? Was he working on intuition, or letting his feelings of wanting her mask the clues he needed to solve this case for Mac.

In the few days they'd been together, she'd thrown him off balance, shattered his usual even temper. Not only had he admitted feelings for Jesslyn that he'd never had for *any* other woman, but he'd let those feelings convince him that she was being set up. Once he'd decided she was innocent there wasn't anything or anyone who could stop him from proving it. She'd turned him on so powerfully he actually felt pain when he thought about pushing her away. He wanted her too much. He'd forgotten all his rules. Now that he had he wanted to throw them out and make up a whole new set or have none at all.

For one night, he'd dropped his icy veneer and the human side of his emotions had told him they could have pleasure and contentment as never before. He wanted to be part of her life. That's why he'd have to stay close and protect her while he found out what was really happening.

He was sure she was being set up. He was also sure that someone could put a good case of circumstantial evidence together and ruin her life. No one could withstand two charges of industrial espionage, even if one hadn't been proven.

On Friday morning, when Jesslyn arrived at work, she was greeted by Carolann and Lena.

"We decided that we don't want you around here today," Lena said.

"Yeah. Go get glamorous for tonight," Carolann added. Then shoved gift certificates in Jesslyn's hand.

She opened them and smiled. Her partners had arranged a day of beauty. A limousine was waiting to whisk her off to Naomi Sims for hair, nails and make-up and then the driver would take her home while she dressed. Palladin, Kaliq and Kaliq's date would come to her house and the limo would return to take them to the Plaza.

"I want my little sister to feel like Cinderella tonight," Lena said. "But just so you don't turn into a pumpkin, take these along."

Jesslyn opened the brown bag her sister thrust at her and laughed. It was a box of crackers.

"Yeah, Cinderella can't get carsick tonight." Carolann said.

* * *

At six o'clock, the limo driver pulled up in front of Jesslyn's door. She felt a little strange with the high fashioned hair style, manicured nails, and what she felt was a pound of make up on her face. She carried two packages from Saks Fifth Avenue.

She thanked the people she passed who commented on how nice she looked. She felt like another person. This wasn't something she wanted to do every day, but once in awhile, it might be nice to feel pampered.

She put a high-protein mix in the blender and turned it on for a minute while she searched for and found a straw. She wasn't going to take the chance of ruining her lipstick, but she was absolutely starving. Jesslyn removed the dress from the bag and laid it across the bed.

She took a bath, but left the door open so the steam filtered through the house and settled on her body for the few minutes she was in the tub.

Carefully, she powdered her body and added her perfume, then went into the bedroom. She slipped on delicate white lingerie, white pearlized stockings, stepped into the white boots that laced up but looked like the old-fashioned buttoned shoes. She carefully put on the Oscar de la Renta's pearl and crystal embroidered silk organza tunic with its silk chiffon skirt. She whirled in front of her mirror. For a brief moment, she wondered if she should wear something that made her look like a bride.

The concierge called to say that her guests were on their way up. Jesslyn took a deep breath and opened the door. Palladin and Kaliq were laughing with a tall, beautiful woman with tawny skin. She wore a black tuxedo jacket, open to the waist but pulled together enough to only hint that she was topless underneath. Her straight black skirt reached her ankles and complemented the high heeled black sandals. She carried her full length sable coat over her arm.

It's a good thing we're going to be in a limo. Otherwise our feet would be soaked by the time we get there, Jesslyn thought.

Palladin saw her first. He was startled for a moment, and then a slow smile crept across his face. She was beautiful. A few tendrils escaped from the curls that were pulled back from her face. Her mouth painted a dark burgundy that emphasized the full lips. He was speechless.

Fortunately his friend was not. "We must be living right, old buddy, to be blessed with two such beautiful women tonight."

Palladin found his voice. "I'm not sure. I think we've died and gone to heaven."

"Hi, I'm Trisha Terrance."

"Jesslyn Owens, would you like to come in for a drink?"

"Sounds terrific."

"Pardon us, ladies," Kaliq apologized. "In the company of such beauty, we've forgotten our manners."

They only stayed in the apartment for a quick champagne toast to the night ahead and they were off to the Plaza.

For Jesslyn, it was exciting and, at the same time, not something she could ever be part of on a daily basis. She didn't know how men and women coped with political mates. The smiles that must have made their jaws hurt, the fake kissy face greetings. The worst were the endless speeches about how "new blood" was needed to put America back on track. She was surprised that they were seated so close to the speakers.

Jesslyn watched as a tall, distinguished looking man with white hair grabbed Palladin in a bear hug, the kind you reserve for family and close friends.

"Mac, this is Jesslyn Owens," Palladin said over the dull roar of the crowd. "Darling, my old boss, Gavin Macklin."

The man took her outstretched hand and shook it limply. "Ms. Owens."

"Mr. Macklin."

"Call me Mac. I guess Palladin will be bringing you to Washington," he said.

"Why?"

"A new administration will be coming in. Palladin might want his old job back."

"Now Mac, you don't even know *if* the administration is going to change. And I don't want my old job back."

Mac's eyes never left Jesslyn's face. "You never know."

His grin seemed forced to Jesslyn. She had the distinct feeling that the man didn't want her anywhere near Palladin.

"No. You don't," she agreed. Mac didn't seem to notice that, while he suggested that she call him by his first name, she had not reciprocated with hers.

Mac rushed off to shake the right hands, schmooze with the right people and she saw his grin was at least genuine. He was playing the conquering hero, and the crowd seemed to love it.

She wondered why he was so phony with her and not

with other people. Perhaps he was a friend of Carolann's and not ready to accept anyone else.

Jesslyn noticed Kaliq and Trisha seemed to be mingling well. Some of his colleagues must have been still on the political beat.

As the dancing began, she was startled to see Frank Mason. He was at a table with a lovely blonde woman, and his red hair clashed slightly with her pink dress. He spotted Jesslyn and waved.

The night wore on and Jesslyn had to make a trip to the ladies room. As she was returning to the table, she felt someone catch her hand. She turned and found herself facing Senator Woodrow Gary.

She was startled at first because he resembled Gavin Macklin. Both men were tall with shocking white hair.

"Ms. Owens. I'd like to speak with you," Senator Gary drawled. While he represented Illinois, he had grown up in North Carolina and still bore the accent.

She tried to pull her hand away but his grip tightened. "Please. Just a moment of your time."

Senator Gary was only forty-five, but his white hair and the lines around his eyes and mouth made him look much older. He led her to an alcove where they could speak without screaming.

Jesslyn stopped trying to twist away from him. "Let me go." The words were soft, but the meaning clear. He couldn't afford to have a scene here. Now. He released her hand.

"I'm not sure what happened, but I understand a diskette was misplaced that was sent to me from your shop."

Over his shoulder, she saw Hank Reynolds standing by the door watching her.

"I don't have the diskette."

"I'm sure you don't. So, I just want to say Mr. Reynolds was out of line and he won't be bothering you any more."

She looked at him for a moment. "And what's the punch line."

"That if the diskette ever turns up you'll mail it to me," he handed her a card.

"Of course, Senator. I want you to get everything that belongs to you."

"Is there a problem here?" Palladin's deep voice surprised her. She hadn't realized he was standing behind her, but she was completely grateful.

"Not at all, Mr. Rush," the Senator said.

"It's been a while, sir. I didn't think you'd remember me."

"Oh, I remember you. Macklin and I may have been on opposite sides about FBI issues, but he had good people around him. Too bad you quit."

"It was time for a change."

"You say that now, but if Mac decides to toss his hat in the ring for Congress, you'll probably campaign for him."

"He'd have to run from Virginia. Why would that bother you?"

"We'd probably come head to head on some issues."

"Then I wish you luck. Mac can be a tough opponent."

"I've been known to be a bulldog about the things I want as well," he nodded and walked away.

His statement seemed more like a warning or a threat. Palladin caught Jesslyn's arm and guided her back to their table.

"What was that all about?"

"Senator Gary told me Hank Reynolds would not bother me again."

"I wonder why?"

She related the happenings. "He was quite gracious about it," she finished. "He said that if I ever found the diskette I should mail it to him."

"I'd sure like to find out what's on it."

"Does that mean you'll rejoin the FBI and relentlessly pursue the lost diskette," Jesslyn teased.

"No way. I'm not that curious."

"You know," she said. "When I first turned around I thought he was Mac."

"Yeah. There was a joke about that," Palladin said.

"Really?"

"That they were more alike than they are different."

"I agree."

Palladin looked down at her. "How long do you want to hang around?"

"I'm ready when you are."

"Then let's find Kaliq and his lady and get out of here."

"His lady? You think it's serious?"

"Yeah. She seems really interested, and it would be an interesting match. He told me she's a chef. She recently left a job at an inn out west."

"They might be neighbors."

"You might be right."

"Is Mac really going to run for office."

"He didn't say. But the Senator thinks he is. I think I saw your friend Frank."

"I don't know why. He wasn't very political at Egyptian Enchantment."

Palladin didn't respond. He made a mental note to get Skip to check out Frank a little more. His gut instinct said that no one climbed the corporate ladder without being political.

As they left the Plaza about thirty minutes later, Kaliq and Trisha asked to be dropped off at the Peninsula first.

Jesslyn didn't say anything when they arrived at her place and Palladin tipped the driver and dismissed him. She waved at the concierge and she and Palladin got in the elevator.

At her door once again, he took her keys and opened the door. Jesslyn felt awkward. It had been a long time since she'd reached this stage of intimacy with a man.

She turned on the lights, hung their coats in the closet, including the long tuxedo coat and walked into the kitchen.

"Would you like a cup of tea?"

"I'd prefer a glass of wine."

"Of course. Red or white?"

"White."

"Es la una de la manaña," came a staccato voice.

"I love your clock."

"I know it sounds crazy, but I couldn't resist it."

He took the bottle of Berringer's Zinfandel she retrieved from the refrigerator and opened it while she got the glasses. He looked around the small kitchen.

"This is nice," he said. "I didn't get a chance to look too closely before you kept running me out of here."

"You were a guest. Guests are not allowed in the kitchen."

"So, now that I'm no longer a guest, tell me about this," he indicated an almond colored antique, claw-foot stove. "How do you cook on it."

"Take a closer look."

They sipped the wine while he took her advice.

He laughed when he found out that it was a modern gas range built to look like an antique. "I'd like to try it out one day."

"You cook?"

"Yeah. You're not the only one who can whip up a mouth-watering meal."

"Actually, I only cook for guests. I stick with the basic food groups."

His eyebrows knitted together as he silently asked for an explanation.

"Eat in, take out, canned and frozen. But my mother made us learn to cook one quick, easy meal. You were lucky I had the ingredients in the house."

"Well, I'll have to do something about your eating habits while your mother is away," he said softly.

She felt the heat rise to her face as he turned to her. "I need you to tell me the truth about something."

"Sure."

"I know you didn't want Carolann to become my partner."

"That was before I met you."

"I know. But someone is investigating my company and I want to know if it was you."

"So you think that I'm trying to romance you through an investigation. Do you have anything to hide?"

"No. Do you?"

"No." The lie almost choked him.

"Could you find out who and why?"

"Probably."

"Will you?"

"Yes," he promised. "And what if you don't like the answers?"

"You don't have to like the truth. Why are you agreeing to find out? What do *you* really want?"

With cat-like speed, he pulled her into his arms. This

was one section of his life where he could be totally honest. "I really want *you.*"

His lips brushed hers a couple of times then his caressing tongue gently pushed apart her lips. A searing flame flashed through her body. It darted through her bloodstream, filling every cell of her body with want and need.

With a groan, Palladin swept her up into his arms. Somehow, she managed to direct him to her bedroom. He tossed her on the bed and came down beside her. He gently helped her out of the silky tunic and skirt. He hung them over a stuffed chair near the bed. He stretched out on the bed beside her while she turned on the soft lighting of her bedside lamp. She felt his hot fingers exploring through her satin bra and panties.

He kept one arm around her as he rolled on his back and began tearing at the tiny buttons on his tuxedo shirt. Once it was open he took her hand and rubbed it down his smooth chest. Then he turned so his body was touching hers.

He covered her face with kisses, then her neck and her breasts. She felt slightly dizzy, but not from the wine. It was from being with Palladin. Here. Now.

"I can't seem to get enough of you," he murmured against her ear, his breath hot and moist. "I've been hungry for you since the night we met."

She could feel his need, different, but just as desperate as her own.

Their breath mingled and the hot sensation of mutual desire spread through them as they lay on the bed.

He explored her earlobe, trailing his tongue downward to the ticklish spot at her neck. That brought giggles from her. He liked the sound and repeated the motion.

Jesslyn trembled and her fingers threaded though the thick dreads as waves of pleasure washed over her just from being body to body.

She felt his body harden and bulge against her and she wanted more. She'd never responded like this before—so quick, so wanton. So out of control that she was willing to say anything, just as long as he kept making her feel on the edge of the unknown for her. She was helpless in her desire. She shifted so she could see his face. His deep chocolate eyes, bright with desire and just as helpless in his as she was in hers. She wanted him, violently, illogically, totally.

She looked at him again and felt proud about the longing she'd created for him.

"I want to make love to you," he whispered urgently. "But I'm not sure if we need more time before we . . ."

"I'm sure."

He inhaled sharply. "Are you ready for this? Tell me now, while I can still leave."

"Yes. I want you."

"What if . . ." he drew a deep breath as her fingers traced the open V of his shirt. "I might not be the best thing in your life right now."

"I don't care."

"What if it's only for one night?"

"Then let's make it the best night either of us have ever had."

He moved suddenly, easily until he was sitting next to her. The muted light from the lamp on the nightstand created unusual patterns across the ceiling.

"This better not be a dream," she grew hot with embarrassment as Palladin chuckled. She'd meant it as a thought, but voiced it loud enough for him to hear.

"No dream could be this good," he told her as he peeled off his shirt.

He caught her hands when she tried to undress herself. "Let me."

She relaxed as he kissed her as he removed an item of clothing. Gone were her white silk panties, garter belt, bra and nylons. She was completely naked by the time he started removing his clothes as he knelt on the bed beside her. His eyes never left hers, even when he fumbled with the buckle of his belt. She turned to him as he asked. "Are you as nervous as I am?"

"You're not nervous."

"No? Then why can't I get this damn belt off."

"You're not nervous. You just need help." She sat up and swiveled around and pulled her legs under her. She pushed his hands away and undid the buckle as she looked at him. She put her arms around his neck. "Do you realize this is the only time we're face to face." She commented about the difference in their height when standing.

"Well, there is one other time . . ."

He stripped off his slacks and briefs in the same motion and reached for her. Suddenly, they were sprawled on the bed and he rolled so she could be on top and not concerned about his weight the way she was about his height.

Her breasts were crushed against the hard plane of his chest. His face was shadowed but his dark eyes glittered in the darkness and mesmerized her with the raw hunger she saw in them.

Jesslyn inched toward him and her thighs brushed his, and she felt the hard bulge of his arousal pressed against her. She froze.

"Come on, Jess," he panted. "You call all the shots."

First, his hands caressed her breasts until they hardened into throbbing peaks. She closed her eyes.

Then she gasped, and her eyes flew open in shock as his mouth replaced his thumbs between her breasts and began trailing down over her ribs, creating rivulets of pulsing heat that flowed through her body. His lips exciting her beyond bearing, and she began to writhe helplessly. She pushed her body upward.

"Easy," he whispered, his tongue teasing her with exquisite skill. She moaned, and he backed to one side, his bent knee pushing her thighs apart.

Her center was a flaming frenzy of need where throbbing heat was building, and she didn't want to lessen the tension that went along with this fire.

His voice came from a distance, velvet soft and tinged with pain. "I can't wait any longer, sweetheart."

Jesslyn closed her eyes and waited, her body twitching and ready. She moved her thighs restlessly, trying to ease the hot ache deep inside her.

He entered her slowly, pushing with gentle insistence against her tight muscles. She could feel herself opening, swallowing him inch by hot inch, until he filled her completely. She moaned and arched against him urging him with words and movements, raking her nails along his sides as she tried to absorb him fully.

Palladin's muscles strained as he thrust into her over and over, until they finally collapsed in ecstasy. Before she fell asleep she heard him say, "Jess, I swear it's never been this good."

"Palladin?"

He heard the question mark in the one whispered word and he almost let his guard down when he looked into her warm brown eyes. Huddled close like spoons, with her head on his chest. She had no idea what she was doing to him, nestled against his groin, showing how much she trusted him.

She had wanted tonight to be different. Her life was finally coming together. She had a flourishing business and a terrific man in her life. Why was there still a frisson of fear twisting through her? What could go wrong?

Ten

Contentment seeped through Palladin Rush as he watched Jesslyn sleep. He'd forgotten all his rules with her. Mac said she was guilty. The evidence strongly suggested that she was guilty. But, for the first time Palladin, was listening entirely to his heart. And that said she was innocent. Now he just had to prove it.

The digital clock by Jesslyn's bed brightly proclaimed it was a little after three in the morning. He'd slept through her other clock's hourly proclamation of the time. He wanted to go back to sleep, but that was impossible. Turning on the light on the night stand, he looked around the bedroom. He hadn't paid much attention the night before. Almost everything in the apartment was old-fashioned, except for the clocks and apparently the suit that she was wearing the first time they met.

The sleigh bed had beautiful white lace covers and brightly covered pillows as accents. Even the huge armoire on the other side of the room seemed to be from another time. Yet he could feel the warmth and love that had gone into her decorating. Despite the difference in the rustic style of his place, he felt at home here.

But he had to get back to the hotel, and for the first time for Palladin Rush, the hardest thing was getting up and going home. He didn't want to wake her, but there was no other choice. He slipped from the bed, gathered his clothes and padded naked into the bathroom that adjoined her bedroom. Her medicine cabinet held an assortment of toiletries, and he found a new plastic shower cap, a bar of unscented soap and another surprise: a heated towel rack.

The cold water pounding against his flesh didn't relieve or change the aches of wanting to climb back into her bed and make love to her again. Still, he had to concentrate on getting her out of whatever this industrial espionage case was and hoping she forgave him for not telling her his original reason for being her constant companion these past days.

Jesslyn had awakened the minute he left the bed, but only opened her eyes enough to see what was going on. She'd enjoyed watching his tight buttock muscles and his long legs as he disappeared into the bath. They were like the rest of him—large, hard, perfect.

She rolled over on her back and looked up at the ceiling. This felt so right, but she knew it wouldn't last. Jesslyn got up and put her robe on. Sooner or later, he'd go back to his mountain. Could passion sustain a long distance relationship?

The door opened and he stepped out fully dressed. The light from the bathroom framing his body.

"I've got to go."

"I know. I'll lock you out."

He retrieved his coat from the foyer closet and they said good-night at the door. He kissed her forehead, knowing if he touched her mouth he wouldn't leave. Then he waited patiently on the other side of the door until he heard the bolt click into place.

* * *

Palladin wasn't surprised to find Kaliq waiting up for him. He was channel surfing.

"How was your date?" Palladin asked.

"It went quite well. No, I don't want to talk about it."

"Not even with your best friend?"

"Not even," Kaliq grinned. "So where do we go from here?"

Palladin shrugged off his coat, tossed it on a chair, and slumped down on the sofa opposite Kaliq's wheelchair.

"She's innocent."

"I believe you. But why pursue a relationship with your ex-wife's partner? That's asking for too much trouble and the fallout could be major."

"She's innocent."

"Fine. Then do we send Carolann to prison? Someone engineered this whole thing, and who else but one of the women could have done it?"

"I don't know. Jesslyn's too straight. Lena talks too much, and Carolann isn't that smart."

"So what's your conclusion?"

"That someone with a lot of power is pulling the strings."

Kaliq rolled over to him. "That could be the biggest problem of all."

"How so?"

"He's seen you with the women and probably had you checked out."

Palladin pulled the band holding down his hair and ran his hands through his hair. "Then he's playing me, and I don't know who he is. But I plan to find out."

The knock on the door startled both men. Palladin

walked to the door while Kaliq positioned himself so when the door was open he couldn't be seen.

"Who is it?"

"Mac."

"Damn!" came Palladin's whispered expletive.

The men looked at each other in surprise and Palladin opened the door. Mac's face was red from the cold and his eyes were blue crystals. He stormed past Palladin into the middle of the room. He and Kaliq looked at each other without speaking and Mac began to pace. "What the hell were you doing tonight? You're supposed to be gathering evidence to help Carolann, but you seem to be more interested in having an affair with Jesslyn Owens."

Palladin closed the door and strolled over to the sofa and sat down.

"Nice to see you, too. Why don't you sit down and we'll talk."

"No. I'll talk. I want you off the case. I want you to go home."

"I thought we agreed to let me call the shots on this one."

"Not when you start cozying up to a suspect. I wanted you to search her office. Instead you take her out to dinner."

Palladin's eyes narrowed. "You having me followed?"

"No. Of course not. Someone was following her."

"Then pull them off."

"I can't do that."

"Mac. You can do anything you want. Pull them off, immediately."

"Not when you're losing sight of the goal."

Palladin whirled and faced Mac. His black eyes flashing

and his tone murderous. "What is the goal, Mac? Finding out the truth or putting Jesslyn Owens in prison?"

"That's just what I mean. You've lost sight of the goal which was to get Carolann out of this mess."

"I always thought the truth would set the innocent free. You used to trust my instincts."

"That was before you started screwing . . ."

"Finish that sentence and you're a dead man."

Palladin had become as dangerous as a cornered wolf. Never had the men disagreed so openly. Even during the times he'd openly defied Mac—going in after Kaliq, leaving the Service, getting a divorce—they had been civil to each other. It had been more like a discussion than a fight. But tonight, the men had become adversaries. Tonight Palladin had threatened the man he considered a second father.

"Something else is happening here," Palladin continued. "I *will* find it. Working with you or alone."

Mac recognized it as the threat and promise that it was. "May I use your phone?" He waited for Palladin's nod before making his call.

"Jesslyn Owens is my kind of woman," Kaliq said. "For a friend, of course," he added as Palladin glared at him, but that only made him laugh, showing strong white teeth in his umber face. Breaking through the tension that had fallen over the room.

Mac finished his call. "Looks as if you have another problem," he told Palladin. "Seems that someone tried to break into your place. The security company has been trying to contact you all day. They went out and checked. Nothing. It's happened a couple of times. Lucky your place is so isolated."

Palladin glanced at his watch. "I'd better get back. I'll call Jesslyn at the shop later."

"What?" Mac barked. "You have to tell her everything now."

"I told you before, my man," Kaliq said. "But you didn't listen. You need to get someone up here with a mop."

"What?" Mac barked.

"To clean up all this water 'cause your *Glacier* melted."

Mac slammed his fist on the wall. "I don't need this now. And one of these days I'm going to wipe that grin off your face, Faulkner." He turned and stormed out, Kaliq's laughter echoing in his ears.

It was too late to call Jesslyn, but he would do that from his home. Within the hour, he and Kaliq had checked out of the hotel, rented a car, and were en route to Palladin's house. Although he was sure no one had gained entry, he needed to check things out for himself. He also needed to talk about his relationship with Jesslyn. Lies didn't work. He probably needed to tell her the truth and help her get out of whatever was going on with her company.

He and Mac would never be the same again. He hoped that the breech would heal enough for them to be friends. How had it happened? How had one tiny woman held his heart captive so quickly? He couldn't believe he'd gone after his ex-wife's partner and fought Mac to keep her. Yet somewhere in the back of his mind, he knew it couldn't last. Nothing for him ever was forever.

The next morning Jesslyn practically danced around the apartment while she dressed. For the first time in months, she searched her closet for something that was business-like and sexy at the same time.

She settled on a silk jacquard two-piece dress with a multicolored floral top and a long purple skirt that complemented her dark skin. As usual, she kept her make-up to a minimum dusting of powder, a few strokes of mascara, and a plum lipstick.

The day went smoothly as Carolann called in sick and Jesslyn assumed it was to be with her mystery man. The receptionist volunteered to handle the deliveries and Lena pitched in with customers. Even Jeff, back from his photo shoot, manned the phones for a couple of hours. Business was brisk, and it was lunchtime before Jesslyn caught her breath. Nothing escaped Lena's sharp eyes when it came to men and women.

"So, how was it?"

"Lena, I don't know what you're talking about, and if I did, I wouldn't tell you."

"That good, huh." She tossed out as she lined up baskets for delivery. Jesslyn's silence didn't disturb her sister's relief and joy that she was over Paul.

"Want to double tonight or are you still into that want to be alone scene?"

"Palladin didn't say anything. Let me see if he's free and we'll join you."

She looked up the number and dialed the hotel and asked for him. She listened and hung up. Her voice trembled, "He checked out last night."

Lena started to say something, but Jesslyn held up her hand. "I'm going to take a walk around. I'll be back in a little while."

All of her life, Jesslyn had to be alone to work through any hurts or problems. Today was no exception. She needed to push it to the back of her mind, as she always did and then take little bits and pieces of it out and deal with it until the pain had been diffused. She'd done that when her career died, when Paul left and now she'd do this with Palladin.

Only this time it was worse than Paul's betrayal. She was so sure that Palladin meant the things he said. That what they had for one night was good. So why wouldn't he want more of the same passion she'd felt?

The noonday crowd mobbed the stores, and Jesslyn found herself spending a great deal of time in the Borders bookstore trying to find something to keep her mind from jumping to conclusions about Palladin checking out of his hotel and Carolann calling in sick. Nothing worked. She couldn't handle it if they got back together now.

If something else happened, why hadn't he called her. She dredged up all the negative signs of a one night stand. He'd never let her come to his hotel. He insisted on picking her up or meeting her someplace. She'd been the one to force the issue and she'd been the one who said it didn't matter when he told her that he didn't believe they were doing the right thing. She'd insisted that she knew what she was doing.

It was after one when she got back to the shop. Lena stood there patting her foot.

"It's about time you showed up. Your boyfriend's called three times already . . . I took the first one, but I let Kathy answer the others."

"What did he say? Why wouldn't you talk to him again?"

The phone rang in the office interrupting her. "You answer it and tell him I said I'm sorry," Lena said and shooed Jesslyn to answer it.

The light was flashing on her private line and she picked it up. "Jesslyn Owens."

"You tell me you're a hard-working business owner and then you take a two hour lunch," came the low teasing voice of Palladin Rush.

"I took a walk around the mall. Where are you?"

"Home. Pennsylvania. But you already knew that I wasn't in New York, didn't you."

"I called you this morning and they said you checked out last night."

He paused. "I can understand you being upset because I didn't call you. I told you. I . . . care . . . about you. How could you believe I'd do that?"

She was flustered now as she twisted the phone cord around her fingers. He sounded so gentle on the phone and she'd expected the worse. "Do what?"

"Treat you like a one night stand." He tried to tone down the anger.

She didn't want to talk about it, but that was exactly how she felt when the clerk said he'd checked out.

"I wasn't expecting you to call me so early. I thought I'd give you time to get to work and then call."

He waited for her to say something. Give him a clue. Was he forgiven? Was it over? No. He wouldn't let himself even start thinking that because he wasn't going to let her out of his life. She was his whether she knew it or not.

"I'm sorry," she whispered. "I guess I thought you'd run for cover."

"I'm never going to run from you. I . . ." He stopped. He'd almost said the three words that would doom their chances. If he told her what he was feeling now and then explained his original mission, she wouldn't know what to believe.

His voice dropped. "I have to see you again. Soon. How about my place this weekend?"

With all her heart, she wanted to say yes, but her head overruled her heart and she refused. "I uh . . . I can't leave the shop. My sister is supposed to go away this weekend and I'm not sure Carolann wants to handle things alone just yet. Why did my sister want me to tell you she's sorry."

"Because she should be."

"Why?"

"I called to explain why we had to leave New York . . ."

"We?" she asked coldly.

"My friend. Kaliq came with me. Someone tried to break in, and the security people insisted I check things out."

Heat rushed to her face as again she'd jumped to the wrong conclusion. "Was anything stolen?"

"No. Probably some kids from one of the neighboring towns. I don't think they were trying to steal anything."

"Just trying to find out how the man on the mountain lives?"

"Probably. But I'm going to have to take care of a few things. Sorry I had to cut my visit short. "Tell your sister I'll make a deal with her. If she trades weekends with you, I won't tell you what she said." If she was a captive audience, she might be willing to listen to his side of the story. She had to listen. She had to give him another chance. They'd been apart for only a few hours and he missed her to the point of almost telling her how much he wanted her.

"You think she'd go for that?"

"Try it. I'll call you later."

"I should be home by eight. I'll see if I can get Lena to change her plans, but don't count on it."

"I have a very nice guest room," he added when she'd paused too long. Even though he felt it would kill him to have her so close and sleep alone. But he'd do it.

"Okay, I'll rent a car and drive up." She didn't want him to think she was afraid to be alone with him. She wanted to feel him next to her just as the previous night.

"Then see if you can leave early Friday afternoon. I don't want you on the road too late."

"I'll call you. And Palladin . . ." She knew it was time to stop hedging her bets.

"Yeah?"

"If I can make it . . . I don't really need the guest room."

"Don't say anything," Lena pleaded as soon as she saw Jesslyn emerge from her office. Lena was alone, as Kathy was out making another delivery.

"How could you?" Jesslyn played the outraged sister for all it was worth.

"Well I was trying to add two and two and got zero. Is everything okay with you two."

"No thanks to you."

"Oh, come on. You thought the same thing. I mean Carolann wasn't here. He wasn't here, and I thought he was trying to tell you that she was with him."

"You didn't say *that!*"

"Is he really angry?"

"Well, he said that he'd let you make it up to him, but it'll cost you."

"Cost me what?"

"He wants me to spend the weekend with him in Pennsylvania."

"How is that going to cost me?"

"He wants me to come up this weekend."

Lena's eyes widened. "You can't mean it. Oh, come on. I finally got Jeff to spring for Atlantic City, and you want me to cancel it?"

Jesslyn patted her sister on the arm. "Not me. Someone you owe, big time."

"Jeff is going to kill me. I already told him you weren't interested in double dating, and that's why you weren't responding to his calls."

Her sister had been surprised that Jeff had tried to contact Jesslyn, but she knew that the man wanted to be around anyone he thought was important. She forgave that little foible.

Palladin Rush was not a happy camper when he got off the phone.

"I hate leaving her like that."

"Yeah, but if you are missing the forest for the trees and the wind from the breeze because you're attracted to the lady."

"I have a feeling that she's going to need me."

"Ha! I can't get over that look on Mac's face when you told him he'd better not try to rush to judgement on her until you were convinced she was guilty."

"You never liked Mac."

"Can't help it. Got an uneasy feeling about the man," Kaliq said. "Did Skip have anything to add?"

Between the calls he made trying to reach Jesslyn, Palladin had called Skip Logan. He gave him what he'd been able to get out of Frank Mason and asked him to check further.

"Skip's getting some strange rumblings," Palladin said. "He says he's going to call in some favors and get back to me."

"Maybe I should do the same." Kaliq decided. "Things get this quiet I say money and power must be talking."

"But why?"

"We find out who, then we find out why."

Eleven

"I want that diskette, Ms. Owens, and I'd suggest you not cause any more trouble. I know your boyfriend is out of town and so is the Senator. Just remember I can get to you before either of them can get to me."

This was Hank Reynolds second call of the day. Now he even mentioned that he knew Palladin wasn't in New York. He must have been watching her or paying someone to do it. She thought of calling Palladin, knowing that he would rush down and maybe get hurt. She didn't want to think of anything worse than him being injured.

"Then, I guess I'd better make a few phone calls . . ."

"No—don't," his tone changed quickly. "You made me look bad in front of a man who loves to make or break careers. Woodrow Gary isn't the kind of man you'd like as an enemy."

"I'm telling you for the last time. I mean it. You call here again and I'm going to see that your boss and Gavin Macklin find out." She bluffed.

"You've made yourself very clear. And, of course, there are other ways to handle this situation. I . . . I won't call you again."

Jesslyn knew that Mac must have some old friends in Washington and Palladin could get him to use them. She hung up feeling proud of herself.

She'd been expecting a call from Palladin and had grabbed the phone on the first ring. She told him that Lena had agreed to cancel her weekend jaunt. She didn't tell him that she'd tricked her into revealing what she'd said to get her into trouble.

"I've got a whole bunch of things planned for us to do. And one of them is to watch my team practice. Maybe you'll take a turn on the ice with us. We won't check you too hard."

"Sorry. My style of ice skating is more in line with Kristi Yamaguchi than Mark Messier."

"Okay," he told her. "We'll let you watch. And, believe me, that invitation isn't extended to many people," he teased.

"I'll be exceptionally grateful," she teased back. What she really wanted to say was that she didn't plan on spending the time with his team. She was coming to see him and wanted as much of that to be without guests as possible.

"Uh . . . Hank Reynolds called me . . ."

"What did he say?" Palladin said in a strained voice. "Never mind, I'm coming down . . ."

"Don't worry," she interrupted. "I handled it."

"How?"

"I told him I'd call the Senator and Mac . . ."

"Mac?"

"Hey, it worked. He said he wouldn't call again. I'll leave here around three in the afternoon."

They said their goodbyes, anticipating the weekend.

Jesslyn cornered Carolann as soon as she came in. They were in the office away from the staff. She waited until Carolann hung up her coat and sat down. She was eager to brag about how she handled their persistent former client.

"Reynolds called me again. This time I told him that I'd tell Palladin, Senator Gary and Mac. He . . ."

"Oh no! You didn't . . ." Carolann's voice was laced with fear.

"Why not?"

"I . . . I was trying to . . . I mean I never expected them to call you."

Jesslyn's heart sank. "He's your client. You expected Reynolds to call you. And then what?" Jesslyn began to pace.

"I thought we could make a deal . . ."

"Blackmail. You were going to try to blackmail this man?"

"He said the Senator needed the diskette for his campaign. I thought some strategy moves were on it. You know."

"So why don't you call Reynolds and give him the diskette, so we can get on with our lives?"

"It's not that easy. We know the diskette exists, and even if we give it back and swear we don't know anything about it, he won't believe us."

"So what are you saying?"

"I just need some time to get . . . some help from another friend."

"You and your friends are going to get us killed . . . oh, my God."

"What's wrong?"

"I missed it. When Reynolds called, the last thing he said to me was that there were other ways to handle a situation."

The mundane life that Jesslyn had come to know came crashing down as soon as her partner admitted her involvement in industrial espionage.

"Where's the diskette?"

"I hid it. If we give it to him, he's going to kill us for sure."

Jesslyn stopped pacing. "We need to get the diskette and hide it some place safe until your friend gets us out of this. Who is he anyway?"

Carolann didn't answer the question. "Okay. What can we do? Where can we go?" Panic marred Carolann's features. She was coming apart.

"We'll get the diskette and go to the police."

"No! No police. Please I don't want to go to jail."

"Would you rather be dead? Where's the diskette?"

"My apartment."

"Lena and Kathy will take care of the shop for a couple of hours. Let's go."

Carolann blinked several times and then agreed. They left Lena trying to ask questions that neither Jesslyn nor Carolann intended to answer, at least not while they were planning an escape route.

Jesslyn didn't recognize the address Carolann gave to the cab driver. And stared at her partner.

"I have another little place where I . . . entertain."

Jesslyn knew that meant this was the love nest she shared with her mystery man. But now she wasn't even curious about who he was anymore. Now she was just scared and only wanted out of this mess.

As they rode, Jesslyn nibbled on crackers and Carolann talked about her life.

"I always had to share things. We lived with my aunt and her kids. I shared a room with my youngest cousin.

She was always getting into my stuff—my perfume, my make up. I hated it. When I was little we lived in Chicago," Carolann continued. "We had this apartment and one day I noticed that I had loose floorboards in the closet. I pulled them up and there was this space. I guess the previous owners had used it to hide something. I started hiding important stuff there. That's how I saved enough to enter that first beauty contest."

"And you won and went on to fame, fortune and blackmail."

They got out of the cab and were about to enter the building when Carolann spied Hank. Neither knew if he'd followed them or waited for them.

"We've got to get out of here," Carolann said. "Come on."

"I think we need professional help. The police . . ."

"The police will only make it worse."

She led Jesslyn through the building, greeting people she knew, so she'd seem normal, and moving into the garage. The apartment house wasn't that far from her own and Jesslyn wondered how she could have lived within walking distance of each other and never run into her.

"This is my car. It was a gift."

Jesslyn stared at the sleek black Ferrari for a moment then looked at her partner. "Honey, if they gave you this, that diskette you're hiding has a lot more on it than somebody's ad campaign."

"We have to get out of here."

"Right. Let's go to Palladin's. He's expecting me to drive up tomorrow, I'll just be a little early."

"Oh, no. Don't involve him in this mess."

"Sorry, but I want someone *I* can trust in on this."

Hank Reynolds stepped out of the elevator but they saw him before he saw them. Jesslyn reached in her pocket for crackers. She'd eaten the last pack in the cab. "I have to drive," she said.

"Not *my* Ferrari!"

"It's that or I'm going to throw up before we get out of New York."

"Okay. Okay." She tossed Jesslyn the keys and they were in the car before Hank walked back and saw them. By that time Jesslyn had pulled the car out and was headed out of the garage.

The arctic February breeze kept her alert since driving in this kind of weather meant keeping your eye on the road. The weatherman was predicting a quick end to the calm they'd been experiencing and that a light dusting of snow would creep into the area in a week. As Jesslyn drove down Interstate highway 80 in the Ferrari, she felt reasonably calm. She wondered how Palladin would feel about his ex-wife and new lover arriving on his doorstep asking for help. She glanced over at Carolann who used the time catching a nap, a sign she hadn't been able to sleep the night before either. Jesslyn began to doubt her real motives for asking Palladin for help, rather than the police. Sure her last experience with them had been unpleasant but wouldn't running look as if she was guilty of *something.*

When she'd used the car phone to call Lena and tell her that they were in trouble and she was on her way to Pennsylvania.

"Don't be so sure that super hunk's going to help," Lena said. "I thought he was Mr. Right until he broke that date and left town. Sounds a little weird that someone broke into his house."

Palladin had explained that they only tried to break in, but she didn't have time to argue the point.

Jesslyn hadn't told Lena about Hank nor did she want to admit the real reason she was behind the wheel. She wanted to see Palladin.

Her face always betrayed her feelings, unlike her partner. Even as she slept, Carolann looked every bit the high fashioned model she once was. Working with her, however, was a mistake that she would not repeat, if they got out of this mess unscathed.

Following Carolann's instructions, she found the narrow cut off to a dirt road with just a guardrail protecting them from the tree-lined slopes. The deserted area didn't bother her as much as the three cars that followed her down the narrow path. An uneasy feeling crept over her until two of the cars peeled away to other equally unusual routes as the one she'd found. She expected the other to do the same shortly, since Carolann complained about the desolate section Palladin had chosen to build his home.

Carolann stirred, her eyes opened and she squirmed in the tiny seat.

"Hey, we're almost there. How long did I sleep?" She asked as she tugged at the snug-fitting skirt of her black Armani suit.

"Only about an hour."

Jesslyn found it hard to believe that they shopped at the same stores. Except for the blue suit she said saved her life, she always headed for the fourth floor in search of classy business wear, while Carolann was in heaven on the second floor with its beautiful but expensive evening wear. Jesslyn wondered if the suit made her slip into the Cinderella complex and flirt with the prince or the "super hunk," as Lena had called him in their phone conversation.

Until that night, clothes had never interested Jesslyn, other than they were well made and easy to keep clean.

"I can see lines in your forehead," Carolann said. "You're gonna get wrinkles from all that worry."

"What if Palladin can't help us?"

"*Then* we go to the police. We use the diskette as a bargaining chip." Carolann chuckled.

"Did you take it out of the basket?"

"No. I exchanged it with another diskette before it went into the basket. My friend was supposed to find out what was on it."

"Did he?"

"No. Once he realized what was on it, he called Hank and made a deal for himself."

"Dare I ask how you got the diskette?"

"I went over and while we were enjoying the hot tub, I got out for a moment and took it from his desk."

The more Carolann explained the more complicated everything got. There was one more question she just had to ask.

"Why did you do it?"

"I'll tell you and you'll get all disappointed."

"Go on."

"Knowing I could pull off something illegal."

She was right. Jesslyn didn't like the answer. Running after thrills always created more problems and yet it was the way your success was judged. Doing the impossible. Beating the odds. Jesslyn knew well what that could mean.

The first year she'd worked for ABLE Communications, she'd been the star at her high school reunion. By the end of her tenure with the cosmetic company, she wasn't even invited to any of the school's alumni functions. The look in her parents eyes hurt the most. No matter how much they believed her, she'd forgotten their warnings. She'd led with her heart and had been betrayed. At least she was getting better. Next time, she'd never trust anyone again. She promised.

Jesslyn said nothing else as she concentrated on the road ahead. Then in the mirror she noticed a Blazer joined the remaining car behind her.

"What kind of car does Hank drive?"

"He thinks it's the thing to drive a Blazer."

"A red one?"

"Yeah." Carolann picked up on Jesslyn's tone and turned in her seat so she could see the cars in back of them. "Don't panic. Other people drive red Blazers." She said in an unconvincing tone.

"Why is it every time you say 'don't worry,' I know we're in more trouble than before?" Jesslyn was sure it was the same car that almost hit her when she bought the suit. No wonder Carolann had been concerned. She knew they were in danger. And she never said a word.

Suddenly, one of the cars shot around Jesslyn and slid in front of her. The other car pulled along side of her. Now she was trapped.

"Where'd you put the phone?" Carolann asked.

"In my bag."

Carolann picked up Jesslyn's leather pouchbag and since the space in the sports car was so limited she stuck the beaded bag she'd been carrying in its place by Jesslyn's side and nervously dialed a number. "I'm getting his machine again." She hung up and dialed another number. "I tried his old beeper number. I'm not sure if he still uses it."

Carolann held onto the pouchbag and from the tensing of her fingers Jesslyn knew the carefree front was just an act.

Nothing else had gone Jesslyn's way, and this was just another dead end. She cringed as the words crossed her mind since they could be taken so literally at this point.

As darkness began to envelop them, Jesslyn knew this was the time to make her move. She pressed down on the accelerator and bumped the car in front of her. Neither of the women wanted to think about the damage to the fiberglass frame of the Ferrari. Caught by surprise, the car pulled over enough for her to squeeze through and try to get on a paved highway. But the dirt road caused the car to slip and slide allowing the Blazer to catch up with them. She couldn't see the driver and just assumed it was Hank Reynolds. He'd probably had another car on the street follow them and wait until he arrived to overtake them.

They hit an unexpected stretch of road and skidded near the railing. Jesslyn fought the wheel as she tried to control the car but its speed made it shift from side to side. Just as she righted the car, the Blazer caught up, pulled along side and bumped the Ferrari. They battled for control of the narrow road. The slippery gravel made it worse for the little sports car, while the four-wheel Blazer did exactly what it was built to do—hold the road.

Jesslyn again found the car heading for the guard rail and turned, forcing her way back to the middle of the narrow road. A fear she'd never experienced before engulfed her body.

"That's it," cried Carolann. "That's it." She pointed to a dusk-shrouded turn-off to the left.

It was too late.

The other car pulled around on the right side and as it passed Jesslyn's door it bumped the Ferrari. The car went into a spin and Jesslyn tried to make the gate up ahead but it was not to be. The Blazer was behind her again and this time not so much as hitting but pushing the sports car to the rail. She heard a piercing screech as the metal guard rail tore through the fiberglass car frame. They had no chance to escape as the car catapulted through the guardrail and flipped over. Then an impact of unbelievable force as the car finally came to rest, against a tree, at the base of the incline. All else faded into oblivion.

Later Jesslyn would recall Carolann's heartrending scream and what she'd seen when the Blazer first pulled behind her. One word across the wind deflector on the front. Written backwards so she could read it clearly in her rearview mirror. *Hellraiser!*

Twelve

FEBRUARY 15

Palladin Rush swung his six foot four, two hundred and twenty pound frame through the doors of the small hospital like a man on a mission. A light sprinkling of melting snow glistened on his dreadlocks as he followed the signs to the nurses' station. The nurse on duty was a bit frazzled and strands of her blonde hair had fallen out of its French roll. She glanced up from the chart she was studying and flinched at the sight of the giant. She couldn't believe a man of his size hadn't made any noise to indicate that he was there.

"May I help you?"

"I'm looking for my . . . wife. Carolann Rush."

Even though they were divorced, he didn't know what else to call her.

She checked the records. "Oh, car accident I'll page the doctor. There's been another accident and Emergency Service is bringing the injured in." She directed him to a waiting room. "The doctor may not be able to talk to you now, but your wife isn't hurt badly and is in a regular ward so . . ."

"I want her moved to a private room as soon as possible."

"Yes . . . sir. We know. We're already getting one ready for her."

Palladin's gaze went to the name tag pinned above her right breast. "Thank you, Nurse Adams."

As he stepped away from the desk he dodged a pretty African-American nurse just coming on duty.

"What do you call that hairstyle?" He heard Nurse Adams ask.

"Dreadlocks. You know that."

"He startled me so I couldn't think for a moment."

"If he's available, he's mine."

"Sorry, I saw him first. Any man who calls me Nurse Adams instead of honey or sweetheart, I'll fight for. But we're both out of luck. He's here to see his wife. Lucky woman."

They forgot him and slipped into their professional roles, as they continued their conversation in hospital jargon.

The room was empty and he realized that the nurse had put him in someone's office rather than a waiting room. That, along with the fact that Carolann was already being moved to a private room, probably meant Mac had pulled some strings.

He'd listened to the garbled message on his answering machine that she and Jesslyn were on their way to his house. Damn! Why? Where was Jesslyn?

Palladin had refused Kaliq's offer to come with him and now regretted it. He needed someone to help him keep things in perspective. To distract him. Then again with Mac on the way it was better that his old friend wasn't here. The two men couldn't be in the same room for five minutes without getting into some kind of argument.

In minutes that seemed like hours, a doctor appeared and introduced himself. Dr. Parker barely came up to Palladin's shoulder and despite the gray running through his blond hair, he looked like a college student.

"I have to tell you that your wife is a very lucky woman," he said.

A second opinion she'd disagree with, but he acknowledged with a slight nod.

"She's banged up a bit, but no broken bones. From what I hear about the car, that's a miracle."

"Can I see her?"

"I'll take you up in a minute. Believe me her bruises are bad, but not life-threatening." The doctor sat behind the desk and motioned Palladin to a chair in front of it.

"I hope that's temporary. She's a model."

"Really? Kinda tiny for a model. But she's going to be fine. You may have to hide the mirrors for about six weeks."

As the doctor thumbed through the charts Palladin took the time to try something he'd learned as a curious child, to read upside down. He saw that she was now in room 305 instead of a ward.

"I think there is something I should discuss with you. Carolann and I are divorced . . ."

"I . . . thought . . ." The doctor stopped.

"What I'm saying, Dr. Parker, is that I will be responsible for the bill, but you'll be paid by check and not an insurance company. I can make that a cashier's check, if there's any problem."

"We'll need you to sign a few papers, but I'm sure there's no problem. Now I understand why she asked for you but we couldn't find your name in her address book. Your friend, Mac, was listed as next of kin?"

"He's been like a second father to both of us."

Dr. Parker retrieved Carolann's purse from a locked drawer in his desk. "Your friend asked me to keep this and only give it to him, but I guess he thought he'd get here first. I'll get those papers."

The beaded bag the doctor handed him was the one he'd given Carolann on their last Christmas together. They'd come up from D.C. to spend Christmas in New York. It was a final attempt to save the marriage. They'd watched people skate at Rockefeller Center, caught a couple of Broadway shows and he'd left her at Bendel's, a chic trendy store while he walked down Fifth Avenue to Saks to get her a Christmas gift. He'd already decided on a thirty-six-inch strand of pearls with a clip on black cameo when he spotted the red and black beaded evening bag. He'd hoped it and the trip would have been enough to convince her to work through their problems, but she'd left six weeks later, almost three years to the day.

Palladin dumped the contents on the desk and spotted the reason for the doctor's hesitation to give him the bag. In front of him, along with a make-up kit, wallet, address book, his class ring and keys were several distinctive foil-wrapped packets.

The doctor returned and Palladin swept the contents from the desk back into the bag.

"I'll take you to see her now."

They left the office and Palladin spotted Mac at the nurses' station and walked over.

"Listen to me, honey . . ."

"Mac, give the nurse a break."

"Palladin!" The man grabbed him in sort of a bear hug. It was an unusual sight since Mac was a little shorter and smaller. "I didn't expect you until tomorrow. I told you I'd take care of it. Thought if it was bad news I could make it easier."

"From all accounts the news is good. But you've got to stop trying to protect me. I don't work for you any more."

"Unfortunately! But we have to talk." Mac looked around and pulled Palladin to the side so no one could see or hear him.

"What's wrong?"

"I think Carolann and her partners are in bigger trouble than I suspected."

"How?"

"Their business."

"We've been through that."

"When I heard about the accident, I tried to reach Jesslyn Owens. Couldn't. Got her sister who doesn't know where she is and I believe her. She insists that they left together."

"We'll find Jesslyn later. I want to see Carolann first."

Mac patted him on the shoulder. "Still in love with her, eh? The Owens woman was just a fling."

"I got over being in love three months after we were married," his voice was cold and his eyes honest. "But I will get to the bottom of this."

"You surprise me. I didn't think anyone got over Carolann."

Mac's soft spot for Carolann was still there. He'd told Palladin over and over he thought of them as his children. He thought they belonged together. No matter what she did, Mac would have forgiven her.

Palladin paced while waiting for the doctor. He spotted

Skip Logan who'd joined Mac at the desk. "What are you doing here?"

"Heard about your wife and thought I should be around for Mac." Logan's face was splotchy red from the weather but his clothes as always were neat. His gray top coat lay over his arm.

"You don't know her well enough to be concerned."

"Au contraire, Mr. Rush," he said. "I do. Better than you might think."

Skip still liked to bait Palladin in front of Mac. Almost as if he wanted Palladin to lose it just once and throw a punch.

"Sorry, she never mentioned you, Lucky. I guess her impression of you wasn't as lasting as yours was of her." Palladin knew this was another way of retaliation. As long as he didn't let Skip get to him. But something else had happened.

Mac stepped between them. "Is there a place we can go to get a little more privacy?"

Palladin led the way back to the doctor's office. He knew Skip wasn't that concerned about Carolann. He'd obviously gotten some information that would make Palladin look bad.

After Palladin had threatened to have him replaced, he'd stopped the usual harassment. He'd done exactly as Palladin instructed. Now something had changed. It was as if Skip knew a secret that he wanted to share. He just wanted Palladin to have to ask him.

Mac cut in, "She's going to be fine."

"Well, there are those new rumors," Skip tossed out.

"What rumors," Palladin asked.

"That your ex and her partner have crossed the line into Federal territory."

"Is that true?" Although Palladin's eyes never left Skip's the question was for Mac.

"Yeah."

"But you said the Owens woman was clean," Skip tossed in. "Did the great *Glacier* make a mistake."

"No. And I'll bet as soon as we talk to Carolann, she'll confirm it."

Palladin deliberately kept himself from appearing surprised. He shrugged. "If I prove your information is wrong, you're going to look incredibly stupid."

Skip grinned. "I got the information from the man you told me to talk to."

"Frank Mason?"

"Yeah. He wants to make a deal and he says he can tie GiftBaskets, Inc. to Senator Woodrow Gary."

"So what does that mean," Mac asked. "Who told you to talk to this Mason?"

"I did," Palladin answered. "But can he prove any of these allegations?"

"He says that Jesslyn Owens has a diskette that can."

Mac looked at his two protégés. So different. So much alike. "Did either of you think about telling me what was going on."

"I just did everything he told me so I could stay on this investigation," Skip explained.

"You've never done anything I told you unless you wanted to do it. And without the diskette, you don't have anything."

"Skip. Palladin. Let's not have this discussion here." Mac called. "I'll talk to you tomorrow."

Skip's jaw twitched at the dismissal but he left without another word just a glare in Palladin's direction.

Skip resented Palladin's money even though it only

traced back one generation. Palladin's father, Brad, hadn't completed college and got a job. He learned to read the financial papers, talk the jargon of "the street" as insiders called Wall Street, New York's financial hub. He realized that his guesses were better than some of the advice of advisors and began putting a little money aside to buy stock. By the time he met and married Abigail Louis, he'd accumulated a small fortune. Abigail was a teacher at the college where Brad attended night school. When Palladin was born his father's small fortune had become a large one.

Palladin inherited his father's skill at reaping the rewards of Wall Street, along with his desire to be the best at whatever he attempted. His parents currently lived in Hawaii, and he visited them from time to time. His last visit was just before Mac called him about the industrial espionage business.

Mac and Palladin left the office and walked slowly back to the nurses' station.

An emergency service crew burst through the door. The doctor left the nurse's station and ran to the stretcher.

"Looks like another victim from that earlier accident. Must have been thrown from the car. Kids were poking around and found her." One of the men shook his head. The doctor bent down to confirm their findings.

When Palladin heard "earlier accident," a feeling of despair came over him. Could it be Jesslyn? He said a silent prayer that it wasn't. He walked over and tried to get a better view of the victim. He couldn't until the doctor stood up and shook his head. That meant she was dead. Palladin saw her face. Chills traveled down his spine, he put his hand to his face and wiped away the beads of sweat that had popped out on his forehead. Something in his training kicked in and he didn't move. He just stared. The woman on the stretcher was his ex-wife, Carolann Rush.

Thirteen

Pain interrupted sleep and Jesslyn tossed from side to side trying to find a place on her body that wasn't too bruised to rest her small frame on. Ever since she got to the hospital, people had been calling her Carolann or Mrs. Rush and asking what hurt and where. Everything and everywhere she wanted to tell them but she couldn't give voice to her thoughts for her interrogators. She was tired of the questions and just wanted them to give her something for the pain and let her get back to sleep. She didn't want to talk or to think. The antiseptic smell tickled her nostrils and she tried to rub her nose only to learn that her right arm was hooked to the IV bag next to her bed. The left arm seemed to be held down by some sort of band. Twisting her head and wriggling her shoulders, she finally got her nose close enough to rub against the pillow and eliminated the itching.

Her mind was so foggy. She knew where she was. She just didn't know *who* she was. The accident she remembered. She'd been in an accident and she was in the hospital. Drugs. That was it. The medication to ease the pain made her forget. When it wore off everything would be back to normal again.

She sensed, rather than saw someone coming toward her bed. Good. She couldn't distinguish if the person was male or female. A whispering voice warned her about talking too much. A voice saying over and over "Jesslyn, don't tell them anything." Then the figure slipped away and she closed her eyes. She didn't want to think, but flashes bounced through her mind. Jesslyn? Carolann? She tried to connect to the names but couldn't.

Downstairs Palladin's face remained stoic but inside emotions ran rampant. Torn between the joy of knowing Jesslyn was alive and the sorrow of knowing Carolann was dead, Palladin allowed Mac to pull him away from the stretcher before he could tell the doctors about the mistake.

Mac made a call, and an hour later for Mac but an eternity for Palladin, a policeman arrived with a copy of the accident report. Jesslyn was driving the car and when the car went off the road, Carolann was thrown from the car because she wasn't wearing a seatbelt and rolled down the embankment. According to the report and the pictures that accompanied it, nothing would have saved her. It was the passenger side of the car that smashed into the tree.

"So people heard the crash, but didn't see what happened," Palladin said as he finished reading.

"That's about it. The police were conducting a routine examination when they found . . ." He couldn't bring him self to say anymore.

Palladin knew they were both hoping that she didn't suffer. Since he'd already claimed responsibility for the driver of the car, there wouldn't be a problem doing the same for the passenger. Still there was one thing that Mac didn't seem to be considering.

Palladin led Mac to the doctor's office where he had gone through Carolann's purse and waited until he closed the door before speaking.

"What the hell is wrong with you, Mac? Carolann is dead. We could wrap this case up. From what I understand, this wasn't just an accident. They had to be speeding when the car went off the road. They were running from someone."

"Maybe they were just driving too fast."

"No. They called me from the car . . ."

Mac interrupted. "Called you? Why didn't you tell me? What did they say?"

"Nothing. That they were on their way to my place."

"And that makes you think this thing is over."

"Why not?"

Mac sat down in the chair next to the desk. "You haven't been thinking straight since you met this Jesslyn Owens. Much as I hate it, I have to agree with Skip. You're involved with the prime suspect and it's totally clouded your vision."

"So what's next?"

"We have to keep the Owens woman from blaming Carolann."

"She wouldn't . . ."

"People do strange things when they're backed into a corner. She and her sister will just say it's all Carolann's fault and probably be able to supply enough evidence to back up the claim."

"What if she was involved?"

Mac's voice dropped and he stared at Palladin. "How can you even say *that?*"

Palladin understood Mac's question. Of all the women Palladin had dated, Carolann was Mac's favorite. He'd even acted as the "father of the bride" at their wedding, since she didn't have anyone she wanted to give her away.

Mac spoke again, "Maybe you're too close now and you should back off and let me handle it."

Palladin let the thought flit through his mind. Was he too close? Was he protecting a guilty person? It didn't matter. He wanted to know who was on the receiving end of this little side business. "I know you want me to stay out of it, but I can't. And the next step is for you to get Carolann out of here."

"How am I supposed do to that, without telling the truth?"

"Never mind." Palladin waited a beat before playing his trump card. "I'll call Kaliq."

"No! I'll help. What do you want me to do?"

He'd known that Mac couldn't let someone else be part of any scheme much less having Kaliq Faulkner helping and Mac waiting on the sidelines. "Find someone willing to claim the body as a family member. Do it under Carolann Evans. We're divorced, and she talked about going back to her maiden name. I'll handle the expenses."

"That'll work. Where should we take the body?"

Palladin felt a sharp pain shoot through him at Carolann being referred to as "the body."

"She doesn't have any immediate family living. We'll take her to Chicago and bury her next to the aunt who raised her."

"What if someone gets suspicious about two women named Carolann?"

"Say they're cousins."

"I can't believe this.

"What?"

"How easily you slip back in the world of arranging things."

"Well, don't count on me to continue this. As soon as Jesslyn can travel, I'm going to take her home with me."

Mac's face turned dark red with anger. "You can't mean that?"

"Why not?"

"What if she's one of the 'bad guys'?"

"She isn't. I've got to make some plans."

"Let me handle it," Mac told him. "If you're going out on a limb for this woman, she must be pretty special. Go home and let me talk to the doctor. I'll tell him it suddenly hit you about the accident and you need to pull yourself together before seeing . . . your wife."

Palladin hadn't thought about that part of it, but until he could get this web untangled Jesslyn and Lena would have to pretend. Getting to Jesslyn and having her pretend to be his ex-wife until they could straighten out the other matter was now a priority.

He walked to the parking lot and climbed into his gray 1980 Lincoln limousine. He preferred his four-wheel drive, but he'd driven the limo because it gave Kaliq the room he needed to sit in the front seat and room for the wheelchair in back. Originally, he bought it at an auction and planned to sell it later, so he never bothered hiring a driver. But somehow, he got attached to it and after Kaliq's accident he kept it around, despite Carolann's urging to get rid of it and if he had to have a limo get a new one. He used it to chauffeur his hockey team around now. The kids loved it.

He picked up his mobile phone and dialed. Four rings later Kaliq was on the line.

"Trouble."

"What happened to Carolann?"

"She's dead." Somehow saying it out loud made it more real than before. Palladin's eyes filled with tears. He may not have loved her any longer, but he had wanted her to be happy.

"Sorry, man. What can I do to help?"

"There's a real mix-up down here. The hospital thinks the woman they brought in earlier is Carolann, but I'm sure it's Jesslyn and Carolann is a Jane Doe."

"What kinda mess is this?"

"I don't know, but Mac still wants to prove Jesslyn's guilt, so I let him think I'm on my way home."

The pause on the line meant Kaliq was probably running a hundred different scenarios through his head. But none seemed plausible. "You gonna leave Carolann in the morgue."

"No way. Mac's getting her out using her maiden name and then we're taking her to Chicago to be buried."

"Looks like you got all the bases covered. Do you want me to go to the Windy City with you?"

"Thanks, man. I was hoping you'd be there."

Palladin and Kaliq said good-bye and Palladin drove the car in the most deserted part of the lot he could find. He got out and headed back on foot. He decided the best thing to do was keep Mac happy—let him think he was following orders while he did what he knew he had to do. They really hadn't put the argument behind them but were pretending it hadn't happen. Sooner or later, they were going to have to sit down and really talk to each other. So he would act as if he was following orders, then do whatever he really wanted to do. And what he really wanted to do was to confirm his guess that Jesslyn Owens was the first woman they brought in.

The reduced staff on the night shift and the emergency just brought in gave him enough distraction to slip back into the hospital. He could see Mac coming down the hall and shaking hands with the doctor. The men were turned, so they couldn't see the elevators behind them. They didn't see Skip come out of the elevator and head for the parking lot. Palladin did and he didn't like it. When Mac and the doctor disappeared into an office, it left the coast clear to make a move. Palladin waited until the nurse turned her back to retrieve a chart and slipped past her. He took the elevator that would put him out of her sight as he pressed for the third floor.

The ride could not have been long but each second seemed an eternity. Palladin knew that once he got past the nurse downstairs anyone seeing him would assume he had permission to be there. Because of the accident, they were probably being more lenient that normal.

He made his way down the hall and entered room 305. He should have known when the doctor mentioned his patient was kind of tiny for a model that it wasn't Carol-ann, but he hadn't. Now he stood over the bed and gazed down.

She was turned on her side. So fragile-looking with her hospital gown peeking above her sheet. Her eyes were closed but he remembered them. Palladin watched her and thought about the last time he'd stood by her bed watching her sleep. Then he hadn't wanted to wake her up, now it was what he wanted the most. He had to be sure she was all right, no matter what the doctor said.

The beginning of what he thought was going to be a new relationship could have been over. He even understood why she was driving the car. She'd probably forgotten her crackers. It would have been funny, but he also knew that it meant she was alive for the same reason Carolann was dead.

He'd call Lena as soon as he was sure Jesslyn was going to be all right. He needed to know that for himself before he would tell Lena. She probably wouldn't like her sister having to answer to the name Carolann, but what else could they do to keep the police at bay.

He and Jesslyn had come so close to finding something beautiful. He hoped it still could happen.

When she wakes up, he thought, everything will be straightened out. She'd need time to recover and he'd take her home with him. He put his hand over hers as he remembered Mac's reaction to that plan. But Mac knew him best and knew that Palladin would do whatever he wanted, and the rest of the world could just wait for answers.

The kick of desire came as a shock to his system making him short of breath and setting his heart to a frightening pace. The woman was in a hospital and all he could think about was getting her out of that bed and into his. He wanted to hold her. Protect her. He didn't believe for one moment she could be capable of something illegal, no matter what Mac said or what the evidence said. He'd find a way to prove she, her sister and Carolann had been duped—probably by the man that he spoke to in the restaurant, Hank Reynolds. He'd have Mac check up on him.

Lena could run the shop. *Lena!* He had to get her here. They had to make plans and schedules. He wasn't going to let Jesslyn go to her apartment. She needed him. After she was better, he'd go looking for the man who ran her off the road and there would be a heavy price to pay for it.

Mac was wrong when he thought that this tiny woman

could play innocent and blame Carolann. Another of Paladin's rules of thumb was that scared people always do what they're supposed to. And he'd known just how to put the fear of God into her—having Kaliq follow them. Pointing out the car and making her worry. But she hadn't run. She faced her problems head on and waited for the result.

"Jesslyn," he called gently. She stirred but didn't open her eyes. He took her hand in his and rubbed his calloused fingers across her smooth skin. He wanted to absorb the pain she must be suffering and take away all the vivid dark blue and purple bruises from her face.

"Oh, darling, please be all right. I need you so much. I need you to forgive me." He could only hope she believed that sleeping with her wasn't part of the lie. If she didn't hate him when she learned the truth, they might have a chance after all, but he wanted the time to let her bond with him while she recovered. He bent over and kissed her forehead. "See you in the morning."

Jesslyn opened her eyes. Another voice. Tender, melodious, someone who cared about her. Someone who needed her. Not the same person who told her not to tell anyone about . . . She didn't know what she wasn't supposed to tell. Ignoring the twinges of pain that snaked through her shoulders she turned so she could see the man.

"Hi," her voice sounded squeaky. She tried to lift her head but spots of light flashed before her and she gave up. "Head hurts."

"It's no wonder," the man said. "You've got a lump the size of Gibraltar."

She couldn't lift her head but she could turn it enough to study the man leaning over her. His lips were pressed together and she knew he was angry. "Mean mouth. I won't tell. Mad at me."

"That's not what you said the last time we were together." He laughed and his face changed.

"You won't tell what?"

"Nothing."

She couldn't see much because when he bent over her he blocked most of the light from the hallway. "Who are . . . you?"

The question startled him. "I could be your doctor." He wondered if she was teasing him or punishing him.

"No. No dreads. No doctor." She coughed.

"Don't try to talk."

"Hurts . . ."

"I know."

"Want . . . go . . . home."

"No one likes hospitals much. I need some information."

"Don't know . . ."

"How did the accident happen? Why were you driving Carolann's car?"

"Don't know . . ."

He wasn't getting anywhere. It would have to wait until the next day.

"Name . . . ?"

"Mine, Palladin Rush?" Damn! She really didn't know who he was. The head injury. Tomorrow she'd wake up and everything would come back to her.

She shook her head. "My name . . ."

Seconds later it dawned on him what she was asking. She didn't know who *she* was. He knew it might be a temporary state. But his cold, logical mind told him that keeping her with him would be the only way to get at the truth. If he let her go she might go back to New York, surround herself with a bevy of lawyers and Carolann's name would be mud if Mac was right about her. Mac would be right in saying Palladin let his body make a decision for his head. She might not like it, but they'd convince her that the only way to save herself was to blame someone else.

On the other hand, if she was innocent and he let her go back to her old life, she wouldn't know who her enemies were. But he had a mountain retreat that could protect her. If necessary that was where he'd take her. Palladin needed her to find the truth and the only way would be to keep her with him. If he made her depend on him for her very existence, he would find the truth and it would free him from Carolann. His mouth went dry as he leaned closer and saw the tears trickling down her face. "Don't worry. You'll know tomorrow. Try to rest and everything will be fine."

"Name . . ."

Her mouth turned down and he knew she wasn't going to let it go. He admired her tenacity. He took a chance. "Carolann Rush."

"Are you my brother?"

"No. I'm your husband." The whispered lie reverberated in his head and the web became more tangled.

Fourteen

"Amnesia! Is that your best answer, Rush?" The tone slipping to sarcasm. Skip Logan was sitting on the edge of Mac's desk while they waited for Mac to return.

"I said she had a mental block, not amnesia."

"And you believe this?"

"The truth is always the best answer, Lucky." Answering the question in the same tone. But using the nickname the agents who didn't like Skip used. He'd always come in second to Palladin. Whether it was professional, academic or personal.

Skip's face reddened and he handed Palladin a report.

"The ex-boyfriend moved to Atlanta just after they broke up. So he's not a factor. At least I can't make the connection . . . Frank Mason's gone into hiding, until we can make it worth his while to come out."

Palladin took the report and then threw his overcoat on the leather sofa next to the desk but chose to sit in the chair across the room and stare out at the gray skies that threatened to release more snow. There were so many things to get in place. Mac was probably sorry he'd called him in on this, but Palladin couldn't let go of the feeling that something else was happening besides the little industrial espionage.

He couldn't say what it was, but he knew that it was

more than his feelings for Jesslyn that made him want to dig deeper.

He leafed through the report. Skip was right. Evidently the man had used his connections and done quite well with his new firm. He'd also married. His wife's family had lived in Georgia for several generations, and it was obvious that he didn't need money or power. At least there was one less possibility.

He wished Mac would hurry with the arrangements. He didn't think he could take much more of knowing that Carolann was being treated as a "Jane Doe" until the "relative" could make identification and claim the body.

"So what are you going to do now? I don't think any of those rules you like to toss out fits this situation."

"Well maybe I'll make up a new one, just for you."

The smile slid from Skip's face and he stood up but at that moment, Mac entered and the men backed off once again. Palladin always felt that Skip might bristle but he didn't welcome a real show of power. It was more a reflex.

"Well, Chief?" Logan asked.

"She doesn't remember anything. For some reason, she thinks Rush is her husband." He glared at Palladin. "I thought I told you to go home and let me handle it."

"If she's got amnesia, where do we go from here?" Skip asked.

Palladin, deliberately ignoring both men, explained. "Amnesia is a misnomer. Its clinical definition is when you forget something immediately before an accident or immediately after. When you can't even remember your own name, it's some kind of mental block."

"Same question," said Logan. "Where do we go from here?"

"I'm taking her home with me."

"Have you lost your mind?" Mac roared. "Did you ever think she may be faking it?"

"If she is, then isn't it better I keep her with me than letting her go back to New York and perhaps getting out of the country when no one's looking?"

"How does the lady feel about that?" Skip ventured.

"I haven't told her yet. I need someone to give her a little push." He looked at Mac and waited.

"Like what?"

"Tell her sister to back up my story."

Mac shook his head. "Who's the head of Security here? I'm beginning to believe that you think I work for you."

"Mac, don't get bent out of shape. I'm sure if you look at it, we all want the same thing—the truth. We're just doing what we always do—lie to get it."

"That's not funny, Rush."

"Most of the time, the truth isn't. Mac, did you find out about Hank Reynolds?"

"He's an accountant with a political bent. He's been contributing to Senator Gary's campaign since the man tossed his hat in the ring."

"What could be on the diskette that would make him threaten the women?" Skip asked.

"Campaign strategies," Mac answered. "It's always good to know what your opponent is planning, so you could counter attack."

"And maybe the diskette was for Senator Gary's eyes only," Palladin added. "What if something on the diskette led back to the leak in the other campaign headquarters?"

"So what are we going to do to link Jesslyn Owens with the diskette?"

Palladin then explained that the doctor said trying to show her familiar objects might not shock her mind back. Too many upheavals in her life had happened within the past five years and the fact that her "cousin" was killed in the same accident where she was injured might mean that the brain has not allowed her to remember the pain. When she can handle it—who knows. She could wake up one morning and be back to her old self. The doctor felt the best plan would be to take her some quiet and serene place, so emotionally she could release the block on her mind and you get the same result without added trauma.

Palladin walked over and looked out of the window. He wanted to tell them about the look in her eyes when he told her he was her husband. She showed no signs of recognition—only fear. He wasn't sure if it was fear of forgetting she had a husband, or of the man who said he was her husband.

Each of the men weighed the idea of her running away differently. Palladin thought that he'd never get to find out if there could be a relationship. Skip wondered if she escaped how he'd look as part of the security team that allowed it to happen, and Mac still planned a way to put Jesslyn in prison or cost her another career and clear Carolann's name.

"Can we link the Senator to anything concerning Gift-Baskets, Inc.?"

"Sorry, Rush." Skip said. "I had the computer working over time on that one. Other than being the recipient of a basket from the company, he hasn't invested money or pulled strings for them."

"When we get back, let's put the computer on the people surrounding the Senator," Palladin said.

But everything would have to wait. They had one somber task ahead of them—flying Carolann's body back to Chicago. Palladin was surprised when Skip insisted on going with them. However, he didn't want to fight one who wanted to pay his or her respects. That night they landed at O'Hare and hired a car service, rather than asking any of her family to pick them up. She'd cut all ties with the aunt who'd raised her and her cousins, but Palladin felt that her surviving relations deserved to know about her death. The weather there was worse than what they'd left in Pennsylvania. Mac, Kaliq and Skip had gone back to the car.

Bitter cold nipped Palladin's face and snow dusted his hair as the wind whipped it around his head as he stood in the cemetery. He wore a scarf around his neck and thought about the times Carolann had teased him about not wearing a hat. She claimed that all the heat from his body was going to evaporate through the top of his head. He remembered the good times of their marriage, but they hadn't lasted. As he paid his final respects, he knew he wouldn't return to the gravesite.

It wasn't that she wanted too much from this life, he thought, it was that she'd never learned that what she put into it would bring the fame and fortune that she wanted. Nothing was given just because she was beautiful. Early in her life, that had been her commodity. Maybe if he'd been a better husband, she would have been satisfied and happy, but somehow he doubted it. He could only make the silent promise that he wouldn't do this to another woman and that he'd clear her name. Only a handful of cousins and second cousins and other fringe relatives joined them as they laid her to rest next to the woman who raised her. The family came out of respect for her late aunt, rather than Carolann. Having burned so many bridges before she left for the bright lights and beauty contests, few of them truly mourned her. He explained he would get a tombstone later.

By late evening, the men were returning to Pennsylvania. The silent ride back was best, as each man had a different view of where they should go next. No one wanted to argue. The snow seemed to have waited until their return, and as they disembarked steady, tiny grains began to fall.

"I'll talk to Lena Carter in the morning." Mac said, as Palladin and Kaliq were getting into Palladin's gray limousine.

Then Mac walked over to his car and climbed behind the wheel. Skip sat on the passenger side. Mac glanced up to see Palladin and Kaliq laughing.

"Hey, I know how to get myself around the city. I have to keep in practice, in case my driver's unavailable."

"Thought the man preferred to have a chauffeur," Kaliq said.

"Well, you never know. Let's go home, so I can get the other guest room ready."

"You're really going to do this?"

"Damn straight. And I'm going to tie up all the loose ends of this little puzzle."

"Sorry I won't be around to see it." Kaliq turned to Palladin. "Got a message from my son about some hang-up in getting the ranch going. Gotta catch the red-eye out of here."

"Anything I can do to help?"

"If there is, I'll be calling."

"Want me to drive you to the airport?"

"Nah. Trisha's going to pick me up."

Palladin shook his head. His friend had always managed to find beautiful women to help him, and he played his inability to maneuver to the hilt. He wondered if there was a woman who could convince Kaliq that he should settle down, or if Kaliq even wanted to after losing his wife several years ago.

"You can't do this!" Lena paced back and forth in front of Mac's desk. "You can't keep me away from my sister! That's impossible. I'll go to the papers and tell the truth."

Gavin Macklin was weary from the trip and the strain of burying Carolann. He was in no mood to be amicable. "Mrs. Carter, you will find that I can do a great many things *you* consider impossible," Mac told her. "Now, unless you'd like to share a cell with your sister, I suggest you cooperate."

"But we didn't do anything. It must have been Carolann."

"Blaming the dead is not going to be a way out." Mac's low-pitched voice didn't hide the anger he felt at that moment.

"Search our office, our houses, check our records and you'll see that we didn't do anything."

"Or that you were very good at covering it up?"

"What's my telling Jesslyn she's married to Palladin Rush going to do?"

"If you don't, I'll have her held as a material witness if nothing else."

Defeated, Lena ran her fingers through her hair and

turned to face Mac. "I'll go along, but in my heart I know one day you'll pay the piper for this."

"Sorry, but some of us never have to pay the piper. Some of us are the pipers," Mac said. "Now let's get over to the hospital and you convince your sister that she is indeed Mrs. Palladin Rush. You can tell her that they were separated for a little while, but she was on her way home when she had the accident."

"I won't do it!"

"Don't push your luck. I'm doing you and your sister a favor. Frankly, I think you both belong in jail."

Lena stepped back almost as if she'd received a physical blow, instead of just words thrown at her.

"Let me talk to the lady, Mac," Palladin said softly.

Lena jumped against the desk. She hadn't heard him come in. "No. I don't want to talk to any of you. I want to see my sister."

"Listen, lady . . ." Mac began.

"Mac. Let me handle it," Palladin interrupted.

The older man hesitated a beat then nodded and left the room, closing the door with a little more force than was necessary.

"Lena, I think you'd better listen very carefully," Palladin said as he strolled over and sat on the edge of the desk next to her. "Someone used your company to sabotage a carefully laid out ad campaign. Now that might not seem like such a big deal to you, but to the company it's catastrophic. And there's more danger. Some rumors are going around that a diskette is missing, and someone is willing to kill to get it back."

Lena's breath caught in her throat. "You mean that it wasn't an accident?"

"Exactly."

"But we don't know about a diskette. This man named Hank was hassling Jesslyn about it."

"Then we have to get to the bottom of it, don't we?"

"I didn't pay attention to what was going on . . ."

"I know that. But now you may be all that stands between your sister and whoever is after her."

Lena shook her head. "I don't know."

Palladin put his hand on her forearm. "We both want what's best for Jesslyn. If Mac presses, he can have her arrested or held as a material witness."

"You can't do that. If you put her in jail and she doesn't know anything, she won't know her enemies from her friends." Lena toyed with the yellow scarf at her throat. She'd worn a conservative moss green suit in anticipation of dealing with doctors. As she glanced down at her brown alligator loafers, she realized she hadn't paid any attention to what she put on when she got the call. She just knew her sister was in trouble and needed her.

Mac had promised to send a driver, and when Skip showed up in the green BMW, she'd climbed in. He couldn't or wouldn't tell her exactly what happened, but gave the same information that she'd gotten from the doctor when she called. Bruises, a deep gash in her leg, but she'd be fine. Lena began worrying when he wouldn't let her talk to Jesslyn.

Even though she and Skip said very little to each other, something told her he, like the doctor, was not telling her everything she needed to know. When they got to Pennsylvania, he'd taken her to meet Mac, instead of going on to the hospital. That was when she knew that something was seriously wrong. She never expected Palladin to be so ruthless about playing with her sister's life.

ONLY HERS
FRANCIS RAY
Bestselling author of FOREVER YOURS and UNDENIABLE
LAYLE GIUSTO
HOME FIRES
Heaven Knows
ADRIENNE ELLIS REEVES

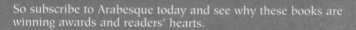

The shock of learning about Carolann's death was nothing compared to the shock of learning how they expected her to help with this charade. Mac had briefed her on the amnesia, but she couldn't understand why he was insistent on her telling the hospital that Jesslyn was Palladin's ex-wife.

"Exactly. And you are the only one who can help her."

"By saying you're her husband."

"I can keep her at my house, away from prying eyes and suspicious minds like Mac's, until she gets her memory back and can take care of herself. But it's up to you." He took his hand from her arm and walked toward the door.

"I'm making this a one time offer. Do we tell her she's my ex-wife or do we let Mac decide what to do with her?"

She hesitated and he reached for the doorknob. "Wait!"

He turned and leaned against the door. He watched as her trembling fingers twisted several strands of hair before she looked out of the window and said, "Okay. I'll do it, but I'm afraid. What if I forget and call her Jesslyn instead of Carolann?"

"Simple. We'll tell her that her first name is Carolann, but she never liked it and everyone calls her by her middle name, Jesslyn."

"Do you lie that easily all the time? Jesslyn was right about you all along."

"What does that mean?"

"Oh, the minute you strolled into her life and ignored Carolann, I pushed her to get involved with you. She kept saying that you had some sort of goal and you were trying to play her." Lena fought back tears as the anger built. "You're like the rest of the men in her life. A user."

Lena gave a bitter laugh. "You're so smooth. That lie just rolled off your tongue. Tell me were you lying to my sister about how you felt about her? She was right. You guys always think that, because you have a little power, it's great to make someone like me squirm. But I know my sister. And if, after all your charades something happens to her, you'll be the one sorry, my dreadlocks-wearing brother."

The threat didn't surprise him as much as the fact she uttered it through her teeth and barely above a whisper. It wasn't an idle threat and Palladin knew she was, as W.B. Yeats put it, as serious as the Ten Commandments.

Never had anyone's words struck him to the core the way Lena's had. He wanted to tell her that he believed in Jesslyn, and yet he couldn't risk too many people knowing how he felt. He couldn't say it was love, but he cared about Jesslyn and he would protect her. Unless . . . unless he came across unequivocal evidence against her, he would get her out of this situation. He'd been away from the Service too long. Even Skip said he'd lost his edge. He couldn't be ruthless anymore. Though he hated to admit it, women were starting to chip away at his veneer. Or maybe it was just these two women. Jesslyn had stirred his passion as no other woman had, and Lena had attacked him in a different way, with one hurtful word after another. But the word that really got to him, she'd hurled like a knife and cut him to the quick—user!

Fifteen

Mac couldn't believe the change in Lena when Palladin called him back into the room. She'd agreed to support Palladin's claim that he was her ex-husband and convince Jesslyn that going to live with him until she regained her memory was the best thing for all concerned.

Lena only balked at running GiftBaskets, Inc. "I really can't do it alone. Jesslyn's the only one who didn't mind how much time she poured into the business. She needed to do something after . . ."

"After she was fired," Skip said, then seeing the anger flash in Lena's eyes, amended it. "After she was asked to resign, she used the business as a way of regrouping. Can't you hold it together for a couple of months?"

Lena shook her head. "I need help. You want me to help you. I need help."

"We'll get someone," Palladin promised. "Skip, what's that organization you used for your father's birthday party?"

"Terrific Temps. I'll give them a call."

"Yeah. Thanks." Palladin remembered the party because it was so unlike Skip to extend him an invitation. Later, he found it was the senior Logan who wanted him around. Then, Palladin was a clean-shaven, close-cropped hair agent who had just been assigned to the incoming president's security staff.

With that settled, Lena was now ready to put on her act. They rode to the hospital, with only Mac and Palladin sharing a conversation. Skip and Lena sat tight-mouthed each staring out of a window on the way from the hotel where Lena was staying to the parking lot.

Ever since the doctor told her that there was really nothing more they could do for her, and she might recuperate at home better, Jesslyn had been waiting for the man with the dreads to come back.

It still amazed her that she knew about world events and sports and so many other things, but nothing about who she was or what she did for a living. The doctor said it was probably from the shock of the accident. He'd even told her about her cousin's death, but still nothing. Why couldn't she remember?

When the doctor mentioned her sister she felt better. Maybe seeing a family member . . . did a husband count . . . he hadn't brought any familiar feelings. What if she never got her memory back? Why would her husband want her to live with him if they were having problems before? Even in her jumbled brain, it didn't make much sense.

"Jesslyn? Are you all right? You haven't said a word since I told you Palladin wants you to come live with him."

Jesslyn, who had been lost in trying to find a connection in her mind with the idea of going to live with the man who said he was her ex-husband, stared at Lena. She was amazed she could accept that Lena was her sister but fought against being divorced. "What? Oh, sorry, Lena—I was just thinking about something."

"Something serious, apparently," Lena commented as she paced by the hospital bed, then sat down next to Jesslyn. No matter how she told herself she was acting in her sister's best interest, she had the nagging feeling she was letting her down with this masquerade.

"You've been distracted ever since I came in. Did you remember anything?"

"No, and that's the real problem. If you trust this man enough to tell me to go stay with him, then why did we break up?"

"You were . . . in a high powered career. You didn't have time to work on your marriage."

Lena had deliberately not let Palladin coach her into a false history. She wanted to answer the questions as truthfully as she could. She was glad she had this moment to see that her sister was well. Except for a few gashes on her leg and cuts and bruises, she was fine. Nothing would require a lengthy stay in the hospital.

"Shouldn't I be going to my place. Near something familiar?"

"I . . . guess it's better if you're safe . . ."

"Safe? Am I in danger?"

"Of course not," Lena stumbled over her faux pas. "I meant safe in that I wouldn't worry about you being alone in New York and getting lost."

"Are you going to come with us?"

"No. I have to look after our best interests. Our shop. It's doing some brisk business, and I think I'm going to have to hire someone."

Jesslyn sighed and tried to bring the business information from the fringes of her memory, but to no avail

"So you need me out of your hair for a while."

Lena laughed. "It would help."

"Am I that bad as a boss?" Jesslyn wrinkled up he nose.

"Sorry. I didn't mean to make it sound like you wer a terror. Although you could be when 1 wanted to d something like go to Atlantic City and there were order to fill."

"Atlantic City? Gambling."

"Right. Did you remember that?"

"No. Not really. I just knew the two went togethe somehow."

Lena shrugged. "That's good. I think."

"So before we leave, tell me something about my life my almost ex, something that will give me a clue as t who I am." When she saw the faint look of fear in he sister's eyes she added, "I hope I'm not putting you i a bad spot."

"You haven't spoiled anything in the least. I'm jus worried about you. Are you sure you're not in any seriou pain?"

"I'm fine—really. A few twinges every now and then and the doctor said I'm going to be sore for a while. H says I must have fainted and that made my body so lim that I didn't try to avoid the accident and hurt mysel even more."

"You are lucky. You always were."

"Are our parents coming to visit?"

"I . . . I didn't tell them anything. They're on this second honeymoon and if I tell them, they'll just come running back here."

"Not that it would do any good."

"It'll be over soon. I just know it. And you deserve to be happy."

Jesslyn felt a twinge of pity for her sister. It was one thing not to remember anything about yourself and quite another to watch someone who loves you worry. She just had to remember and soon. If she didn't feel she was getting the best at his house she'd just demand that he take her to hers.

"What do you know about this man I married?"

Lena didn't know whether to tell her about the bully that made her come here and lie or give her as much of Palladin Rush that she knew.

"He's very tough. He tends to think the world should see things his way and that causes a lot of trouble."

"Did it cause problems in our marriage? Was I afraid of him?"

"You never discussed that with me, but truthfully I never felt you were in any danger. He's a lot bigger, but as far as I know, he'd never hurt you . . . physically."

Jesslyn was relieved. If she was being forced to stay with him, she wanted a weapon but didn't know how to ask for it. Now that Lena had convinced her not to worry, she just wanted to get out of the hospital. She almost missed the beginning of Lena's story about Palladin.

"We met him at a party and he was checking you out from the second you arrived," she said. "You had kind of a whirlwind courtship and got married. But you were busy climbing the corporate ladder, and you just grew apart."

Jesslyn leaned forward and studied her sister. She wore casual clothing, a cameo with a black woman hung around her neck. Still, she was dressed to go out and now Jesslyn felt she had ruined that. Now she tried to think of other things besides Palladin Rush.

Heat rushed to her face and she tried to hide it but it got worse when she heard someone yelling in the distance. "I'm fine, Lena—really," she repeated firmly, forcing a smile. "And I'm not worried about the shop."

Lena cocked her head and stared at her sister. "Could it be that you're wondering what Palladin will expect of you if you go live with him."

"Yes. What if one of us wants to reconcile and the other doesn't?"

"I don't think you should worry. You may both want to reconcile."

"Would that be good?"

"That would be great. He's pretty terrific looking. And I hear his house is fabulous. It's some kind of unique place. I think it was going to be a corporate retreat."

Jesslyn was still having trouble reconciling her busted marriage with a man who seemed to have it all.

"So when do we tell him that we've agreed to go with him?"

"I think he's finalizing your hospital bill."

Jesslyn drifted back into a dreamless sleep that only lasted for the time it took the nurse to leave the room and walk back to her station. Jesslyn stirred and moaned. She tried to postpone opening her eyes because somehow her body knew that consciousness would bring pain. She didn't want to face it. The medication was wearing off, and her body was like one big toothache. Everyone kept talking about the miracle that she hadn't broken anything, but her back hurt and she had seen the cuts on her leg. The cuts would require plastic surgery at a later date, or she would always have to wear opaque stockings. She couldn't understand why some words meant something to her and the most important like her name had currently vacated her memory bank.

She shifted to find a comfortable position that only made it worse. She wouldn't ask the nurse for any pain-killers. She'd just keep telling herself over and over that the pain was gone. It would be a sort of hypnosis, and soon she would feel as good as she said.

Images popped into her head like the lights from a flashbulb. A black Ferrari. A woman with light brown eyes. Pretty woman. A red Blazer. Then she heard far away screams. The car was sliding down a hill and a tree was in the path.

It was frightening that somehow she knew she'd seen all these things, but she couldn't put them together or put names with them except for the man who said she was his wife. She wouldn't have believed him, but a memory of kissing him popped in her mind every time she saw him. He came to the hospital and . . .

Her eyes flew open. Now she knew where she was and a slight fear accompanied that knowledge. She looked around the hospital room. Although her body ached with every movement, she pulled herself up to a sitting position and put a pillow from the side of the bed she hadn't slept on behind her. She wriggled until she was facing the window. The only thing she could see were snowcapped trees. That seemed to go on until they faded into the horizon. Just looking at them gave her chills.

Palladin's mountain. And she was going to stay at his log home.

She could hardly remember how she'd ended up in

this bed. She wore a long white ruffled silk nightshirt and it seemed to feel right, but she didn't remember changing from the opened-back hospital gown.

She tried to recall everything that had happened after she'd been admitted to the hospital. There'd been all those questions—questions she couldn't answer because she'd had no earthly idea of who she was so how could she know what happened with a car. "The Ferrari," she said aloud. "That's what they were talking about." The brief flash of memory was gone so she still didn't know what happened. Mac. She remembered him from the hospital, yelling at her until Palladin asked him to leave. He didn't believe her. Everyone else called her Mrs. Rush or Carolann, but he called her Jesslyn. Finally, she'd asked and he'd satisfied her curiosity when he explained that she didn't like Carolann so they called her by her middle name. She had flatly refused the suggestion of staying in the hospital a few more days.

She giggled when she remembered the bulldozer Palladin turned into when she told him she didn't want to follow the doctor's orders. He'd simply said, "I own a mountain and you're coming to stay with me." Despite not really knowing who he was, she felt safe enough to nod when the doctor asked if she really wanted to leave.

She was glad her sister was coming with them. Somehow, it was comforting to know you had more family than just a husband.

She'd spent a night in a hospital room while Palladin had made travel arrangements. Lena said she would go to Jesslyn's apartment and pack for the trip. Jesslyn tried to imagine the apartment but a snake, a boa, flashed in her mind, and she shook her head to wipe out that image. The morning before leaving the hospital, another man came to visit her. He was in a wheelchair. When he left, Lena kept talking about his good looks, his diamond stud earring and his pet, a falcon. Jesslyn admitted to herself he was impressive, but she found herself drawn to Palladin.

The next thing Jesslyn had known, she'd been dozing in the back seat of a limousine, her sister next to her with Palladin Rush in the driver's seat. And, again, she'd felt safe.

Now, as the medication wore off she felt her mind was clear and she began to formulate her own questions. One she'd over heard Lena ask Palladin. "Who would want to kill her?"

She looked at her hands. Her nails were very short as if she worked with her hands. She didn't want to put anyone else in danger. If someone did want to kill her, then maybe this mountain was the safest place to be.

Jesslyn gasped as she saw the log home sitting on the mountain with lights on the top floor blazing and throwing patterns across the snow. In the darkness of the car, she turned to Lena. "Have you ever seen anything like this?"

"N . . . No," she answered. "We didn't do much socializing while I lived in Michigan."

"I'll give you a tour tomorrow," Palladin said. "I think it's best that we all get a good night's sleep."

He pulled into the space under the deck and parked the limousine. "Stay in the car until I check the house," he ordered. He went inside, leaving Jesslyn and Lena to talk.

"Why can't you stay a few days?" Jesslyn asked. "Maybe you can help bring my memory back."

"Not that I don't want to, but someone has to run the store and keep us out of the poorhouse."

"You'll call me every night, right?" Jesslyn made no attempt to keep the fear out of her voice. She was in the middle of nowhere, with a man people told her was her husband and, while she hadn't recognized Lena as her sister, she wanted her to stay around. Yet she knew it couldn't happen.

Palladin returned and led them through the mud room where they deposited their heavy coats and boots. They entered the main house and again the women nodded to each other in astonishment. The home had four bedrooms that were divided by the great room, with the main focal point of a huge stone fireplace in its center that stretched past the second story of the house. The room also divided between the sitting area and the kitchen and dining area as well as acting as a support for the stairs on either side that led to the second floor.

"Now I know why you laughed when Jeff called you a black Abe Lincoln," Lena told him.

"Who's Jeff," asked Jesslyn.

"He's a guy I date."

Jesslyn wanted to explore the magnificent structure from every angle, but although she'd spent a week in the hospital, she felt her eyes closing. Hoping no one noticed, she started for the stairs.

"Uh huh," Palladin stepped in front of her. "You can barely stand up. You need rest."

"I've been resting for a whole week. I didn't even get to go to my partner's funeral."

Palladin's brows knitted together as he looked at Lena.

"I had to tell her something," Lena said.

"Guess so," he finally said.

"I feel badly that I can't really mourn because I can't even see her face clearly in my mind."

"Don't worry, sis, it'll come back."

"So, let me get you settled." He signaled for them to follow him and walked across the room and opened the door in a corner. He left them to retrieve their luggage.

The room Jesslyn looked over had eggshell walls and a couple of blue and beige area rugs. The pattern in the rug was carried over in a lightly stenciled pattern down each wall. The night tables on either side of the bed matched a standing wardrobe closet near the window. Somehow, though Palladin had said on several occasions that she never lived in the cabin, she felt at home.

This room called to her, but as she explored a little further, she found a Jacuzzi in the full bath that adjoined the room. Obviously, this was the master bedroom.

The minute she walked into this room, she knew it was hers. She loved it, with its enormous maple wood canopy bed and creamy white material wrapped around the top. It had an elegant, romantic look. The bed was so high from the floor that it required a little step stool next to the bed for Jesslyn to be able to get in the bed. Six stark white pillows neatly stacked against the headboard and a quilt of many colors was tucked under the mattress that made Jesslyn want to crawl in and not worry about her mental block. At the foot of the bed was a large Thomasville chest that probably housed more linen. The room wasn't too feminine nor too masculine, but a blend that both could enjoy. Jesslyn wondered what other women might have stayed here.

Palladin returned with the luggage and set it down by

the bed. Jesslyn noticed they were only her bags and did not include the tiny overnight duffle bag that had belonged to Lena.

"I can't take this room," she told him.

"Why not? I think it's pretty terrific."

"Right, and I won't put you out of your bedroom."

He ran his fingers over his mustache and beard. "Come with me."

She wanted him to take the luggage, but for a big man, he moved quickly and the women had no choice but to follow.

He crossed the great room and opened a door. "Take a look." He stepped back.

Lena, more curious that Jesslyn, stepped forward into the room first, then Jesslyn came in and looked around. The bed was even larger in this room and the decorations in browns and muted greens were clearly of a masculine nature.

"My bedroom."

Lena was now on the other side of the room and opened a door. "Yep. It has a Jacuzzi even bigger than yours," she told Jesslyn.

Looking chagrined, Jesslyn turned to Palladin. "Do all the bedrooms have their own spas?"

"Umm huh," he nodded.

"Mine, too?"

"Yes, Lena, yours, too. Originally this was going to be a lodge and conference center. The owners fell on hard times a few years ago and had to abandon their plans. When I bought the tiny cabin that sat here, I found the plans and decided that it should be a conference center. When it was finished, I just didn't want another house."

"So I have a pretty rich husband. Was I going to get a lot of money if we got a divorce," she asked. She was trying to jog her memory.

"No," he answered.

"Prenuptial agreement?"

"Iron clad," he said.

Before she could dwell on that thought, her sister was looking at the view above the bed. "Wow!" she said. "Seeing stars like this must make for some interesting nights."

Jesslyn agreed and tried to hide a yawn.

"I saw that," her sister said as she entered the room.

"So did I," Palladin added. "Go to bed now."

As much as she wanted to defy him, her body simply wouldn't cooperate. She went back to the room she'd been assigned but didn't bother to unpack. She was suddenly so tired that her eyes wouldn't stay open. She pulled a nightgown from the overnight case she'd put her things in from the hospital and went into the bathroom. She washed her face and stared at her reflection. "Please, please let me wake up tomorrow and know who I am," she told the image.

She used the step by the bed and climbed up and scurried under the covers. She was asleep before she could raise another thought about who she was.

Lena and Palladin sat in front of the fireplace as they worked out a schedule for the shop. He expected her to handle most of the functions but would supply a support team that would make it easier. He didn't tell her how many favors he'd called in to make sure that the shop would be there for Jesslyn's return. Once that was settled, he poured her a small sherry but didn't take one himself.

"She's better off with me."

"That's what you say now. I'll be in New York and there's no telling what could happen here."

"If you're trying to allude that once you leave I can slip into Jesslyn's bed, let me remind you that there are penalties for that sort of thing."

"How close are you and my sister?"

"I'll let her tell you when she regains her memory. Good night, Lena." He left her sitting there and went to his room. After taking a shower and trimming his beard and mustache, he crawled into bed. He generally slept nude, but made a mental note to pull out some pyjamas now that he had a house guest.

Sixteen

The next morning Jesslyn was shocked when she opened her eyes and focused on the digital clock by her bed. Her drapes were drawn so the room was still dark and yet the clock said it was 11:36 A.M. She sat up and looked around. She didn't know what she was expecting, but this wasn't it. Her wish from last night hadn't been fulfilled because she still knew absolutely nothing about herself.

The difference in the room showed that someone had come in and unpacked her bag. The closet door was ajar and she could see her clothing hanging neatly inside. The dresses were rather long and with much detail, and she wondered how her old-fashioned style had attracted a man who seemed to prefer the casual look.

She grabbed a pair of leggings and a long blouse, then looked in the dresser drawers and found her underwear. She showered, dressed, and minutes later, she was headed for the kitchen. The fireplace blocked her from view and she was astonished to hear Palladin warning no, she thought, threatening Lena.

"She's going to need the business when her memory comes back, and it had better be there. Don't try to charm any of the financial people out of money. They report to me. And believe me, it's not worth the trouble to break any of my rules."

Lena was listening but not looking at him. Somehow Jesslyn knew that her sister was afraid. What could this man hold over her? Even in the hospital, Jesslyn wondered why he wouldn't let her go back to her apartment. Wouldn't the things she'd lived with since their break up be more likely to help her remember? What else was going on here? She had no time to think as a deep voice said, "Good morning, Jesslyn. What would you like for breakfast?"

Feeling a little stupid at getting caught eavesdropping, Jesslyn came forward and sat next to her sister. "I think I need to take it easy. I'll have some tea and toast."

He nodded and turned to the stove to retrieve the hot water. As he held it over the cup he asked, "How do you take it?" Embarrassed because she didn't know the answer, Jesslyn was relieved to hear Lena give the instructions to make it an herbal tea. Palladin complied and then popped four slices of bread in the toaster.

As promised, Palladin gave them the Cook's Tour and then fixed a snack as Lena packed for the 7:15 P.M. train back to New York. At the station, the women were teary-eyed, and he gave them some time to be alone before getting Lena situated on the train and hugging her goodbye.

They were finally alone. It wasn't as if Jesslyn expected Palladin to pounce on her as soon as Lena left; it was simply the thought of being alone with an attractive man who used to be your husband. Correction, who was still legally your husband. She fought the inner recesses of her mind for some sort of recognition, but as she left the bedroom, after being forced to take a nap to regain her strength, she found none. When she'd initially balked, he told her in that deep, "I-mean-it" voice, that he didn't have a problem stripping her clothes off and putting her to bed naked.

After her nap, she felt a little better, but sad after no flashes of memory came. She slammed her hand against her night table and decided to look around again. The house, so familiar to him, was alien territory to her. When she'd asked him if she'd ever lived there, he shook his head. "You don't like isolation." She took a slow tour of the house and the inside seemed more magnificent that the outside.

Jesslyn thought of the interior as a house without walls. The living room, dining room and kitchen were divided more by paint, space and furniture settings. In the living room section, she saw a bookshelf that blended in with the white pine wall covering. Under the last shelf were baskets that contained a myriad of magazines from financial to computer to travel to almost anything she could think of at that moment. She decided on a travel magazine. It was amazing that such a large place could seem cozy because of the towering two-way designed fireplace that also acted as a room separator between the living room and dining room. A good supply of wood enabled them to use the hearth for most of the heat and to conserve fuel. Most of the furniture was oversized and comfortable for someone as large as Palladin, yet not too overpowering for Jesslyn to enjoy. Since he was in his office catching up on things, it gave Jesslyn a chance to do a little rearranging while she waited for him. The tufted ottomans were the size of a coffee table and she pulled one of them near the fireplace and sat down to peruse the magazine while waiting for him to return.

A physical therapist had designed a series of Tai Chi exercises for Jesslyn to help her get back in shape while avoiding all the bouncing around that aerobic exercises were based on. She would start those exercises the next day. She fell asleep while making those plans.

Palladin studied the sleeping form and steeled himself against picking her up. Despite his righteous indignation at Lena's suggestion that he might take advantage of Jesslyn, it was exactly what he wanted to do. Evidently, she hadn't told her sister they'd become intimate, or Lena would never have left them alone. Bringing that into the foreground of his mind made him even more aware of how easily he reacted to being near her. He hoped that Skip and Mac found something to clear her now that he'd told them about Hank Reynolds. He hoped he could hide his reactions from Jesslyn and he hoped like hell that she remembered that she still wanted him. Never had he wanted a woman so much. He fell asleep after admitting that cold showers weren't what they were cracked up to be.

They spent a lazy day getting acquainted and talking about whatever they could find that prevented them from talking about their relationship. Later, she curled up on the oversized chair in front of the fireplace and leafed through magazines while he took care of some financial accounts for a client.

The table was set for two, but the size of the serving dishes seemed to indicate it was for a small dinner party. Palladin obviously had a healthy appetite. Why wouldn't he need a lot more food to fuel his large body, she thought, as she settled in at the other end of the table and paused. She noted the real china, the silver and the candles.

"Uh huh, don't even try it," he told her. He stood by the stove holding a large frying pan.

"I beg your pardon."

"If you think you're going to be waited on, think again."

"I . . . don't remember how to cook, or if I ever did," she said, then a wide smile appeared.

He remembered the time in her apartment when she explained the four basic food groups—eat in, take out, frozen and canned. Her antique-style refrigerator was filled with items that could be thrown in a microwave. Palladin had never considered that cooking. Even in the Service, he'd been known for his gourmet meals. There were so many other things pulling at his life, Kaliq, Carol-ann, the fact that he liked financial counseling work, and that he was just burned out from trying to do it all.

At first, he thought he'd go back to the Secret Service, but after he got involved with the cabin and the feasible way to make it pay for itself, he had changed his mind. His hair had gone through several lengths during the change, from the very short brush cut at the beginning of his sabbatical to shoulder length to the just-below-chin length that seemed to be right for him.

He studied Jesslyn. In so many ways, he admired her. She'd taken the proverbial lemon and made enough lem-onade to last a lifetime. For a moment, he wondered if that grin on her face as she said she didn't remember how to cook was real or not.

"Well, in that case, all you have to do is take orders. In fact, that might be a good way to deal with you. I'll just tell you what you used to do and then you'll just obey."

Palladin bit his lip and stared at her while thinking of the possibilities. The ones he wanted to happen couldn't. When her memory returned, and he was sure it would, she would hate him for taking advantage of her.

Jesslyn studied his face for a moment. He meant obedience in the kitchen. At least, that's what she hoped he meant, but maybe that was another way to help her memory. He could just tell her what to do and sooner or later it would just come back to her naturally. Their eyes met for a brief moment and both knew the other had produced a fantasy thinking about that statement. And each was afraid it might come true.

"What can I do to earn my supper?" That didn't help eliminate the fantasy going on in her head, but he didn't seem to notice anything inappropriate.

He opened a drawer, found a sharp knife and handed it to Jesslyn. "Peel those cucumbers and slice them in half, lengthwise and get rid of the seeds."

Palladin saw her look down at her hands—as if she didn't recognize them. As she performed the little task, he noticed her hands, also. Her nails were now short, unpolished, not the lacquered paste-ons from before. Most of the women he knew had a standing weekly appointment for a manicure. He made a mental note to call Lena and get Jesslyn's personal appointment book. They'd never been able to find the pouchbag that she'd been carrying the night of the accident. It might still be out on the road. Jesslyn was driving, and Carolann's bag was wedged down on the driver's side, so it was only natural that the people who rescued her assumed it belonged to her. So many questions remained unanswered and would continue to linger until her memory returned.

Jesslyn watched as he put a large cast iron skillet over a low flame on the stove and then pulled out another pan. Dumping butter in that one and putting it on another low flame.

While she performed the simple task she noticed a large bowl filled with an odd mixture. "What's that?" she asked, turning up her nose.

"Tabbouleh. Sort of an herb salad. It's something I make when I'm tired of potatoes or rice."

"What's in it?"

"Bulgur, mint, scallions, lemon juice, cayenne pepper. Oh, sprinkle some salt and freshly ground pepper on those cucumbers."

Behind his back, she made a face, then picked up a fork and gingerly took a small portion and tasted it. It seemed grainy, tangy. Different, but not bad. She put the fork near her plate and continued her task, flavoring the cucumbers and slicing them.

"How was it?"

She smiled. "Okay."

With a cat-like movement, Palladin scooped the cucumbers Jesslyn had just finished and dumped them in the second skillet. At the same time he added a small amount of oil to the first skillet.

"You're pretty handy to have around the kitchen."

"Why is it that if a man isn't married, people think he only eats out of cans and boxes?"

"Oh, some guys are exactly like that."

"And some women are worse. Was Paul that type?"

"Who?"

"Never mind."

"Tell me." Her voice developed a slight edge.

"A guy you were seeing." He'd hoped for some recognition, but as he studied Jesslyn's face he knew the name hadn't helped her memory problem.

"Does he know where I am?"

"No. Uh . . . You guys broke up a while ago."

When he glanced over his shoulder, he saw tears forming in her eyes. "What's wrong?"

She slammed her hand down on the table. "What kind of woman am I? I screwed up my marriage, and now I find out I have another busted relationship to my credit."

Wrong again, Rush. He thought to himself. Mac had been so sure about Jesslyn Owens. She was going to use Carolann as a way of redeeming her reputation, but that wasn't what he saw in this woman.

"Maybe it's the men and not you."

"Right!" Obviously, she was not convinced.

The slight whiff of smoke from the other skillet demanded his attention, and he pulled it off the fire to let it cool a bit. He wasn't sure he could offer her any comfort without telling her the truth. He put the pan back on the fire then added four pieces of salmon fillet.

Jesslyn had pulled herself back together by the time the salmon was finished and watched as Palladin put the salmon on a platter and the cucumbers in a bowl. He lit the candles and turned down the lights. On another occasion, it might have been something to do to set a romantic mood, but tonight he just wanted Jesslyn to relax and feel comfortable in his house.

As dinner progressed, Palladin struggled to find something they could talk about. Funny, he never thought about how difficult conversation is with someone who's missing several years from her life. What she thought of as a current event, he thought of as history. What she knew about music would now be considered classics. Her favorite TV shows had been canceled and replaced by ones with strange sounding names and actors she didn't know.

He did notice that none of the things she knew was personal. She talked about everything she could remember almost as a spectator who flipped through life as one would when changing channels on TV.

The thought of TV reminded him he hadn't listened or watched much of the news since the accident.

"Sorry, I need to catch up on a few things," he explained to Jesslyn as he pressed a switch near the table and a wall slid back revealing a television at least 50 inches that was already set to the All News Channel.

"Today in Chicago, the fast rising career of Woodrow Gary, the Senator from Illinois took a turn for the better," the woman was saying.

Jesslyn saw Palladin's face take on a fierce expression as he stared at the screen. He obviously recognized someone. "Do you know them? Do I know them?"

"Yes. The tall man on the left is Hank Reynolds. The gray-haired man is Senator Gary. We met him at a fund-raiser in New York."

". . . Senator Gary had been beleaguered with rumors of money problems for his Senatorial race, the charge that the Senator had contributions coming from shady sources, but when pressed, his accuser could not supply any proof." The camera showed a thin, slightly balding man running from the reporters. He turned, shook his fist at them and yelled "Charisma isn't everything if you're a crook. I had the evidence, but I don't have it now. When I get it, you'll see."

"And?"

He waited for some recognition and when it didn't happen he let it drop. It meant another phone call to make tonight.

"He seems familiar, why?"

"He's one of your clients." It was enough of the truth, without trying to scare her about the man.

They watched the news for another hour, and he found himself enjoying being a teacher. She was like a sponge. One minute he'd tell her something and the next she was asking all the right questions, digging deeper for answers. Remembering them or learning them. He didn't know, but the fact that her eyes danced as she grasped a subject made him talk more than he'd expected.

"I'm going to take you to a hockey practice tomorrow."

"You know the Flyers?"

"Not a professional team. My little guys."

"What do you do for the team?" She asked.

"Buy them uniforms, skates, coach, whatever."

"Do they have sponsors?"

"A few. So you know hockey, eh?"

Jesslyn smiled and tried to explain. "I guess so. I know what it is, some of the players but I still don't know *how* I know."

"Probably a memory flash."

"Well, why doesn't it flash on telling me more about me?"

"Give it time."

As they finished dinner and lingered over the 1993 Louis Jadot Puligny-Montrachet Chardonnay, he realized that no matter how much he loved his solitude, he'd missed conversations like this. He'd had dinner at a woman's house and enjoyed letting her show off her domestic skills, but he'd never invited a date to his house for dinner or anything else. Most women hated the isolation of his place, anyway.

While she'd managed to eat one piece of salmon, a spoonful of salad and several cucumber slices, she'd watched Palladin eat two pieces of salmon, half the salad and the rest of the cucumber slices. He didn't just eat to fill his stomach. He was a man who enjoyed savoring the meal.

"I don't think I could eat anything else," Jesslyn said.

"Really. Well, I think you're a chocoholic."

He went over to the refrigerator and pulled out a flat pie pan. "I made this a couple of days ago."

She looked at it and was lost. A toasted coconut chocolate ice cream pie.

"I think you're right. And I think something in my stomach just moved over to make room for a piece of that."

After dinner, when they were relaxed enough and Jesslyn felt bold enough she asked, "Would you help me try to remember something?"

"Sure, what?"

"Our lives together. Would you kiss me?"

Palladin felt cold fingers down his spine and for a moment couldn't answer. Then he simply said, "I don't think that's a good idea."

Jesslyn hadn't told him that she remembered when he came to the hospital. She remembered him saying that he needed her. Deep inside she felt that he meant it. After all, he didn't know that she could hear him. She looked around at the care he'd given in putting his home together. That kind of man would take care of a relationship in the same way. He wanted her back, and she wanted to be here. She'd find a way to make him admit it.

What else could he say? The truth. That if he kissed her he wouldn't want to stop there, and he didn't want her in his bed thinking she was his wife. He wanted her there knowing full well who she was and why she was in his arms.

"If I had the accident on the way here, aren't we still . . . close."

"Not that close. We talk and you ask for help with your finances, that's all."

"Then why can't I live with my sister while I'm . . . recovering?"

"Because it isn't safe . . . yet."

"Doesn't the woman in your life have anything to say about this arrangement?"

"There isn't a . . . no she doesn't."

Jesslyn smiled and looked back at the TV. He'd almost said what she suspected. He wasn't involved with anyone and that meant she still had a chance to get her husband back. She had to get some information from her sister that would help. The accident had given her a second chance, and she wasn't going to blow it this time.

"Can you entertain yourself for a little while? I'll be in my office."

"Sure." She stood up and began to clear the table.

"You don't have to do that."

"You cooked a great meal. I'll do the dishes." She busied herself with loading the dishwasher, as she'd seen him do the night before. Within minutes, the kitchen was clean and Jesslyn was browsing through the stack of magazines by the fireplace, pulled the large ottoman nearer and got comfortable thumbing through the ones about the infinite variety of log homes. It was amazing how this place could seem so large and yet be so homey.

Palladin dropped the phone in the receiver and sat there. He didn't believe in coincidence, and the idea of Hank Reynolds being a client when Jesslyn's business has been targeted for industrial espionage was highly suspect. Kaliq had agreed with him and would spend a few days hanging out in New York, probing the Internet and contacting old friends. He'd be back in Pennsylvania in a few days.

He knew he wasn't just in his office to catch up on things or get someone to help with his investigation. He was hiding. If Kaliq found out, he'd never hear the end of it. He was afraid of someone sixteen inches shorter and one hundred and twenty pounds lighter. What was it about the Owens sisters? Lena had thrown down the gauntlet at their first meeting, and now Jesslyn asked him to kiss her. His log home was almost eight thousand square feet and was starting to shrink. The knock on the door made him feel the house had just gotten a little smaller. Where was Kaliq when he needed him?

"Come in."

She opened the door wide enough to see him at his desk but didn't enter the room. "I know this is off limits, but I need to ask you a question."

"Yeah?"

"I don't like the clothes my sister packed. Could you take me shopping?"

"Okay. There are a lot of great outlet stores around."

She nodded and disappeared.

A wide grin spread across his face. The solution to cramped quarters no red-blooded American woman could resist—shopping!

Seventeen

After feeling smug for about three minutes, Palladin realized his mistake. When they left the hospital, she had Carolann's handbag. She thought the money and credit cards belonged to her, and with Carolann's death, he had canceled and destroyed them. He grabbed the phone and dialed Lena's number.

"When Mac first called me and wouldn't let me see her, I canceled all her credit cards. I wasn't sure what you guys were up to," a sleepy Lena told him.

"Okay. Have you gotten any replacement cards?"

"A couple. I'll send them."

"Okay. Thanks."

"But I know what you should do for this particular shopping trip."

He waited and when she didn't continue, "Lena?"

"It's your plan—you foot the bill."

The distinctive click and the dial tone left no doubt that Lena Owens Carter would only go so far in this deception. He dropped the phone back in its cradle and went to find Jesslyn.

He knocked on the door and Jesslyn gave him permission to come in. She sat in the oversized bed with several of the pillows propping her up as she leafed through a news magazine with several more scattered on the bed. She looked both innocent and sexy.

"I have a morning workout with my team. I can come back and pick you up after breakfast."

"I'd like to see the workout."

"Sure." Palladin smiled and left. He was surprised, since women who liked sports usually preferred the professional kinds. Jesslyn was different. And it was a difference he liked.

"I guess we should leave after breakfast tomorrow. You don't have any credit cards, so we'll use mine."

"Okay. And I'll write you a check. I still have money in the bank, don't I?"

"Why don't you just let it stay there until you get back to . . . yourself?"

She nodded and reached for another book. He watched as the movement caused her nightgown to slip from her shoulders and as her fingers touched the book she revealed the top of her breast.

"Good night," he said and made a hasty exit, closing the door before he heard her response.

That sight meant a restless night for Palladin. When Carolann had been brought to the hospital, she didn't have a purse. His mind replayed as much of the accident as he could piece together from the police report. Mac had called in a few more favors and only a tiny mention of the accident had appeared in a local newspaper. If Carolann had been thrown from the car, as they believed, then there should have been another purse—Jesslyn's. He'd ask around and see what turned up. He thought about it and decided that if anyone found it, they wouldn't associate any of the names in the paper with the accident and would probably keep the money and throw the bag away.

As they prepared to leave, Jesslyn asked, "Don't you have another car besides the limo? We don't want people to think we're celebrities, do we? Where's your chauffeur?"

"When I bought the car I thought it might be an investment. There were a lot of corporate clients in Philadelphia and New York that I'd be able to start someone out in business. Then I found out it's a great car to take my team around in."

"Well, the limo it is. Should I sit in the back?" she teased.

"Don't even try it." He opened the passenger door and waited.

"You're no fun." She said, as she sat in the limo and swung her legs inside.

The trip to the Franklin Mills Mall would probably be an all day excursion. He'd deliberately selected it, rather than Strawbridge or Clothier.

But first it was off to the ice rink. Jesslyn was surprised at how many little guys there were vying for spots on the team. They practiced skating forward and backward. Each took a turn being the goalie and trying to prevent Palladin from scoring. Jesslyn was amazed at the quickness of a few of them.

Palladin was in control. When two of the boys decided to have a hockey fight, he stepped between them.

"You can play on the team and not fight, or you can fight and you're both history."

The youngsters glared at each other and decided that hockey was better than fighting. He seemed so at ease with children, nothing like the tough facade when he spoke with adults.

After practice, it was time to shop. At Franklin Mills, each area was given a color and called a neighborhood. They'd entered into the Green Neighborhood and began to walk through the mall. They roamed through using some, but not many, of the coupons from the book each shopper was given.

Jesslyn was drawn to the Saks Fifth Avenue outlet in the Blue Neighborhood. Roaming through designer's discounts made her think of Palladin.

They went next door to T.J. Maxx, and she found some casual clothes that suited her current lifestyle. Three hours and two trips to the cash machine later, they were in a restaurant in the Red Neighborhood.

"We could have gotten something from one of the fast food places, you know," Jesslyn said.

"I thought you'd rather sit down to a full meal and rest. You must have a black belt in shopping."

"Hey, don't blame it all on me. You're the one who insisted on getting me a TV-VCR and all those tapes."

"My collection runs to history and old movies."

"I can't believe with a TV that size you don't have more tapes."

"Hey, Easter's coming up and you haven't seen *The Ten Commandments* until you've experienced Moses parting the Red Sea on it."

The smile left her face for a moment, and he knew she was thinking that by then if her memory returned, she wouldn't be spending Easter with him.

* * *

As they drove back she explained, "I'm going to use one of the books I got as a journal. I've been having some flashes of memory and I want to write them down. Maybe together they'll trigger something."

He tried to make it sound casual, "What kind of memory flashes?"

"Nothing specific. A flashlight in my face. Someone calling my name."

"What's the other book for?"

"An expense account. I'm going to pay you for all those clothes you bought me."

"Don't. Call it a gift."

"No way. You're my financial advisor, not my husband. You can't buy me things."

He laughed at the way her stubbornness came through, even though she didn't remember anything. It had taken that sort of determination to fight back when most women would have hidden or taken a low profile job after being called a thief.

He admired her tenacity, her strength and he wanted her to stay with him, but it wouldn't work. He, Mac and Kaliq had thought they could have it all, but none of the women could handle it. Palladin liked a woman who could take care of herself, and that woman would hate my solitary lifestyle, a Catch-22 and all of that.

The gray-haired man slammed his fist on the table. "What kind of incompetents are running things." He glared at the other three men sitting with him.

"I don't know, sir," said Hank Reynolds. "He keeps her so isolated that we don't know if she has her memory back."

"A simple thing like getting a diskette from a little tramp, and you guys blow it."

The men were not going to argue, but one was brave enough to offer a suggestion. "You're never going to get her to come forward unless you move Palladin Rush."

"Then I guess I been overpaying you guys. People out there want to open my empire to the scrutiny of the electoral college. If that happens, gentlemen, and you could have prevented it, I'm going to see that you all pay."

The meeting room was small and the people who were present knew they were in trouble. As Hillary Rodham Clinton called the strategy room the "War Room," Senator Gary had called his "Takeover Squad." He expected every one involved on the planning to hire the best people for the job. Someone wasn't doing that. He would only issue one warning. His reputation as a career-breaker was one he worked hard to keep. He was a dangerous man with dangerous friends.

"Gentlemen, I'm giving you fair warning. If that diskette surfaces, and I have to explain it. I'm going to make sure that you're going to be doing the same thing."

As Palladin pulled up to the house, he was surprised to see Mac's car parked out front. They greeted each other. Skip was driving and Palladin introduced Jesslyn to him.

"I need to talk to . . ."

"Jesslyn," Palladin supplied.

"Ms. Owens," Mac amended.

Palladin led them inside, and after seeing that they were comfortable, went to get the packages out of the car. He silently cursed the tension he felt in the room.

If only Mac could get to know her. Give her a chance. He'd know she couldn't do anything illegal.

"Ms. Owens, I need to know if anything has come back to you."

"Were we friends?"

"Once."

"But you don't like me now." She sensed his hostility.

"That's not true."

"Yes it is. Are you mad at me because I left Palladin."

"I did advise against it, but you never listened to me."

"I don't think he likes us to fight. So why don't we put on a good face for him?"

Mac grinned. "You're absolutely right."

When Palladin returned, he noticed the relaxed atmosphere and lifted an eyebrow to Mac questioning it.

"Jesslyn and I are trying to get to know each other again." Mac told him. "I think it's a great idea for her to write down what she remembers. Keep me informed?"

"Sure." Palladin promised.

The discussion turned from the problems to the shopping expedition, and although Palladin invited him to stay over, Mac insisted he get back to New York and left.

"Well, I guess you're glad now," Palladin said.

"What do you mean?"

"While you were playing hostess, you didn't get a chance to unpack the goody bags."

She grinned. "You're right."

While she unpacked the clothing, he set up the TV-VCR and adjusted it for the best view from the bed.

He noticed one bag remained on the bed. "What's that?"

"Personal things I picked up while you were touring the electronic section."

Something in the way she said "personal" made him not want details. After testing one of the tapes in the VCR, he left the room.

As soon as he did, Jesslyn reached in the bag and produced several pairs of matching bra and panty sets. Red, purple, green, strong vibrant colors that her complexion demanded. She remembered the saleslady's reaction to the next item she pulled from the bag. The white satin and lace peignoir set. "Are you buying that for your honeymoon?" the woman asked.

"No. Just for seducing my husband."

"Honey, ain't no way that can't work."

Palladin used his shoulder to hold the phone while he threw together a quick meal. He planned on fixing something light, since they weren't really hungry.

"When are you getting in?" He was saying as Jesslyn came into the kitchen and began setting the table.

It was amazing how they'd fallen into a routine and were less and less shy around each other in the few days since she'd left the hospital. He looked for signs of fatigue during the whole day, but had found none. The idea of shopping seemed to give women extra strength and endurance.

When Jesslyn started to get up from the table after eating, her leg muscles cramped and she sat down quickly.

"Damn. I knew I shouldn't have let you run all over that mall."

"I didn't run. I took it easy. I rested between stores most of the time."

"Right!" he said, as he got up and came around the table. Not waiting for her to respond, he pulled the chair back with her still sitting in it, scooped her up into his arms and carried her to her bedroom.

"Get out of those clothes, I'll be right back."

"For what?" she asked and then smothered a giggle.

"Don't get smart. Put on something so I can give you a rubdown."

"A massage?"

"A rubdown." He said again and left.

By the time he returned, she'd slipped into a pair of loose-legged PJ's. She lay back on the bed and let him stuff pillows under her legs then he started massaging her legs. Alternating, he rubbed from the ankle up the calf to the knee until he could tell by her relaxed facial muscles that the cramps were leaving.

"Doing too much," he told her. "But I hear that, if this happens, the only way to get used to it is to do the same thing the next day."

She hadn't opened her eyes, but her groan told him that she wasn't that anxious to hit the mall again.

"I think I'll just walk around the house."

"Good idea. But don't go down by the barn. I haven't been able to shore it up yet."

"Okay," she kept her eyes closed and relished the feeling of his long fingers moving up her legs. Working to make her comfortable. Allowing her to fall asleep.

Kaliq had come over for Palladin's lunch and charmed Jesslyn with his wit.

"Jesslyn are you all right?" Palladin interrupted. "You haven't touched your food."

"Well, darlin'," Kaliq said. "I can understand that.

First you have a terrible accident and then you have to eat Palladin's cooking."

"What's that supposed to mean? I'm a good cook."

"Yeah, if you like strange sounding food. Personally, give me a good old-fashioned steak, so rare that the cow is still attached, and I'm a happy man."

Jesslyn laughed. "How'd you get stuck with Julia Child junior over there for a friend?"

"Errors of a misspent youth. He was my roommate at Harvard."

"Was he always into strange food?"

"Nah. He used to eat like a real human. Then he decided to get healthy."

"If you two don't stop talking about me as if I'm not here, I'm going to pull out that Middle East cookbook I have and really fix it so you can't pronounce what you're eating."

Kaliq winked at Jesslyn. "That threat is much too serious to test."

"Yeah, let's change the subject before he really gets mad."

They sat down and Jesslyn had to admit each time he'd fix something, whether she could pronounce the name or not, it had been delicious.

Kaliq told her about his work in Wyoming.

"I'm afraid of falcons," Jesslyn admitted.

"Then you must come spend some time with me and Namid."

"Namid?"

"It's Chippewa for Star Dancer," Palladin explained.

While Palladin busied himself outside for something, Kaliq had a chance to find out how things really were.

"No problems living here?" He asked.

"Not so far. Palladin's been great."

"And no memories?"

"I get flashes sometimes. A Ferrari. A woman with light brown eyes. And Palladin."

"Has anyone told you about these flashes?"

"I know that the car is the one I wrecked. The woman is my partner who was killed in the accident."

Kaliq was quiet for a moment. He watched little drops of snow slide down the windows in the front of the house. "Do you know why?"

"Someone wanted to kill me?"

"Yeah. Would you rather be in the hospital."

"No. I'm glad I'm here instead of the hospital. I don't think I could feel safe there."

"Palladin will guard you with his life, you know that, don't you?"

"I do and I believe he will."

"Then why do I get flashes of you now. Sitting in a beat up old car?"

Kaliq knew exactly why she had those pictures in her mind. Because he had agreed to get involved for an old friend. He was glad that she wasn't looking for an answer for the second part of her question. "Well, gotta go."

He headed back to the small cabin on Palladin's property.

The weather, Jesslyn noted, was still threatening everyone with sunny days backed by snow flurries. As she continued to look around, she knew Palladin was justifiably proud of his beautiful home. He was a man who chose solitude but opened his house to friends and Jesslyn hoped that if they didn't get back together, they would remain friends.

Left alone together again, Palladin and Jesslyn decided

on a game of chess. It took a long time to play out before he won.

"You're good," he said to her.

"You're better right now."

"What's that supposed to mean?"

"Oh, that when my memory comes back, I might be able to beat the pants off you."

"Well, that's one way to get them off."

She turned away, and he shook his head letting his dreads sweep around. "Blushing at your age, tsk, tsk." He kissed her on the forehead before he left. Then went out to take care of some other menial task.

All day she'd thought about him, about the kisses they must have shared, about how bitterly disappointed she'd been when he hadn't even tried to carry those kisses further. She'd had trouble falling asleep wondering what she would have done if he'd really kissed her and worried because maybe the reason he hadn't wanted her was that he had found someone else, and as soon as she got her memory back, he would ship her back to New York and get on with his new relationship. That would be the one thing she couldn't fight. If he didn't have a woman that he was madly in love with, they had a chance. If he did, well, she wished he would tell her, so she could get on with her life. Somewhere behind his eyes, he was living in a tough world and not willing to let anyone in.

There was one other problem. Jesslyn remembered, or thought she did, making love with him—recently, not years ago, even though he said the marriage had been over for years.

She felt the underlying warmth Palladin had and she wanted to be with him. There was something she couldn't explain. Intuition? Maybe. But she felt as if she'd met her soul mate.

Palladin sat in the office adjoining the house and wondered if he'd explained the situation to Kaliq enough. Surely the man understood that if he stayed over, there would be no chance for anything to happen. Kaliq liked her just because Jesslyn brought out another side in Palladin, a side that would fight Mac to keep her safe. But knowing what they shared before and now being with her when she couldn't remember was torture. He didn't know how many more cold showers and brisk walks in the cold he could take before coming down with pneumonia. How could she do this? He looked at her and he wanted her. She called his name and he wished it was in the heat of passion. He had been able to walk away from every woman in his romantic life except this one. And it wouldn't work. When she got her memory back, she might want to come and visit him, but he wanted more. He wanted her to stay with him. Just him for a few weeks, months, years, whatever it took for this passion to subside.

Jesslyn combed through some more magazines, planning to take several and read herself to sleep. She walked into her bedroom, threw the magazines on the bed and headed for the bath. She was feeling much better after the massage Palladin had given her the night before but decided not to mention it unless he did. She soaked in the Jacuzzi for fifteen minutes, dried herself off and put on a shimmering blue nightgown. Then she remembered the IOU's she'd written in her notebook. She slipped on a robe, grabbed them and headed for Palladin's office.

She tapped on the door and waited until he said she could enter. He was going over a financial report and he didn't look at her. She carefully looked at him, however. His locs were pulled back with an elastic band forcing them to lie flat against his neck. He'd trimmed his mustache and beard and didn't look quite as rakish as he had earlier. He didn't wear a tie and his white shirt was opened two buttons down allowing wisps of hair from his chest to peek out. He looked up at her, his black eyes studying her body, "Muscles cramping?"

"No," she said a bit louder than she wanted to. "I just wanted to give you these."

He looked at the slips of paper in her hand and was about to refuse, but then he looked at her and her face said it was important that he take them so he did. Carelessly tossing them in the "in box" on his desk. "Does that make you happy? Are you satisfied now? You owe me money."

"Yes."

She started to leave, then caught sight of the beaded handbag she'd brought home from the hospital. He had dumped the contents on a table opposite his desk and searched through it. Palladin hid a smile knowing how embarrassed she would be when she found the condoms, and he was right. As soon as she recognized them, she tried to put them in the handbag so he wouldn't see them. Unfortunately, the quick movement sent everything else scattering. She struggled a moment longer and closed the bag. She left the room but barely had time to close the door before Palladin burst into laughter. And she felt the heat rise in her face.

Eighteen

"I want to go for a walk," Jesslyn announced to Palladin the next morning. She tried not to notice his chest but couldn't help it. Despite the morning chill, he was shirtless as he worked on the fire. His broad back showed no signs of goose bumps, and yet Jesslyn could feel hers as she rubbed her arms. The mountain road couldn't be navigated, so she was stuck until enough snow melted and the truck could be used. Then she would insist on returning to her life away from him. She wriggled her toes in her bright, pink fuzzy slippers.

He obviously hadn't heard her. His tight jeans rode lower as he stoked the fire in the living room fireplace. A feeling of desire rippled through her, followed by embarrassment She felt a little like a Peeping Tom as she watched the muscles disturb the smooth bronze skin with each motion of his arm.

Realizing that he wasn't even aware she'd spoken, she cleared her throat and repeated her statement.

"Sure," he said without looking up. "A stroll after breakfast would be good for us."

"I don't want 'us' to do anything. I want to go for a walk. Alone."

Palladin rose and turned to her. "It's kinda dangerous, if you don't know the area . . ."

"I said a walk, not a trek. I don't plan to do too much. What, am I a prisoner?"

"Of course not But in your condition . . ."

"I've got amnesia or a mental block or whatever they want to call it this week. I'm not an invalid."

"Calm down. Don't forget to dress warmly and don't go too far."

She glared at him and stormed from the room. Taking her frustration out on the closet door and dresser drawers, she assembled her selections on the bed. Grateful that whoever packed for her had included thermals. When she'd asked about getting her clothes from New York to Pennsylvania, Palladin just said "a friend" had packed them. She wondered for a brief moment who it could have been then went on with her dressing. After the thermals, came black stirrup pants and then a heavy black sweater. Fifteen minutes later, she slipped her feet back into the bedroom slippers and tossed a short, beige down coat she'd found in the closet. A bright yellow scarf was in the pocket. She threw the coat over her arm. Somehow, the coat didn't bring any degree of familiarity as the other things she'd put on. She'd get her boots from the mud room and go out that way.

As she returned to the living room, she was surprised to see that Palladin had donned a red and green plaid shirt but had not buttoned it. He sat in the recliner by the fire and had pulled another one up for her.

"I made you some hot chocolate," he said, indicating the tray on the coffee table.

She wanted to give a snappy remark, but it would have been in poor taste for such a nice gesture. "Thank you," was all she managed as she walked over and picked up a cup then sat in the recliner after tossing her coat on the back of it. She took a sip. "Cinnamon?"

"I thought you'd like to try something other than the café latte I've been forcing on you."

"It . . . it wasn't so bad. I was starting to get used to it."

He laughed and showed strong, white teeth. She couldn't help noticing how straight they were. Did this man have any physical flaws?

"I apologize for making you feel as if you were under house arrest, but I am worried about you."

"I know, but somehow I don't feel like the hot-house flower people keep telling me I am," she told him. "Sometimes, I think it's better if I go back to New York and try to put my life there back together." She saw the flash of light go through his eyes. "I'm not going." He seemed satisfied until she added "Yet." Then the light flashed again.

"What if I never remember?" She didn't know what she wanted him to say. Maybe that she could stay until she did. Maybe that he wanted her to stay, even if she did remember.

"You will."

"But what if I *don't?"*

"Let's take it one day at a time for now."

His logic again—she hated when he refused to think about alternatives. He'd been like this when he insisted she come live with him rather than stay in New York. It made sense. She hated things that made sense. She wondered if that was from her memory or her circumstances. She looked at him and found that he was staring into the fire as deep in thought as she'd been. When her gaze started traveling to the open shirt and the tiny, black curls that made a deep V across his chest and narrowed at his waist as it disappeared into his jeans, she knew it was time to take that walk.

She wasn't strong enough for it to be a long walk, but she had to get out of the house before she did something stupid. A thought flittered through her mind of ripping his clothes off, but since she was several inches shorter and a hundred pounds lighter, he'd have to be a willing participant. "I'm really getting punch drunk," she said aloud. She glanced at him to see if he'd heard her. Fortunately, something else was on his mind as he stared into the fire.

The plan was to walk to the gate at the bottom of the path and back. Just spend some time away from Palladin Rush.

She stood up and put on her coat. She pulled a bright yellow wool scarf from the pocket and wrapped it around her neck then zipped up the jacket. She admitted to herself that he was a great looking man and she must have lost her mind to have messed up their marriage. When her memory came back, she would know what she'd done. And she'd fix it. She couldn't let him get away again.

Palladin looked at her and she noticed a grin spread across his face. For some reason, he was laughing at her, and she'd been seriously enjoying looking at his body and speculating on their relationship. And he looked at her as if she was a joke. Anger spread through her blood like wildfire. She had to get out of here.

"Don't say it!" she warned him.

"What?"

"Whatever the 'don't' is that's on the tip of your tongue. Just let me alone."

"If you insist."

His lips were pressed together and she couldn't take any more. She wanted to know what caused that smirk so she could say something smart to wipe it off his face.

"Oh! Go ahead," she continued. "What's the 'don't?"

He stood up and turned away from her. Then stifling a giggle he said, "Don't forget to put on your boots."

Heat washed over her face as she realized that thinking about his body and enjoying sitting in front of the fire with him had distracted her so much that she forgot she was on her way to the mud room to get her boots. She didn't have to look. She was still wearing those fuzzy pink slippers. There was nothing she could do to wipe the smirk off his face or get her boots on. She would have to undo everything, since she'd wrapped herself up so tightly she couldn't bend over.

Palladin turned back and their eyes met. He walked over and lifted the scarf and tugged. She had no choice but to follow him. He led her out to the mud room and pushed her down on the bench. Then, in swift movements, he pulled off the slippers and slid her feet into fur-lined boots, laced them tightly, then stood up and took her hand. He led her to the door and couldn't resist.

"Don't stay out too late." He said as he closed the door before she could say anything.

She stomped down the steps and onto the path before she realized she wasn't in any condition to walk so fast. At this rate, I'll be too tired to walk around the house, much less try for the gate, she mused.

Inside, Palladin Rush took in a deep breath and let it out slowly. This wasn't working. The more time he spent with Jesslyn, the more he believed in her and the more he wanted her. He was becoming more aware of her as each day passed, more comfortable with her in his house. Somehow, she sensed what they had before and it was what she was looking for. But he couldn't lie again. Palladin decided to call another doctor. No matter how cold he acted, she saw through him. Jesslyn thought that her husband wanted to reconcile and didn't know how. What would happen if she never learned the truth? He knew the moment she entered the room earlier. Before she said anything about taking a walk. He felt her presence, her warmth. He'd continued working on the fire to keep from facing her and . . . and what? he thought. Taking her to bed. Telling her the truth. Both. Neither. For the first time in his life, he'd lost sight of his goal. Jesslyn Owens fascinated him with her innocence and her sensuality. Kaliq had been right. The man once called Glacier didn't exist any more. He'd never been this out of control. In a 7600 square foot house, he felt as cramped as he'd been in his 600 square foot studio when he was in college. Only then, it was a pleasant cramped feeling. In case she decided to go near the gate, he switched off the alarm.

"Mac was right," he said aloud. "I should have let him handle things."

Twenty minutes later, he was dressed in warm clothes, having decided that Jesslyn had walked enough.

After walking down to the gate, Jesslyn decided not to return to the main house but do a little exploring that had been a "don't" on Palladin's list. Feeling defiant, she walked toward the barn he said was going to become a mini spa. The huge red clapboard building did look as if it was on its final stand, so she decided not to go inside just take a little peek.

The weather had warmed up considerably as she walked,

and she began to enjoy the feeling of being alone in what was truly a winter wonderland. Tiredness washed through her, but she fought it off. She liked the idea of being surrounded by old, tall trees rather than old, tall buildings or even new, tall buildings. *Peaceful,* came to her mind. Then she heard a tiny crack. She turned quickly. Nothing. She turned back in the direction of the barn and a few steps later she heard it again. *Palladin!* He was following her. *Damn the man.* Probably practicing his old Secret Service tricks.

"Okay," she muttered aloud. "I'll just see what happens when I go to your old barn. What are you going to do when I break one of your rules."

She tromped through the snow forgetting how tired she'd felt only minutes before. She stepped toward the barn and found that the snow in that area was deeper than she'd thought. She found herself sinking and snow filling her boots, and seeping through her stirrup pants. Forcing herself forward, she made it to the barn. But the effort took more of her strength. The snow was melting in her boots and sending cold chills all through her body. Jesslyn took a deep breath and slumped against the barn door. The house seemed miles away. Berating herself for pushing too hard and wanting too much, she looked down the path she'd formed, hoping Palladin wasn't too far behind her. Right now, she'd settle for one of his lectures after he helped her back to the house and she got out of her wet, cold clothing.

"What the hell are you doing?"

Palladin's familiar, deep baritone voice made her jump against the barn. How had he gotten behind her?

"You imbecile! You scared me. What's the matter with

you? Following me. Scaring me." Her breath came in short spurts as she practically spat the accusations at him.

"Get a grip, honey." He told her. "I don't know what you're talking about."

She was so angry, she reached down and picked up a branch.

Palladin stepped back, "Don't!"

"I'm sick of you and your 'don'ts'," she said, as she threw the stick.

He didn't bother trying to avoid the missile, just let it bounce off his chest.

"If you're finished with your hysterics, we can go back to the house."

He turned and started away from her.

"Where are you going?" She wasn't sure if he wanted her to walk back to the house by herself.

"To the house . . ." he stopped and turned back to her. "There's a path behind the barn that leads to the house. How do you think I got down here?"

"You weren't following me?"

Palladin walked back to her. "What are you talking about?"

"I . . . I didn't see anything but I felt . . . I thought . . . someone was behind me."

Palladin scanned the area Jesslyn indicated. Nothing seemed wrong. Had disarming the system allowed an intruder on his property? Unlikely. Why? He was the only one concerned about Jesslyn Owens and what she knew. Or was he?

Rather than alarm her, he simply said "Follow me."

She started after him but couldn't resist defying him one time. As she went by the barn she pulled the rickety door open as far as the chain would allow it. She froze.

"Oh my God! No! No!"

The light streaming in from above highlighted the only thing in the barn. A red Jeep with one word across it—"HellRaiser!"

Nineteen

Flashes of memory. Still pictures turned to moving ones. She knew *everything.* And she was in danger.

Jesslyn ran toward the path. She didn't know where she was running. It was just pure instinct. The flight or fight mode of all human existence. No match for Palladin's long strides she tried to run in a zigzag pattern but she couldn't escape.

Not wanting to hurt her, Palladin caught up with her and tackled her. Rolling to the side so he wouldn't fall on her. She struggled to get free. Her small fists pounding against his chest. It would have been funny, except he knew how frightened she was. He grabbed her hands and pinned her to the ground. Then in one fluid move stood up, pulling her with him and threw her across his shoulder in a fireman's carry. He walked back to the house ignoring her screams. The weakness from the accident took over and she went limp against him.

Instead of going through the mud room, he used the front door and walked depositing Jesslyn on the sofa in front of the fireplace.

"Now listen," he told her. "We're the only two people out here and I'm bigger, so we do things my way. Got it."

She nodded. Trying to figure out how she was going to contact Lena and get help.

He told her how someone tried to kill her twice using a Jeep that looked like his.

"I want to take you into the barn. I want you to look for damage. That's where I always keep it. When Mac said that Carolann had been in an accident, I took the limo."

She watched him. Her eyes said it all: fear and anger.

"You may not believe this, but I'm all that stands between you and whoever wants you dead. Remember I could have gotten rid of you anytime."

That got through to her. Jesslyn knew that Mac and Palladin could call on all sorts of resources to make her disappear. Why keep her around and risk her memory returning. Besides, along with the return of her memory came the feelings she had for Palladin Rush. She knew in her heart that the man who she loved wasn't a killer.

Her eyes told the new story and Palladin relaxed. "We can't tell anyone that your memory's back."

"My sister . . ."

"Her phone might be bugged."

He could see the tiredness in her face and he hated what he'd done and yet it was the only way he knew. "Why don't you take a nap."

"I'm going in the bedroom, but I'm not going to sleep. I'm not that stupid."

She stalked into her bedroom. Palladin began making calls but his first one was a setback. He learned that Hank Reynolds had been found dead behind the wheel of his car. It was labeled a suicide, but Palladin knew better. Someone was tying up loose ends, and Jesslyn could be the next in line.

"You're awake," he said.

"How very observant of you."

His mouth twitched at her sarcasm. "Ah. Back to your usual sunny self, I see. I was beginning to worry about you. You've been so . . . cordial and agreeable."

Jesslyn looked grim. "You can stop worrying. I have a few questions for you, and I won't be so polite if I don't get some straight answers."

He nodded, his smile deepening. "I'm at your service."

"Is my sister in danger?"

"No, but telling her might change that. Even if the phone isn't bugged, I don't think she could continue her concerned sister act if she knew you were okay."

She nodded and he could tell she was looking at the situation with her logical businesslike mind.

"Before you start your questioning, is there anything you need? Food, water, pain medication?"

"No medication," she answered quickly. "I want to keep my head clear. It's been kind of frightening to know there was something in the gray matter and not being able to call it up."

"All right. But don't hesitate to ask if you need something. There's no reason for you to suffer unnecessarily while you recuperate from your injuries. I tried not to add to them when I tackled you."

"I don't think you did. At least, I don't feel any worse waking up now than I did this morning."

"That's a good sign. What's the first question you want cleared up."

Jesslyn really wanted to know if he'd come into her life solely to destroy it, but she went to her second question instead. "How soon can we clear this mess up and I get my life back to normal."

Palladin said, "I know you miss the hustle and bustle of Manhattan and I'm trying to get you back. But I don't have a time frame. Maybe a week? Maybe a month?"

He could tell she didn't like that answer. She came closer and sat down on the ottoman. He studied her as she seemed to be a little shaky. "You're sure you wouldn't like to rest a while longer?"

"Well, I guess that means I have to make the best of it."

It wasn't the answer he expected, nor the one he wanted.

"I'm hungry," she said, as she glared at him. "Feed me."

He chuckled and held out his left arm. "I can't have you spreading word that I allowed my guests to starve. It would do irreparable harm to my reputation as an attentive, gracious host."

Smiling at his teasing, she placed her right hand on the crook of his arm, determined to hide her lingering weakness from his too-sharp eyes. "Consider yourself on probation. Punishment will be your restriction to the bedroom."

He lifted his gaze from the hand resting on his arm to her face, his smile enigmatic. "I'll keep that in mind," he murmured.

"I guess you don't understand what it was like to see that Jeep. You've never been scared. You must have thought I was crazy running when I had no place to run."

"I understand more than you know," he told her. "Why don't you find something to amuse yourself with while I find something to whip up."

* * *

You wouldn't know you've never been scared. She'd thrown the words at him, but he did understand. Palladin understood her fear. He'd experienced it when he realized that the woman registered as his wife was Jesslyn. He knew the only way to protect her was to let them continue thinking that she was his wife—and that she didn't remember anything. As he always said, fear would make you do what you should have done in the first place.

He was even scared now, scared to reveal his true feelings. Oh, yeah, he knew what it was to be scared. He was more than a little nervous right now.

He should have gotten to Hank Reynolds when he had the chance. He'd failed her, but he was going to get her out of this mess and then he was going to let her go. He knew he'd have to push her away. She was going to fall into that situation that patients experienced with doctors, convinced that they were in love with their saviors. It wouldn't be real.

He went into the kitchen and studied the contents of his refrigerator for a few minutes, then made his decision. He threw together some low-fat vegetable enchiladas, black beans and rice. He combined some fruit, added a few jalapeños and let it stand while he fixed a dessert of baked bananas in rum, an attempt to make the meal festive and healthy at the same time.

Jesslyn was suddenly sorry she'd revealed that much to him. She wanted to appear strong, tough and capable. Fear was something he probably had never experienced. Mac and Kaliq both said that he just took charge when he learned about the mixup with Carolann. He'd always come up with the answer. Even when she got her memory back, he didn't just run off to Mac and tell him. He ran down the possibilities of solving the other issues. That meant he needed a strong woman to go along with him. Not one who whimpered at the first sign of real trouble.

"You know I can protect you, don't you?"

"Yes. But I've been living this lie. Trying to get my 'marriage' back and then I find out that we're not married. That you thought I was a crook and you were going to put me away . . ."

"Hey, I never said that."

"No, but be honest. Didn't you feel great when Mac came to you and said he needed you."

Palladin didn't answer and she continued. "That grand ego. You just come in like Peter Falk in *Columbo* and see things that no one else sees and ask questions that no one else thinks of and *Voila!* I confess and end up in jail and Carolann gets the business. What do you get? Carolann?"

He started toward her and she took an involuntary step backward. He stopped. "You're right. I felt great. And, in a couple of days, I thought I was back in a sort of Secret Service mission. But you're wrong where Carolann is concerned. I never wanted her back. I just didn't want her to be in any trouble. I owe her . . ."

"What? What do *you* owe her? She didn't like leaving Washington's social whirl, so you had to keep her happy wherever she lived? Are you still in love with her?"

He was glad the fireplace in the living room threw out a lot of heat, so she didn't know he'd broken out into a cold sweat from thinking about the answer to her accusation that he still loved Carolann.

He went into the mud room, put on his boots and grabbed his hunter's jacket. He had to get away. He walked down toward the barn from the back way. He needed a few minutes to be alone. He sat in the Jeep. It couldn't have been coincidental that someone with a Jeep like his had pushed her car off the road, even though he'd convinced her that it was. Nor did he believe that someone had borrowed his Jeep, since there were no scratch marks on it. Someone had deliberately used a Jeep exactly like his. Who had done it eluded him, but the why was obvious. Someone wanted him to take the fall for it. If Jesslyn hadn't lived, he would be a suspect

Jesslyn understood she'd pushed him with her accusations about Carolann, but what else could she think. He told her their relationship couldn't be long term, so obviously he wasn't in love with her.

Even if he wasn't in love with her, he'd protected her She owed him an apology and then she wanted to go back to New York. He wanted a mistress, someone who allowed him to set the pace in the relationship. She wondered if she was fighting with him because she wanted more. She wanted him to say that he loved her. If he did she wouldn't hesitate to have a commuter marriage, but she couldn't stay here wanting him the way she did When he hadn't returned in an hour, she went to bed She couldn't keep her mind on a story so she opted for the news. Senator Gary—the Senator had been touted as the Republican's John Kennedy. He was charming and well-spoken. Jesslyn only noticed that he reminded her of Mac, with his gray hair in the same sleek style. This time he was criticizing the head of the FBI over the way things were being run. The Bureau came under his attack often, and this time was being accused of failing to protect a witness. The man had been run down on a busy street by a car.

Hours later she heard a noise. What had happened? She got up and didn't bother throwing a robe over her thin nightgown. Palladin's room was on the other side of the house, and as she came out of her room she knew that was where the groan came from. She heard it again. Not a groan, but a yell. As if he were in pain. Palladin needed her.

Without thinking she ran to his door. It was slightly ajar. She listened but heard no other voices. The yell, however, had become a groan. She pushed the door open, and as she stepped in, she heard him again.

"You can't blame me," he said. "No. Carolann, it's not my fault."

Hearing him calling to his dead wife made her stop. She was right in leaving. He was still in love with Carolann. She turned to go, but he yelled again. "Look out Kaliq!"

She took a deep breath and walked to the bed. Moonlight streamed across his face and his dreads were in disarray, scattered across the pillow and some across his face. He tossed and turned as if the nightmare was getting worse.

He sounded as if he was in so much agony that she didn't care if it was over Carolann. She just wanted his pain to stop.

She went over to the bed and touched his arm, lightly, at first then shook him. "Wake up, Palladin. Wake up!"

Palladin came fully awake, his eyes bright, his mind alert. "What do you want?" He growled at her.

"I . . ." She started to leave. He was probably upset at being in such a vulnerable position.

"Wait! Don't go . . . please." He caught his hair with both hands and brushed it so it hung behind him.

"Yer . . . yes. You . . . screamed . . . for Carolann."

"No. I didn't."

"Yes, you said . . ."

"I know what I said. I've had the dream before, and someone has had to wake me up."

From the way he said "someone" she knew he was talking about a past lover.

"Come here." He held out his hand. She paused for a split second before putting her hand in his. He pulled her down until she was sitting on the bed with her back against his chest. She could feel the hair from his chest through her thin nightgown.

"I told you once that I owed Carolann. Let me tell you why."

"You don't have to tell me anything . . ."

"Yes, I do. So just sit still and listen."

He pulled her close, she pulled her legs up on the bed and found it easier not to look at him.

He knew what the dream was about, but it had been months since he'd had it, and maybe if he talked to someone he trusted it would subside. Whatever happened between them as man and woman, he did trust her.

"Before I went into the Secret Service, I was part of a rescue team and I still maintain those skills. Kaliq was a journalist. He got caught in hostile territory and I thought the powers-to-be were dragging their feet about going in and getting him."

"So you went."

"Mac and Carolann were furious when I told them that a few members of the team had contacted me. But I had to go. It took us a week. We went in and got him out, but unfortunately, not soon enough to save his legs."

"Is that what caused the riff between you and Mac?"

He smiled. How could he tell her that *she* was the reason for the riff between them.

"It was the prelude to the end of my marriage. Carolann was pregnant at the time . . ."

"Oh my God!"

"Yeah. She lost the baby during that week and we never got back to trusting each other."

Now she understood why Carolann said that Palladin "owed" her. "Did you have that dream while you were still married?"

"A couple of times."

"So Carolann knew your Achilles heel, and she used it."

"The thing is I knew I was being used and I couldn't stop myself."

"Guilt," she said, remembering what Carolann had once told her.

"So that's why you were so protective of her."

"Until I met you."

"Do you have these nightmares often."

"Not as much as I used to." He didn't want to tell her that just thinking about losing her had triggered it.

"Well, if you're okay, I'll go back to my room," she said.

"Don't go."

"I don't want . . ." she started but couldn't say it—

that she didn't want to make love. She did, and if she stayed the night and he asked, she knew she would.

"Sleep with me. And I mean sleep as the operative word."

She wiggled until she was under the cover and lay there until she thought he fell asleep.

Twenty

The next day, Jesslyn got to see what hockey practice was really like. Palladin's team worked hard, and with each trying to out skate the other, a pushing match began between two of the larger boys. Palladin got between them and grabbed the shirt of each and held them apart

"You're supposed to be teammates. What are you going to do? Fight each other and have the other team laugh at you?"

"But Mr. Rush, he's always hogging the puck," one boy finally said.

"So, that may make him a bad team player, but is fighting going to help?"

"Hey, I'm not a bad team player. I just want to win."

Jesslyn understood that after. Being fired from Egyptian Enchantment, she wanted to win at anything to make them sorry and perhaps see that she couldn't have been the one who sold the information or even condoned such an act.

"Sometimes boys," Palladin said releasing them, "wanting to win so badly can make you lose. Now you might score a goal this time. But what if you miss?"

The boys looked at each other and mumbled an apology. They spent a few minutes on the bench at Palladin's direction, and Jesslyn saw them working together the next chance they got to be on the ice.

As a treat, they joined Palladin and Jesslyn for breakfast.

"You his lady?" one of the other boys finally asked.

She looked at Palladin, who seemed to be ignoring the question. Jesslyn wanted to know the same thing, but just explained that she and Palladin were friends and she was staying with him while she recovered from an accident.

The rest of the day was spent discussing the boys' grades. There was a hard, fast rule that no one with less than a B average could be on the team.

After they left, Palladin explained that the boys were smart but not using that brainpower, so after the hockey club got to go to a few things like a Chicago Bulls basketball game and Disney World, they had such a long waiting list of boys who wanted to be on the team that they ended up forming two teams. There were a couple of dropouts when academics became part of the prerequisite, but for the most part they held their own.

The day seemed to fast forward into night, and Jesslyn didn't object when he took her hand and led her off to his bed. She'd undressed and slipped into a nightgown and they'd barely settled in their spoon-style positions before her eyes closed and she drifted into a deep, relaxing sleep.

She awoke to find herself alone. Palladin was a man of habit in so many ways. She knew that he was jogging down to the small general store to get the Sunday edition of the *New York Times*. The only paper that was delivered by mail was the *Wall Street Journal*.

Jesslyn, in all her twenty-eight years, had not encountered a man like Palladin Rush. She knew he backed off whenever they were getting close and she knew it was because of the child he'd lost with Carolann. He'd never said he wanted more children, but after seeing him with his little hockey team, she knew he did. The problem was that he seemed to want them right away, while she hadn't even thought about having a biological clock, much less on whether or not it was running until now.

Since her fiasco with Egyptian Enchantment, she'd secretly dreamed of being a big success and having them sorry they used her as a scapegoat. And now, when it was within her grasp this new problem of industrial espionage and her feelings for Palladin were giving her serious doubts.

If she didn't try to regroup and expand her business, she'd always wonder *if* she could have made it work. If she chose her business over Palladin, she might wake up one morning and have nothing but ledgers and cash flow statements to keep her warm.

Shaking her head at that thought she found a solution. If he asked her to stay, she would. If he didn't, she wouldn't bury herself in work but make time for a full social calendar. She owed it to herself not to get so wrapped up in business that she didn't look for someone to share her life. She couldn't imagine anyone filling it as full of joy as Palladin, but she wasn't going to hide from the chance that she could be happy with someone else.

She stretched and glanced around at the room. It fit Palladin. Everything was designed to accommodate a man of his size. From the obviously custom-made bed that she needed a stool to stand on before she could climb on to it to the armoire on the other side of the room that was at least seven feet tall and four feet wide. Instead of feeling overwhelmed, she felt cosseted. In the time they'd been together, she'd never studied his bedroom. During the time she'd lost her memory she'd avoided the room, and after she'd gotten her memory back they'd spent more time in what she'd come to consider her bedroom. Though curious, she never crossed the boundary from being a good guest by snooping through her host's personal belongings.

She wanted to stay in the warm cocoon Palladin's bed had become but nature convinced her otherwise. She sat up, swung her legs over the side and squirmed around until her foot found the little stool by the bed so she could use it to get down. Then she crossed the house to her bedroom, showered, dressed in leggings and a long bulky sweater. Jesslyn padded barefoot into the kitchen and began making tea and setting the table for breakfast.

"I was hoping you weren't going to get up so early," Palladin's voice startled her and she dropped the sugar bowl which shattered on the terrazzo tile floor scattering grains of sugar along with shards of glass.

"How can you do that?" she screamed. "I didn't hear you come in."

"Sorry," Palladin said as he put the paper on the table and walked over to retrieve the broom and dustpan. "Don't move."

He swept the sugar and glass up then took a wet mop and brushed over the same place, hoping he'd gotten rid of all the glass. He then picked Jesslyn up and carried her away from the area. "Go put your shoes on."

"I hate shoes."

"You'll hate getting a sliver of glass in your foot even more. You can make coffee for me while I shower."

She didn't like his orders, but she obeyed, and by the time she'd returned, Palladin had put sugar in another sugar bowl that matched the creamer.

"I liked the pattern so I have a couple of extra pieces," he explained when he saw her raised eyebrow.

She set the table and made the coffee while waiting for him to shower and change clothes. She started separating his sections of the paper from hers, amazed at how quickly she'd fallen into that pattern.

When he returned, he was dressed in what she thought of as his college-boy casual look: his beige turtleneck under a tartan long sleeved shirt with a button down collar and fresh jeans.

They added toast and scrambled eggs to the breakfast menu and sat down to enjoy their meal. Just as they finished, the buzzer sounded to alert them someone was at the gate.

"Yeah," Palladin's voice didn't hide his annoyance. He listened a few moments then pressed the button to shut off the alarm and barked for the person to come up.

"Logan wants to talk to me," he explained to Jesslyn.

She nodded. Although she didn't get a feeling that Skip disliked her as much as Mac did, she wasn't comfortable around him. She jumped up and started cleaning the table.

Palladin went out to meet Skip and by the time the two men reached the living room, Jesslyn had fled to her bedroom. She glanced at the bed she hadn't slept in and sighed.

Every time I think of us as a couple, something happens to remind me that we aren't, she thought. She'd rummaged through the magazines Palladin had bought the day before when he was jogging.

There was a hard rap on the door before he opened it and demanded she join them.

"I thought he wanted to talk to you," she mumbled.

"I want you there. Just don't react when he mentions things you should know, but since you have amnesia you don't."

She didn't see a heavy coat, so she assumed Skip had come through the mud room. His short blond hair was a little tousled from the wind and he seemed uneasy in his dark brown pleated trousers, beige shirt and a brown tweed V-neck cardigan.

Jesslyn sat in the chair by the fireplace but the two men chose to stand. "What's on your mind, Logan?"

Skip hesitated as he looked at Jesslyn then back to Palladin. "I'm getting some conflicting information on your . . . on Carolann."

"Like?"

"Well, you gave me her address and she still holds the lease, but no one in the building remembers her staying there for more than one or two nights in any given month."

"So she has another place." The conversation was going downhill, as far as Palladin could tell, but he held back his temper and let Skip ramble on.

"I checked with Mac, and he had the same address."

"So check with someone else."

"I can't find anything else on her. That's the crazy part. Then I spoke with Lena Owens and she had this same address."

"Did you try under Evans?"

"No. That's next"

"So, what do you want?"

"I want to make sure that, if I uncover some information that leads back to your little roommate over there, you'll use it."

Jesslyn had watched the two men with their little shadowboxing number. She curled up on the sofa and opened a large volume of *Black History* that was on the coffee table. As she suspected, Skip's reluctance had something to do with her, but the actual vocalization of her fear shocked her and she let out a gasp.

"Why don't you let me worry about her!" Palladin said.

"Good. I just don't want you to get bent out of shape when I start investigating."

"Go for it. Pull out every skeleton in the closet you can find."

"Even yours?"

"Mine, Mac's, the president's—I don't much care, as long as you get to the bottom of this."

"I'm glad you feel that way."

"Does Mac know you're here?"

"I don't tell him everything I do or every place I go."

"Is that all?"

"For now."

Skip nodded at Jesslyn and left. Palladin followed him out and after making sure he was no longer on the property, turned on the alarm again.

"What was that about?"

"A declaration of war."

"Really?"

"On both of us."

"Why didn't he just call you?"

Palladin laughed. "I could say it's a Man-Thing."

"And I could throw this book, and considering your size and my size, I could probably strike a vital area of your anatomy."

"He was issuing a challenge that he was willing to take me down as an accessory or even the mastermind to this industrial espionage business."

"And he had to come all the way to Pennsylvania."

"It's not 'all the way.' He was probably visiting his family. He's from Philadelphia's Rittenhouse Square section."

"Ritzy."

"Very."

"So what do we do about his threat?"

"Nothing."

"He wants you on the same side of the courtroom as he wants me, and you don't want to do anything."

"He won't lie. He won't manufacture evidence, and we aren't guilty, so we don't have anything to worry about."

"I don't think it's that simple . . ."

"I don't want to discuss this."

"Well what do you want to discuss?"

"How about a vital area of my anatomy."

Before she could comment, he'd pulled her to her feet, lifted her in his arms and was striding purposefully to his bedroom. He couldn't believe how easily he lost control and yet he knew that once she got her life back this would be over. Yet he couldn't stop his raging need for her. Once in the privacy of his bedroom, he dropped her on the bed and came down beside her, remembering his size could hurt her without meaning to.

Jesslyn trembled and burned as Palladin's hands began stripping her clothes and stroking her skin. She'd never felt this aroused before. She'd never let go the way her sister always said it happened—that you stopped caring about the past, the future and lived for the hot, erotic moment that reduced a man and woman to such a basic need.

They separated only because they realized it was easier to undress themselves than play the game of helping each other. Their need was too great to indulge in fun. They needed to be very serious this time. In seconds, they were naked and pressed tightly against each other.

Over the past few days, she'd known that they would end up this way. How could they not want each other when they were living in the same house and getting to know the people under the facades. At least she was getting to know a little about him. There was a part holding back, refusing to commit. But now all she could think of was the yearning in her soul crying out only for the pleasure he could give her.

He urged her into position with touches rather than words. Her body became limp—pliable. He almost exploded the moment he was inside her, but he found the edge of his sanity and held on. Determined to give more pleasure than he got, he felt he lost that battle just as he won everything else.

Later, as she rested, he slipped from the bed and got the *Times*. He crawled back under the covers and they separated the paper into their favorite parts as she started to do before Skip arrived.

"I guess the Senator from Ohio is preparing to make a run at the White House." Palladin's tone indicated that he did not look forward to that decision.

"You know every time I look at him I think of Skip and Mac."

"Skip *and* Mac?"

"Yeah. Skip's blond and Mac's gray, but in a black and white photo you can't really tell what color the hair is."

"Umm . . . mm."

"What?"

"Didn't you say that Carolann talked to the Senator once?"

"Well I heard her on the phone but later she said the Senator wasn't the one she was talking to. She got really bent out of shape when I asked if he was her mystery man."

Palladin pulled her closer to him. He wanted their bodies touching. He wanted the memories, even though he knew he'd be tortured by them after she left. Other people may be able to have commuter marriages, but he knew what that was like. Sooner or later, you missed an important event. And while she'd say it didn't matter, it would. And those things chipped away at a relationship. It had happened with Mac. It had happened with Kaliq. And it had happened with him. He really believed that there were some men who always fell in love with a woman who needed more than a husband.

He was so lost in thought he only heard the last part of Jesslyn's sentence.

". . . like the one Skip drove today."

"What?"

"I don't know if I should be angry or just annoyed. You weren't listening to me."

"Sorry. What did you say?"

"That the day I almost got run over by the Jeep I saw Carolann talking to a man in a green car . . ."

"Like the one Skip drove today." Palladin finished. "I'm missing something and I know it. When I thought that the kids used the Jeep for joyriding, I didn't want them to get in trouble, so I didn't report it. Mac knew a couple of kids in the area and asked me not to. Now we know that someone else 'borrowed' it."

She stared at him for a moment. "You don't think it was Skip? He's married."

"Right, and Carolann said that I'd be really upset about it."

Jesslyn nodded. It wouldn't be the first time a woman used her ex-husband's enemy as a way to punish him. She knew that he meant he was missing something when she and Carolann were run off the road. He'd left his car near the hockey rink, so again it could have been joyriders who returned it. The person who forced her off the road knew what he was doing.

"If Skip drives for Mac, does that mean he's taken some of those anti-terrorist driving techniques?"

"We all did. In fact, one of the guys liked it so much he took more courses and quit to become a stunt driver in Hollywood."

"What are you going to do?" she asked.

"Nothing for now. I wondered why Skip wanted to stay on this case after I threatened to have him removed." Palladin said more to himself as he remembered how frantic Skip was to stay on the case. "I need proof. But once I get that proof . . ."

He didn't need to finish the sentence. Jesslyn knew Palladin wanted someone to pay for the attempt on her life and for Carolann's death, and he'd have no problem watching Skip pay.

Twenty-one

"I love your name. How did your parents decide on Jesslyn?"

Her cheek resting against his shoulder, she smiled. "My dad was into African-American history and wanted to name each child after someone he admired."

"Lena, as in Lena Horne?"

"Right. With me he was hoping for a boy and with the last name already Owens . . ."

"Jessie Owens—the Olympic star."

"But I came along and my parents knew that I would be the last child they were able to have, so they found the name in a book and *voila.* Except that only one person ever called me 'Jessie'. I was in the eighth grade, and this little boy I had a crush on called me Jessie. He was tall, for his age, and was a bit of a bully, but for some reason I liked him. He then said it was a boy's name and that I looked like a boy."

"Petite doesn't mean boyish."

"No, but I didn't get curves till my senior year of high school. Anyway, he said I looked like a boy, and I said I also hit like one."

"You didn't."

"Oh yes, I did. I gave him a fat lip. My teacher told

my mother and I spent the next four weekends confined to the house."

"Was it worth it?"

"No one ever called me Jessie again."

He laughed as he pictured this tiny girl taking on the school bully. "It suits you."

"And your mom picked a name that meant fighter."

"Actually, that's not quite the truth. I looked it up and learned its origins before I asked her how she picked it. I was so proud of what it meant that I told her. Then she confessed that she really picked the name because, when she was a kid, there was a TV show about a man named Palladin. She said the show would start with him dressed in white and attending the opera. Then he'd get a message and in the next scene he'd be dressed all in black. He was a hired gunfighter."

"I hate to say this, but I think your name suits you, also."

"Hey, no one hired me. I volunteered my services."

"Okay, you're a volunteer gunfighter."

"I can get you to take that back."

He caught her and began tickling her. They rolled around on the bed and before she knew it he'd pulled her beneath him. "Now take it back,"

"What if I don't."

She knew he was going to kiss her, and it was what she wanted also.

They were startled by a voice from the door. "What exactly is this?"

Still laughing, they sat up to find a very angry Kaliq Faulkner staring at them.

"It's not what you think," Palladin said. He realized that only Kaliq could have gotten in with the code. But he was astonished and ashamed that he hadn't even heard the car. If he was missing things, he'd probably also missed clues. And for what? Now that she had her memory back, the woman couldn't wait to get off his mountain and back to the bright lights.

Jesslyn scrambled to pull her nightgown over her legs and slid off the bed as she headed for her bedroom.

"He'll explain everything."

"Not everything. Meet me in the living room in fifteen minutes."

She could hear Kaliq coming to her defense as she closed Palladin's door. "I can't believe you'd take advantage of her. I should never have left you alone."

She didn't hear any more, since she'd reached her room but knew that she should do what Palladin asked. Meet him in the living room and help him explain that the situation had changed.

She washed up quickly in her bathroom and slipped on a flowing red quilted robe she'd gotten at the outlet. She put her feet into a pair of leather sandals and ran her fingers through her short hair, relieved that her casual style didn't require a lot of effort. She settled for a touch of plum eye shadow, a little blush and a quick swipe of mascara, figuring that would make her appear a little healthier looking. She wasn't exactly pleased with her battered-looking reflection, but she knew it could have been worse. She wasn't complaining.

As he'd promised, Palladin was waiting in the next room with Kaliq—a much more contrite Kaliq.

Palladin was sitting in an armchair in the living area, sipping a cup of coffee, but he stood when she entered.

"Kaliq, my dark knight. Thank you for coming to my rescue," she said.

"Only you didn't need rescuing."

"But if I did, it's nice to know that, even though he's your friend, you didn't want him to do anything wrong."

"Well, you'll be happy to know Jesslyn," Palladin began, "that Kaliq has volunteered to go to New York and tell your sister in person."

"Don't worry. I'm sure she'll be relieved but willing to continue this little farce," Kaliq added.

"My sister can be quite an actress. But could you smuggle my bookkeeping files to me. I don't think she's much of a storekeeper."

"Sorry." Palladin said. "We can't take a chance. We don't know who was involved."

"All Carolann would tell me is that *you* were going to be very upset when you found out about the new man in her life."

Palladin turned to Kaliq. "While you're in New York, see what you can find out."

"I'll go tomorrow. I just came by to pick up a change of clothes and I'm going back to the Inn by the Lake."

"What is so interesting at this place?"

"The scenery."

A half hour later, they were alone again. Since the mood had been broken, they chose to go to their respective bedrooms and get some sleep.

Palladin was gone when Jesslyn woke the next morning. Once again, he'd prepared breakfast for her and left it in the refrigerator. She'd just finished dressing in a pair of khaki shorts and a black T-shirt when the phone rang. It was a message for Palladin. Senator Gary was inviting him to a campaign function. Jesslyn thought the voice sounded familiar and meant to tell Palladin about her message in the hospital warning her not to tell anyone. But when Palladin returned from his run, he had several of his little hockey munchkins and she forgot to say anything about Senator Gary's voice.

"We're hungry men after a quick practice, and I'm supplying the food," Palladin told her. His little team scrambled for seats at the dining room table, and before she knew it, Jesslyn was helping Palladin serve up steaming oatmeal, toast and hot chocolate.

After that, they played a few games, and Jesslyn wondered if he was using his team to put distance between them. With her memory returned, he no longer wanted to be alone with her, especially after the previous night.

As soon as the kids finished and the dishes were in the dishwasher, she grabbed a pair of sunglasses because of the glare off the snow, bundled up and hurried outside. It was another gorgeous day in a winter wonderland, and she had no intention of spending it indoors.

She'd teased Palladin a little about being a hermit, but there was some merit in being all alone on a mountain with time to reconsider your life. This is what it must have been like when he first bought it. During the next two hours, she found out exactly how that felt.

Another feeling came over her. What if she stayed with him? The idea of really getting to know someone would certainly happen if there were only one other person to talk with. Kaliq had been saying that he'd have to return to Wyoming again if they didn't hurry up and solve this puzzle. In Jesslyn's mind, things only got more tangled as they progressed. She sighed rather wistfully and wondered why she, who'd never minded her own company before, was suddenly wishing for companionship. She couldn't even delude herself that it was just anyone's companionship she craved.

She wanted Palladin. And the extent of that wanting had her walking even faster, as though to escape a hazard she didn't quite understand.

She toured the entire mountain and even took a second look at the Jeep in the barn before starting back to the main house. Her thoughts remained fixed on Palladin and the night she'd spent with him, the things he'd told her about himself, the insights she'd gained from those glimpses of his past.

Jesslyn realized that she had never been in love, not even with Paul. She'd never had or felt capable of having the strong passions that her friends seemed to feel for their lovers and spouses. She'd felt smug and superior because she'd never allowed anyone to turn her into such a vulnerable, emotional wreck. No one had ever mattered so much to her that she couldn't walk away without regrets when the relationship ended, or made her feel as though her heart would break if her feelings weren't returned.

She was beginning to wonder rather nervously if she was setting herself up for her first taste of heartache. This meant, of course, that she simply couldn't allow herself to fall in love with Palladin Rush. She'd enjoy being with him while it lasted, savor the time they spent together, but she wouldn't love him. She nodded once, decisively, satisfied with the strength of her conviction.

She looked up from her sober contemplation to find

Palladin standing some ten feet ahead of her, his dreads blowing in the breeze. His lazy smile made her wonder if she was as firmly in control of her emotions as she'd believed herself to be. All it took was a smile from him to have her quivering like a tightly strung bow, a heartbeat away from throwing herself into his arms and flinging caution to the wind.

Palladin was looking more dangerous to her all the time.

As though he'd sensed Jesslyn's restlessness, Palladin went out of his way to keep her busy during the day. He introduced her to his financial operation, from personnel management to maintenance to purchasing and accounts payable. He showed her his plans and ideas for future properties, such as resorts, and seemed to value her opinions and suggestions. They talked until late in the evening, cheerfully argued politics, religion, philosophy, arts and literature.

To the obvious fascination of his employees, Palladin was rarely away from Jesslyn's side during those days, though her presence didn't appear to affect his performance of his job. To Jesslyn's delight, he seemed able to concentrate totally on his responsibilities and enjoy her companionship at the same time. She didn't want to interfere with his duties, but she was very glad he seemed to enjoy being with her as much as she loved being with him.

It was only when she mentioned an idea for a "financial gift basket" that Palladin's smile faded. He promised to help her with it, but at the same time knew that she was feeling homesick and he'd have to let her go when the time came. Thinking about leaving gave her an oddly hollow feeling, but she refused to dwell on it. She'd face that later, because whoever was responsible for Carol-ann's death remained out there. And when Palladin found him—and she was sure that he would—it would be safe for her to leave Palladin's mountain.

Twenty-two

They were awakened by the phone. Palladin answered it on the second ring, which led Jesslyn to believe that they had both been pretending sleep.

"What do you want?" He paused. "Okay come on up."

Then he turned to Jesslyn and said, "Skip Logan wants to talk to me about something."

He buzzed Kaliq's cabin.

"Just wanted you to know that Logan's on his way," he paused. "No, I don't know what he wants, but I'll get back to you. Better be prepared to take a trip, if it's important."

Minutes later, Jesslyn and Palladin had each slipped into a thick terry cloth robe and found a comfortable place in the living room as they listened to Logan's car approaching.

Skip looked a little frazzled. His hair was almost stringy and looked as if he'd been running his fingers through it constantly. Even his clothes had the been slept-in look.

"We took your advice," Logan said. "We checked around and found another apartment under Carolann Evans. The police are getting a search warrant for it tomorrow. But I think we should go in tonight."

Two sets of eyes stared at him not quite believing what they'd heard.

"Why?"

"Look Rush, frankly I think you and your ex-wife and your new . . . girlfriend are all in this together, and Carol-ann got scared. That's why she kept coming to see Mac. But I'm afraid that if it keeps up, you guys are going to get him in trouble."

"What makes you say that?"

"Sooner or later, she's going to get her memory back. I'll find out what really happened."

Neither Skip nor Mac knew that Jesslyn had regained her full memory. Palladin had only mentioned flashes every so often.

"Have you already been there?"

"Yes."

"What did you find?"

"Just this." He held out a class ring from Harvard.

"Probably mine. She used to wear it around her neck. So what's the problem?"

"I know I missed something. I also knew that if I called you it wouldn't help. But if you saw me, you'd know we have to team up."

Despite how the men felt about each other, they had a deep love and respect for Gavin Macklin. They would work together to save him. Palladin held up the ring and when Jesslyn put her hand out, he gave it to her.

"That's what you meant when you said you knew her better than I thought?" Palladin asked Skip.

"She came on to me a couple of times and I bought her a drink—when she would visit Mac."

"And she told you how rough it had been living with

me, how I had promised to take care of her and left her when things got rough."

Skip's face turned red and he began stuttering.

"Don't let it bother you. It's standard for her. Of course, when I met her, it was her aunt who didn't take care of her."

"So it's a routine."

"One that seems to work," Jesslyn added. She wanted to say "with men," but Carolann had told her how the people at Egyptian Enchantment had treated her, and with her own experience with them, Jesslyn bought the story also. This probably was why Mac didn't like her. Carolann had made her the villain in their trouble as partners. Jesslyn knew that too many things happened that would need someone with money and power, but who could do it and why? Palladin and Skip agreed to meet the next day but not tell Mac anything.

Jesslyn met Mac at the front door later that morning and let him in. She didn't want to alarm him that Palladin and Kaliq had gone to meet Skip without him. It was easier to pretend she didn't know what was going on with the investigation. She told him Palladin and Kaliq were at hockey practice. And they would be back in an hour.

After she made him a cup of coffee they sat on the wrap-around porch.

"So I understand you have some memory flashes. How did that happen?"

"I just saw something that looked familiar and things started to flash through my mind."

"How convenient that it was after Skip Logan came up with a new suspect."

Jesslyn ignored him and twirled the chain around her neck. Out of the corner of her eye, she could see Mac staring at her. He seemed almost frightened. She couldn't imagine why.

Jesslyn got up and walked over to the window. "I love this view."

"So you planning to become the next Mrs. Palladin Rush?"

"I don't think so."

Mac's head snapped up. "I thought that Palladin was protecting you because you were the love of his life."

She shook her head but did not look at Mac. "More like his sense of justice. He knew I was in trouble, and he was just determined to keep me safe."

"Humpf, more like he had an itch and wanted to scratch it."

"I can't believe that you don't know him better."

Mac's lips curled as he said, "He's like any man. A woman turns him on, and he has to be with her for a while. I'm surprised that you didn't think of it as a forever thing."

"Guess I can't assume at this point anything more than wanting my own life back as soon as my memory returns."

Jesslyn hoped she could stall Mac a little more. That way, he wouldn't have a chance to stop them from breaking into Carolann's apartment.

The need to know routine was wearing thin. If he was wrong, Mac would tear a strip off Palladin for not believing in him. And the idea that two of his most respected former agents were going to break into an apartment would probably kill him.

Then a thought occurred to her. What if Skip was the guilty party. It would mean he'd lured Palladin and Kaliq to their enemies. Maybe she was just getting paranoid about everyone and everything.

The phone rang and she answered it to find her sister on the other end. Disappointment came through her voice.

"Hey don't shoot the messenger!" Lena said. "I just thought we'd talk for a while."

It dawned on Jesslyn that Palladin asked Lena to call. In casual conversation, she could give all the right tips.

"You remember Mac, don't you?" she said. "He's here babysitting me while the others are off playing hockey."

"Palladin called and wanted me to make sure you're ok."

"Oh, don't worry, I'm fine."

"Well I'm going to call back in half an hour, okay?"

"Sounds good to me. If you can't find it, call me."

Mac waited for her to hang up. "How's your business going?"

"I can't wait to get back. My sister's terrific, and I'm glad she was there to take over but it isn't her first love, I don't think, and she probably could use my help."

"You guys ever have sibling rivalry?"

"No. She's eight years older, so we never got the chance to hang out until we were past the rivalry stage."

"Lucky. I never had any relatives. Palladin and Carolann were my family."

"And Skip."

"No. He was more like an employee than family."

* * *

Palladin walked over and stood by the door leading to the bedroom. The rose and beige theme played out again. The brass bed with a beige quilt covering it and neatly arranged pillows in beige trimmed in rose. Different from Jesslyn's, yet the same city-like furnishings. He wondered how long it would take before Jesslyn grew bored with the rustic qualities of his place. The only thing that seemed out of place was the state of the art computer. He hadn't recalled Carolann ever wanting to damage her lacquered nails on a keyboard. He checked the system and everything seemed pretty normal. Nothing but programs were saved to the hard drive and he remembered that Jesslyn mentioned an argument about a missing computer disk, but a search of the desk proved fruitless.

"What I can't get over is this place. It looks like a page out of a magazine." Kaliq waved his hand around indicating the sunken living room/dining room combination. The room was divided by color. The rose colored walls served as a backdrop. The color from the walls was picked up on the rose, beige and tan area rug where the yellow pine colored table and chairs sat.

The black wrought iron chandelier hung directly over the table. Along the wall was a long buffet table with china, silver, and napkins at one end and serving dishes and utensils at another.

"Too . . . neat. I need to check with building management. Who cleans this place?"

"Guess the doorman would know."

"Let's talk to him."

In a matter of minutes, they were confronting the doorman.

"We want to know who cleans apartment 433 West?"

"I . . . I . . . don't know . . ." John began fumbling

with the gold braiding on his navy jacket He stopped to hail a cab for a man leaving the building, pocketed the tip and reluctantly answered questions.

"What do you mean you don't know?" Palladin's voice dropped but still had a dangerous edge. Before he could answer, Skip joined them.

"What's the deal?"

"We're just finding out who would know something about the people who work here," Palladin answered.

"And finding out that our friend here is a little short on filling in the blanks."

"I . . . I don't know. I've only been here a couple of weeks. This isn't my regular shift . . ." The man tried to assist another person leaving the building, but Skip helped her.

"When we talked to you before you said you'd been working for the building for five years."

"I have . . ." The glares he received from all three men made him hurry on. "I worked weekends. The old guy, Sal, retired and I got his shift . . ."

"Where can I find him," Palladin cut in.

"He lives in Astoria with his daughter."

Two hours later Palladin, Kaliq and Skip were being served rich hot coffee and talking to Sal. Carolann used a service, but different people, so he'd only been able to supply them with the name of the company.

"Yeah, I remember her," he said when Skip showed him the picture that had incensed Palladin at the hospital. The one with Skip, Carolann and Mac. "Always wondered why she only had two boyfriends. Pretty lady like that."

"Two? What did they look like?"

"One young, red-headed guy. One old, tall guy. And there was a shorter man."

"Could you be a little more specific?"

"The guy in the picture with her. Used to come to see her a lot. Bring her flowers . . ."

Palladin didn't hear the rest of the Sal's recollections. He was staring at Skip. They both knew at that moment that one of Carolann's visitors was Gavin Macklin.

They managed to thank him and get out of the house without alarming him about their investigation.

"Mac! I've got to get home. I left Jesslyn with him."

"So what?"

"She knows where I am and why. One slip, and Mac will start putting the pieces of the puzzle in place."

They thanked Sal and were back in their car when Skip announced. "You can't go back yet."

"What?"

"If the Owens woman slipped up and told him anything, he'll be ready for you. If she didn't, I don't know how we can get people in place to take Mac out of that fortress you built."

"Never thought I'd say this," Kaliq spoke up. "But he's right. We have to do this carefully."

"They only thing we have is that Mac and Carolann were having an affair. We need something to link Mac to the operation."

"I always said that she wasn't smart enough to pull this off by herself." Kaliq shook his head.

"I think I know who the other guy is?"

Two pair of eyes stared at Palladin.

"Frank Mason."

Skip took out his notebook and flipped back and forth until he found it.

"Have him picked up. Let's see if we can scare the truth out of him."

Palladin let the information run through his mind. "You suspected Jesslyn?"

"Up until ten minutes ago, when we talked to the doorman."

"You were in her hospital room."

She was right. Over and over, Jesslyn had insisted that the man in her hospital room the night of the accident reminded her of Mac.

"Carolann contacted us just before she bolted for your place. Man, I thought I'd have a heart attack. When I saw the crash survivor, it was the Owens woman. Then Mac suggested we wait to see what you could come up with."

All of his machinations had been in vain. No wonder Mac kept urging him to let Jesslyn take the fall for the stolen property. With her history, everyone would have condemned her. Mac would be in the clear. No one would be able to tie him back to the theft.

Palladin waited until Skip escorted Frank Mason into the room. It was amazing at the favors you accumulate over the years, he mused. He was grateful that Skip had them. The man blanched and took a backward step only to be pushed forward by Skip.

"Doorman says he's been around quite a bit since Carolann moved here."

"Hey! What's going on here? What about my rights?" Frank protested.

"The only right you have now is to talk or die." Palladin's voice was almost a whisper.

"You can't . . . I want to go back to my cell. My lawyer's on the way to bail me out."

Skip patted him on the shoulder. "Haven't you heard. Someone bailed you out just before your lawyer arrived and you left in a green BMW."

Palladin added, "At least that's what your lawyer was told."

Frank's face reddened and his breath came in short gasps. "What are you guys trying to do?"

"Get at the truth," Palladin said softly.

"What do you want from me?"

"The name of the person who set all this up."

"I don't know . . . I swear. Carolann and I would meet here and exchange information, but I haven't seen her. Ask her. She knows. Really. She knows." He began to tremble.

"Carolann's dead."

"No! She can't be."

"She is. Now talk!"

Frank loosened his tie. "It was Jesslyn Owens . . ."

The words were barely out of his mouth when a stinging backhand from Palladin sent him crashing into the wall. Then Palladin grabbed him by the tie and pulled him up until he was on his toes.

Skip was shocked at first at the violence coming from the man they all knew as Glacier, but did nothing. As Palladin tightened his grip on Frank's tie, Skip stepped in and pried the men apart.

"One more lie and I'll leave you alone with him." Skip told Frank.

"No. That's . . . he wants to kill me," Frank sputtered.

"Right. Now do you talk, or do I take a coffee break."

Frank looked from one man to the other. There was nothing he could do but tell the truth. He had no doubt that Skip would leave him, and that Palladin might not kill him but make him wish for death. He knew there was something lethal about the man.

Slowly, he explained how he and Carolann stole the ad campaigns from Egyptian Enchantment. They never expected Jesslyn to be blamed. The plans had already been sold, and Carolann said that Jesslyn was smart and would land on her feet.

"So you and Carolann were having an affair." Skip said.

"No."

"You weren't lovers?" Palladin questioned.

"No. I'm not in her league. She and I were partners. Nothing more."

"All I did was drive the Jeep. I wasn't supposed to hit Jesslyn. I was supposed to scare her."

"Where did you get the Jeep?"

"From Hank Reynolds. He got it from his boss. That's why he could get the plates that said Hellraiser."

Knowing there was nothing more that Frank Mason could tell them, Skip led him out and said he would return him to his cell and then come back so they could search the place again.

"Then where do we go from here?"

Palladin smiled, "I didn't want to share this with Skip, but when Carolann was a little girl, she hid everything of value in a box under the floorboard of her closet."

"And you think old habits die hard?"

"I'm betting they do. We never found her little scorecard book she said she kept and I know for sure she kept one."

"Ever get to read it?"

"No. I respected her privacy. Sometimes it's better not to know."

The men entered the bedroom and Palladin tapped around the floor until he found a loose board. He got a knife from the buffet table and used it to pry up the board.

"Damn!"

"What is it? What did you find?" Kaliq couldn't see around his friend to know what he'd discovered.

"The motherlode. Her diary, a couple hundred thousand in cash and a computer disk."

Palladin tossed the bag of cash and the diary in Kaliq's lap and headed for the computer. He turned it on and as soon as it was up and running he tried a couple of applications until he found the one he needed. He slipped in the disk and waited.

Twenty-three

By that time, Kaliq had joined him and was watching the screen. When the images came on the screen, it wasn't an ad campaign. It was a payoff record for a Senator from the Midwest, one who'd been touted as presidential material. It was the one that Mac had helped elect by providing information on his opponent that led the man to withdraw from the race citing health problems, Senator Woodrow Gary.

"That's what scared Carolann," Kaliq said. "Being married to you, she knew enough to realize that this wasn't just industrial espionage. Mac was using the security firm to gather information then selling it to the highest bidder. He and the Senator were planning a run for the White House."

"And Mac would get what he always wanted."

It had been so easy to make it appear that Mac and Senator Gary were on opposite sides. When Senator Gary was elected president, he'd appoint Mac as head of the FBI, and it would appear to all concerned that the new president had crossed party lines to get the best man for the job. If Gary lost, Mac would probably still be the best contender and then he could feed Gary information to help him win the next time.

"What's that?"

"To run the agency. He'd be the president's appointee."

Jesslyn sat in the rocking chair and twirled the chain watching the ring attached to it circle her finger and then reversed the motion until the chain unwrapped several times before Mac spoke to her.

"You're driving me crazy doing that."

"Sorry, I just keep wondering what's keeping Palladin and Kaliq."

"If you think that Palladin is going to get you out of this because of a few *romantic* evenings, I can assure you that isn't going to happen."

"I didn't do anything but choose the wrong partner."

Jesslyn knew that Palladin wasn't comfortable with Skip's suggestion that they not tell Mac what they were doing. She was so nervous that she wanted to share the possibility with someone. Still, each time she and Mac had been alone, he had bordered on rude.

After a few moments of thinking about telling him about the second apartment, she decided not to say anything. It would be more fun to see his face when she was cleared of wrongdoing and his beloved Carolann was proven to be the thief.

"How are things with you and Palladin?"

"Fine."

"What are you going to do when this little adventure we're all sharing ends?"

"I haven't decided." She told him. What she really meant was that Palladin hadn't decided, but she wouldn't let anyone, other than her sister, be privy to that information.

Mac took out a notebook and thumbed through a few pages. "What did Carolann tell you?"

"Nothing. Maybe she kept a diary?"

The older man smiled. "Probably like Marilyn Monroe. Everyone swore that she kept a little red book and wrote down everything, but no one's found it yet."

"Maybe they don't know where to look."

"And Palladin knows where to look for Carolann's?"

Jesslyn's eyebrows lifted as she noticed the edge in Mac's voice. "If it's the same place she used when she was a kid, he might."

"What's that?"

"Palladin's class ring." With trembling fingers she peeled the tape on the ring away as she told him about the other apartment. "He gave it to me." She held up the ring in her hand. She'd gotten all the tape off. "Umm . . ." she said. "Class of 84 . . . no this isn't his ring. This must belong to another of Carolann's friends. This says class of 64."

As she said it she got a chill from the base of her spine all the way up her back. She looked up to find Mac staring at her. "Oh, my God!"

Mac faced her and pulled the gun from his shoulder holster. "I guess we all know the truth now. You and Palladin. Rolling around in the snow. Having fun when Carolann was dead. If I could have kept you two apart, I would have been home free. Woody and I would be running the country. But you know that, don't you?"

Jesslyn didn't say anything. When he mentioned the snow she realized that someone had been following her that day. Mac. And what he thought was "fun" was when she got her memory back. They were fighting, and he thought it was a prelude to lovemaking. The man missed the signals. Now Palladin was walking into a trap and she didn't know how to stop him.

"Dammit, man! I left Jesslyn alone with him," Palladin said. "I've got to get home."

"Not a big problem, Rush. But first we have to straighten things out here."

Palladin started toward the door, his eyes daring Skip to try and stop him. "I'm going home. And I'll take care of Mac alone, if I have to."

Skip started to block his path, but Palladin's eyes narrowed into tiny slits and in a voice just above a whisper said, "Try and stop me."

Kaliq rolled his chair near the door. "Think about it, man. You can't just go back there like nothing happened. Mac's gonna take one look at you and who knows? He might decide to kill Jesslyn like he did Carolann."

Palladin ran his left hand through his dreads. "What do you want me to do, just sit here?"

Skip's brows knitted together as he looked at Kaliq then Palladin then back to Kaliq and shrugged his shoulders asking the silent question.

"The man's in love. Having a little problem getting perspective on this?"

"With the Owens woman?"

"She has a name," snapped Palladin. "Stop calling her the Owens woman as if she's not a person!"

Palladin started to pace like a caged panther.

"No wonder Frank Mason said he'd tell everything, if we promised to keep Palladin away from him," Skip observed.

How could he have missed the signs? If it had been

anyone but Mac, he would have known before he found hard evidence. Now, because he hadn't, Jesslyn's life was in danger. There was no way to warn her. He had to pretend that the information from Skip had led them on a wild goose chase.

In the short time that Skip and Palladin had learned they were on the same side, a plan formulated. Not that they would ever be friends, but for the first time they wanted the same thing.

Palladin laid out the plan pure and simple. He was going in alone and no one was to try and stop him. He agreed to a wire so they would know when it was safe to come up and arrest Mac or storm the place if Palladin failed.

"I'll kill him." Palladin ran his fingers through his hair, tossing his dreads out of the way. "If he does anything to her, I'll kill him."

"He won't." Kaliq saw the glittering anger and tried to get Palladin refocused. "We have the evidence. He probably knows it."

"Skip, I need to get home fast," Palladin said.

"I'll make some calls."

After Skip left, Palladin turned to Kaliq. "A joke, isn't it? All while we were in the Service, Mac wanted us to learn to work together. We never did. Now when he needs it the least, he gets his wish."

"Yeah. Looks like Skip got his wish, too."

"What wish?"

"Well, everybody knows Skip hated that you were always so in control."

Palladin smiled and took a deep breath. No one had ever made him lose it the way he had when he learned that Jesslyn was with the mastermind. "I mean it. I'll tear Mac's heart out if he . . ." the thought of what could happen stopped him from saying it out loud. It was just understood. "He must have been laughing his head off every time I ran around trying to prove that Jesslyn was innocent."

"I don't know about that. He was pretty shocked when you kept insisting she was innocent."

"I guess he thought it would be quite a joke. I would be off in left field and he'd have all the answers."

Kaliq rubbed his hand across his face. "I think what he really wanted was for you to point out all the loopholes in his escape plan."

"Sure, then he could cover them up and no one would be the wiser."

"Guess he forgot the power of true love."

"Don't even go there. It can't happen."

"Does your family know they're getting a daughter-in-law?"

"They aren't."

Kaliq wheeled around. "What do you mean by that? You're going crazy thinking about what might happen to her. You've put everyone on notice to let you handle things. Now you say you aren't going to marry her?"

"My place is a great vacation for her. Hers is the same for me. But to try to combine those worlds . . . no way."

"Does she know that?"

"She's living some fantasy right now, but it's turning into a nightmare and she'll be glad to get back to New York."

Kaliq opened his mouth to argue but Palladin's eyes told him it wouldn't do any good—at least not right now.

Ten minutes later, Skip returned. He had arranged for a car to take Palladin to the helipad on the Met Life building. He would follow with Kaliq and meet with the police in Pennsylvania. The men shook hands and Palladin left.

Once downstairs, a police car was waiting and, with sirens blasting got him to the Met Life building and within minutes he was on his way. He prayed for the first time in ages.

In short minutes to the pilot, but long ones to Palladin, they landed a mile from his mountain retreat. They knew that Mac would hear the copter, but as long as it sounded as if was headed in a different direction it wouldn't make him panic. Palladin would simply hike back to his house and climb up the rough side of the mountain.

All the features he considered important were now playing against him. He never expected to be the one to try to breach his own security system. How could he get there without being seen? Even if he did, what about the alarm. He knew Mac would turn it on, and if he made one mistake, it could cost Jesslyn her life.

He turned to Kaliq. "See if you can keep him interested in the bottom of the hill while I try to come up the other side."

He hadn't done much climbing since he'd returned from visiting his parents in California. The still early darkness of late winter also worked against him. He didn't know if he could still make it and he certainly wasn't dressed for it. He wasn't dressed for climbing, but he had to do it. Jesslyn's life depended on it. He took off his gloves so he could get ready.

He tossed off his coat and stripped down to his shirt and jeans. Wrapping his gun in plastic and using his shirttail as a kerchief he tied the gun and then put on his vest and buttoned it, forcing the gun to stay trapped between his body and the vest. Then he put his gloves back on and began the climb. The biting wind of March laced through him, but he shook it off. Carefully, he stepped on the rocks. His fingers grew cold and numb after only a few minutes, but he only noticed that he'd scraped a fair amount of skin from his sides when he stopped to take a breath. He deliberately channeled his thoughts to the pictures they'd found in the apartment.

They were the kind that you put the camera on a timer and jumped into a quick pose. Carolann and Senator Woodrow Gary, naked, locked in a passionate kiss. He wondered if Gary knew the pictures were being taken or if Carolann had had a hidden camera, thinking it would protect her. The man campaigning on family values had a mistress. How long had the affair being going on? Then there were those of Mac, along with Gary and Carolann. How long had he been used by the two people he trusted most.

As he reached the top of the mountain, he kept low to the ground and crawled to the structure. He cursed the huge windows that gave him the view he loved so much. They now left him vulnerable.

He made the decision. He would have to let Mac catch him. That way, he could be on the inside and maybe convince Mac that it was over and better to give up and make a deal. He was sure that there were connections that the government would be willing to bargain with him to find. Another of Palladin's rules fell by the wayside.

Fury swept through his body like a forest fire. He wanted to just go in and rip Mac apart with his bare hands. Setting Jesslyn up to take the fall for his and Carolann's thefts. He could only hope that he didn't kill the man before the people Skip called could get there. Mac didn't know it, but right now his best friends were men who only wanted to arrest him. Given a choice, Palladin would find relief in tearing out Mac's heart, rather than sending him off to prison.

He had to test the door. He remembered showing Jesslyn the alarm system and maybe she'd been smart enough to turn it off.

Wiping sweat from his brow, he stepped back from the door to the mud room, picked up a rock and tossed it at the door. If the alarm went off, he could hide by the garage and let Mac think it was a malfunction. He held his breath and tossed the rock. Nothing. He tossed another rock, this time at the window. It wasn't on.

He grabbed the doorknob and braced himself again for the alarm, just in case Mac had redirected it. Then he turned the knob and let out a deep breath. It wasn't on. Mac had made a mistake. With speed that belied his numb fingers he stripped off his wet clothing and into another pair of jeans and a shirt.

The wire taped to his chest reminded him to give the signal that he was inside. The taps from his fingers could be heard by the people gathered at the foot of the mountain, but not by the people in the other room.

He put the gun next to him on the bench and did the hardest thing he'd ever done. Waited. Now that he was inside and knew there was no imminent danger, he needed to get warm.

When he was ready, Palladin slipped behind the pillar between the kitchen and dining room. He saw them. Mac patiently holding the gun and talking to Jesslyn.

He told himself that Jesslyn would be fine. He just had to wait until the time was right.

At the front of the property the team was assembling. Kaliq arrived and found Skip as well as some men and women from the local police standing by a can where a fire burned brightly. "Where is he?"

"He went up the other side of the mountain. Why?"

"No reason." Kaliq rolled his chair closer to the fire and tossed the diary in.

"Hey, was that a piece of evidence?"

"Mixed company," he nodded to the women officers, "prevents me from telling you what it was a piece of."

"Might make a good story."

"It's a 'needs to know' kind of thing. No one here needs to know."

Twenty-four

"You don't have much to say, Jesslyn."

"Well, saying 'how could you' sounds too trite."

Mac shrugged his shoulders and walked over to her. "I expected you to fight. Go down kicking and screaming."

"Happy to disappoint you."

His eyes narrowed. "You're too calm. What did you do in there, turn off the alarm?"

Jesslyn turned her head. Mac used two fingers to bring her chin around. "Yeah, that's what you did. But it won't work."

He suddenly grabbed her arm, dragged her to a standing position and pushed her toward the kitchen. He found the panel. "Never thought I'd need this code. That's the only reason I don't know it, but you're going to give it to me."

"No, I won't."

Mac stood behind her and put the gun to her head. She closed her eyes. "Don't worry," was his next comment. "I won't kill you." He slid the gun down the side of her face to her rib cage then further down until the barrel was pressed against her thigh. "Do you know how painful a bullet in the leg can be?"

Jesslyn opened her eyes. She knew he was serious,

and she knew she could not handle physical pain. She didn't pretend to be brave or dare him. And she knew he could see the fear in her eyes at the thought of having a bullet in her leg.

"You'll pray for death. If Palladin's on his way here you've got plenty of time to hurt. Your choice."

She ran her tongue across her dry lips. "Twenty-four nineteen, thirty-seven."

He punched in the numbers and watched as the red light came on signaling the alarm was set. Then he ushered Jesslyn back to the living room.

"Did you hire someone to have me murdered?"

"Yes."

"Why? You were peddling your little secrets all over town. Why kill the goose that lays the golden eggs?"

"Simple. If Carolann could have gotten a larger share of the business, then maybe we would have gone on the way we were—maybe even found a way to ease you out and take over completely. You had a nice little corporate client list, but you wouldn't let go."

"Why didn't you just start your own business? Why did you want mine?"

Mac shrugged. "Think about it. How long did it take you to build that list? If you hadn't stepped back on that curb when you did, everything we planned would have worked out just fine."

"And with the way Lena felt about business, you'd just play white knight and buy it from her."

"Now you're beginning to see the big picture. Most people don't pay attention to little operations like yours. As long as you don't become a high spender and call attention to yourself, you can go on for years manipulating these guys who think they can run the country."

"He's going to stop you."

Mac didn't answer. Jesslyn knew he had the upper and. She could only hope that Palladin had enough ense not to walk into a trap. That something in that partment told him what was really happening. Nerves nade her body crave for movement. She got up and valked toward the door.

"We had another plan for Lena with you out of the vay."

He was anxious to tell her how clever he had been. he faked indifference until he finally decided to tell her.

"Plan B was to keep her around for a silent partner, ne who would take the fall if anything went down.

"But Carolann got greedy when she realized what was n that diskette.

"She wanted to play in the big leagues, but didn't have he guts when it came down to real trouble. She would ave told Palladin everything."

Jesslyn bit her lip and thought about what it must have elt like for Carolann. She'd stepped on so many toes uring her modeling career that she didn't have any riends. There wasn't anyone she could turn to but her x-husband.

The phone rang. Mac nodded for her to answer it. They new it was Palladin. She picked it up and gave a trembly reeting, paused and stuck the phone out to signal Mac t was for him.

"I didn't want it to happen this way," Mac was saying.

He pleaded his case, asking Palladin to understand ow it felt to be so close to his goal and then have it natched away. Mac turned away from Jesslyn. She acked up till she was near the kitchen and bent down o pull the cover off the alarm. She worked quickly. Palladin had to be able to get to the house. He'd take ca of Mac. All she had to do was make a way for him enter.

She eased back into the living room and sat down.

Mac slammed the phone down. "He's worried abo you. He'll be here in twenty minutes or so."

"He'll kill you."

"What did you do to him?"

"I'm not the one who betrayed him."

"He never would have doubted my word that Carolan was the victim. He was all set to send you to prison. B he fell in love!"

He made "love" sound like the ultimate evil. For hin that was probably how it felt. She smiled, knowing th would make him angry and distract him.

"Carolann was at least beautiful. I don't know wh he sees in you."

"I guess it's that 'eye of the beholder' line."

He came closer. "You're not even smart. You think didn't notice you sneaking off to the kitchen while I wa talking to your boyfriend."

Jesslyn backed away. He took another step toward he "I suggest you put that alarm back on. Or I'll go bac to Plan A." He lowered the gun until the barrel was poin ing at her legs.

Keeping her distance from Mac she returned to th kitchen and lifted the panel. He followed her and watche as she punched in some numbers and the red light cam on again.

Now they could only wait. After ten minutes of silenc Jesslyn had to ask, "Where are your ethics?" Sh couldn't understand the man who supposedly had bee like a second father to Palladin and even to Carolann.

Mac snorted. "Ethics. Yeah. I'll tell you about that. I ive them my life's blood. Put together a team and then ecause they want Rush and he wouldn't play the game, 'm out. He could have moved up, been a contender like Colin Powell. Then, when I wanted the Bureau, they vould have given it to me. When he quit, it made it look s if I couldn't hold my team together."

"I thought *you* quit?"

"Well they had to give me something. So they let me esign, take my pension and they even got me the job as ead of security for a top firm. Oh, the government was o good to me, but they didn't give me what I wanted nost."

"To be head of the Bureau." Palladin's voice startled oth Mac and Jesslyn. She started to him then looked own at the very lethal handgun he was holding.

"What? How did you get in?"

"I live here, remember?"

"You couldn't have disabled the alarm." Mac started o bring the gun around to Palladin.

"Not a good idea. Put the gun down, Mac. I didn't ome alone." He didn't mention that the alarm wasn't n. Mac must have forgotten to set it.

"You aren't going to shoot me. We've been through oo much together."

"Is that why you had an affair with my wife? I saw he pictures."

"You don't understand. We needed you and you be-rayed us."

Although he kept the gun on his target, Palladin vanted to find out the whole truth. "What are you talking bout?"

"I wanted the president to put me in charge of the

Bureau. But I'd only get it on one condition, that I g
you to stay. How many black men could have been a
that level of power. We wouldn't have had to worry abo
elections. We'd be the ones that they wanted, no matt
what party was in the White House."

"And you call that a betrayal?" Palladin couldn't be
lieve he'd been so wrong about a man he considered
second father. All these years, he'd been getting even fo
what he considered a betrayal. He shivered at the though
of the kind of man Mac really was with the kind of powe
that being head of the FBI would give him.

"Are you okay, Jesslyn?"

She nodded, then noticed the blood dripping on th
living room floor. "You're bleeding," Jesslyn's concerne
voice made him smile. He nodded for her to get the fir
aid kit.

"I'm not as good at climbing mountains as I was.
scraped a good portion of my skin off."

"I guess you need a lot of practice?"

"Don't turn toward me, Mac. Put the gun down o
the floor, gently. Now!"

Mac watched her walk to the bathroom. He shifted
little but knew he couldn't move too much.

"You'd shoot me? Not even try to work somethin
out?"

"Do it!"

Mac seemed to waiver on whether or not he shoul
try to escape. Palladin moved closer. "Don't make m
shoot you, Mac."

Jesslyn breathed a sigh of relief as Mac lowered hi
weapon, but the sigh turned into a scream as he quickl
reversed directions and pulled the trigger.

Years of inactivity spoiled his aim and he missed. Pa

ladin rushed forward knocking Mac down and the two men fell to the floor, stumbling into Jesslyn and taking her with them. Mac held on to his weapon, and as they wrestled, he pointed toward Palladin. Jesslyn jumped up and her movement forced Mac to try to get off a shot. Too early and wide of his intended mark, he did claim one victim—Jesslyn.

She felt a bursting pain in her hand, looked down and grew weak as she watched blood pouring from the wound. Holding the mantel on the fireplace she could only be a spectator as Palladin let out an unintelligible roar. There was another shot before he wrestled the gun away. He raised the gun and brought it down solidly against Mac's head. Both men stopped moving.

Then, uncharacteristically, Palladin raised the gun and was about to hit Mac again until Jesslyn shouted his name and he snapped out of the white-hot rage and stopped with the gun in mid-air. He lowered it to the floor as he collapsed on top of Mac.

Slowly, Palladin rolled over and got to his knees, leaving Mac on the floor. He pulled the gun out of the unconscious man's hand. Jesslyn ran to him and they stood there holding each other for a long, reassuring minute.

He got some rope and tied Mac to a chair while Jesslyn got the first aid kit. He bandaged her up, as he explained that no bones in her hand were hit, but she'd need stitches. He called Kaliq who'd been sitting at the bottom of the hill waiting until the right moment to call in the cavalry. Once Palladin removed the wire, they'd been afraid to do anything that might jeopardize more lives.

"It's about time, my man," was all Kaliq said when Palladin cut off the alarm and called him to say it was safe to come up.

While they waited for the local law enforcement and the FBI, Mac regained consciousness.

"Why?" Palladin's soft request to his mentor was barely a whisper. Mac and Jesslyn knew he wasn't talking about the thefts, but the affair.

"You betrayed me. Me and Carolann. It gave us a sort of bond."

"What are you talking about?"

"You made promises to both of us and you broke them."

"You blame me for your busted career, so you have an affair with my wife?"

"It wasn't like that. She needed someone. She needed you to think more of her welfare than running off to some godforsaken rescue mission. I wasn't her lover. I was her friend." Mac looked down. "I was the one who was there for her. I took care of Carolann better than you ever could."

"The lady was no hothouse flower who had to be pampered. She didn't need you."

"She did! I was the one who found the evidence that she'd smuggled from Egyptian Enchantment, and I gave it to her so she wouldn't go to jail. You ran off to some godforsaken country to rescue that crippled friend, and I was the one who held her hand after the abortion."

Color drained from Palladin's face. Jesslyn could only stare at the man.

"Abortion?"

"You wouldn't stay with her. She didn't want the baby. She didn't want any children, but you did. And she got pregnant for you. And you betrayed her. All for this stupid mountain retreat."

Jesslyn felt tears roll down her cheeks—his child.

Carolann had vengefully destroyed his child. Mac knew it and let her hold it over Palladin's head. She saw Palladin's eyes glaze over. She saw the granite-like facade take over.

"Doesn't matter, Mac." Ice dripped from every word.

No explanation would satisfy the protégé who'd become like a son to him. All this for money—money that he wouldn't see. She shook her head at the thought of giving up so much for so little.

The FBI arrived shortly after ten that night. The temperature had dropped into single digits, making the road up to the house slightly treacherous. Palladin and Jesslyn were exhausted by the time the agents carted Mac away. In the hours, before the men arrived, Mac made two attempts to explain what had happened with Carolann. The steel-like glare from Palladin's dark eyes silenced him each time.

Later, when Kaliq, Palladin and Jesslyn were trying to put things in perspective, Palladin wanted to find out why it was so easy for him to get into the house.

Jesslyn was curled up on the sofa in her robe. She'd insisted on showering and changing into a gown and robe because she felt the doctor could work better than if she was wearing the tight turtleneck sweater.

He'd put a couple of stitches in her hand and had given her a clean bill of health, otherwise, before he'd left.

"Really, it wasn't bad," he told Palladin. "No more than when I have to stitch up those little rabble-rousers you call a hockey team."

But for all his reassurance, Palladin shivered every time he looked at her hand.

"How did you manage to turn off the alarm?" Palladin asked.

"I didn't. I got Mac to do it."

Kaliq rolled his chair over so he could look her in the face. "How did you do that?"

"I knew if I turned the alarm off he'd make me turn it back on. The only way you know the system is on is that little red light."

"I'd better sit down. I don't think I'm going to like hearing this." Palladin crossed over to the sofa.

"I turned the alarm off and switched the bulbs and then turned it back on. So when Mac thought he was turning the system on he was really turning it off."

"Brilliant, my lady," Kaliq took her hand and brought it to his lips.

Delighted with Kaliq's appraisal of her skills, she looked at Palladin and cringed. His black eyes were shooting angry sparks that felt like daggers against her ego.

"I'm not tossing accolades at the way you risked your life," said Palladin. "You could have gotten yourself killed. Don't ever do that again."

"Well, it wasn't my fault that you don't know how to find me a safe bodyguard."

"You don't need a bodyguard. You need a keeper."

"Wait one minute . . ."

"Children!" Kaliq interrupted them. "You mustn't fight over this."

"You're right," Palladin agreed. "But she scared me. If Mac had noticed . . ." He couldn't finish that thought.

"I'm sorry, but I wanted to help."

Palladin pulled her from the seat opposite him and into his lap. "I guess I'm feeling the pressure of something happening to you. The FBI will be here in the morning to debrief you. So you'd better get some sleep."

The knock on the door startled everyone.

"Damn! I forgot to reset the system." Palladin walked to the door and threw it open. The tall, voluptuous woman standing there stunned him for a moment. "Trisha, I wasn't expecting you."

She swept in with the rolling hip motion that models used on Parisian catwalks. Her thick, shoulder-length red hair would at one time need to be tamed with a hot comb, but she wore it natural. The bright mass of color bore blond streaks that complemented her golden brown skin.

"I thought Trisha and I would spend the night at the inn rather than here."

"You don't have to do that." Jesslyn knew why he'd arranged to leave. He wanted to give Jesslyn and Palladin some privacy.

"I will see you two tomorrow," he said, ignoring them. "And I'm not doing this just for you." He nodded in Trisha's direction. "I certainly want to get to know this woman better."

"Before you run off, I need to talk to you," Palladin said.

"Don't you need to talk to your lady?" Kaliq answered. "We'll be back tomorrow."

"You first. The lady's next."

Jesslyn watched the men adjourn to the den, but she wondered if she should read anything into the fact that Palladin had used the term "the lady," not "my lady."

Twenty-five

The radio and the TV weatherman had predicted more snow the next afternoon. Jesslyn wondered what it would be like to be trapped here till spring, just the two of them. It would give her time to show him that she could live in his world. She could handle a few trips to the city and back here. The bandage on her hand was only slightly uncomfortable. The bullet had passed through a fleshy part and nothing in her hand was permanently damaged. She did wonder if the injuries her body had suffered in this past month meant her relationship with Palladin was jinxed, but she was willing to risk it.

Maybe she could split her ballet tickets with a friend. Maybe she could bargain with her sister for more time away from the shop. It all depended on whether or not he wanted to continue the relationship. He'd never used the word "love" but that didn't mean he couldn't feel it. She'd just have to ask him.

She and Trisha had talked and were now raiding the refrigerator. Trisha's question about jam brought her back to the present.

"You need what?"

"Don't tell anyone, but I'm a closet junk food junkie. Every now and then, instead of wanting the Inn's specialty of Plum and Almond Potstickers, I crave a peanut butter and grape jam sandwich."

Jesslyn laughed and glanced toward the den.

"Are you going to be staying here or going back to New York?"

"That's the million dollar question. I don't know. Right after he found out his wife was having an affair with his mentor, he just got sort of quiet."

"Kaliq's asked me to come to Wyoming."

"Are you going?"

"I don't know."

Jesslyn shook her head. "Here we are, two successful businesswomen. Great futures and we're waiting for two men to decide our futures."

"No. We're letting them decide their futures. Do they want to be happy with us or alone and miserable."

"I like your thinking. Make me one of those," she said indicating the sandwich Trisha held, "I'll find the liquor and we'll drink to that."

The women got comfortable and Trisha asked, "Did you like being part of a case like this?"

"No. I was scared most of the time. Not once did I feel that adrenaline-high that people talk about." She shivered. Palladin had told her that was what she was experiencing and the reason she wanted to make love. She knew, however, that she was not on an adrenaline high. When Palladin had held her close and told her that everything was going to be all right she'd just been relieved it was over and had no desire to ever try the cloak and dagger world again.

"Kaliq mentioned Carolann . . ."

"Yeah. She loved it. She used to brag about being with a man who could be at the center of an attack on the president. I think she wanted someone to try something just so she could brag that her husband prevented it or got shot trying. I don't think she cared which."

"If you stay around . . . give me a call. We'll do lunch, as they say among the corporate elite."

"Even if I don't stay, I'll keep in touch." Jesslyn promised.

"Thanks. I might need someone to talk to sometimes."

"What else do you do besides hide in closets and eat peanut butter and grape jam sandwiches?"

Trisha's eyes lit up. "I collect chess sets."

"I play chess." Jesslyn found it easy to talk to Trisha. They seemed to find common ground, even in hobbies.

"I read somewhere that it made you a better strategist. So I learned just for that reason." Trisha explained.

"I read that also. But I learned because all my friends were going out for cheerleading in high school to get boys, and I joined the chess team to avoid them."

Palladin and Kaliq were jolted to find the women sitting in front of the fireplace with a glass of bourbon in one hand and a peanut butter and grape jam sandwich in the other and laughing.

"I don't think we want to know," Palladin said.

"Right. And you thought I'd stopped living dangerously," Kaliq murmured.

When they left Jesslyn asked, "How did you know not to come back the normal way? We never got around to talking about that."

Relieved that she wasn't drunk, angry or both, he explained.

"You were right about that apartment not being a place

where anyone really lived. It was where they met as lovers and where they planned using your business to transport stolen information."

"Why me? Mac kept talking about Frank being arrested. Why?"

Palladin pulled her down on the sofa beside him and wrapped his arms around her. "Frank was part of it."

"But he was the only one who didn't treat me as if I was a leper."

"Unfortunately, that's also what made me suspicious of him."

Jesslyn struggled to sit up but couldn't get away from his vise-like grip. "Because he was nice to me there had to be something wrong?"

He lifted his hand and turned her face to his. "Think about it. Rumor says you sold out to another company. Why would anyone on the fast-track stay in touch? We both know that the slightest taint in business makes people desert family. Why not friends?"

She remembered the night she and Palladin met. Frank told her that her company was being checked out. That there were rumors, but not what they were exactly. She now understood why.

"He wanted me to find out about Carolann. No one knew about Mac."

"And if you didn't go screaming to the police somewhere, you'd be roped in as an accomplice."

Jesslyn shook her head. All the time she thought she was fighting back from disgrace, someone was trying to drag her down into something far worse that being suspected of industrial espionage. She would have been part of the real thing.

"How did I get so susceptible?"

"Because it wasn't the first time Carolann and Frank had used you."

Jesslyn's eyes widened and she gasped. There was only one other instance it could have happened. This time when she pushed at his chest he released her. Then she walked over to the pillows in front of the fireplace and sat down. "Are you saying *she* ruined my career at Egyptian Enchantment?"

"Yeah. I have proof you can use."

"Why?"

He stared at her. Why not? It would vindicate her—make all those people who didn't believe her into losers. Each would pretend he or she wasn't the one pointing the finger but find some excuse as to why they never came forward to Jesslyn about it.

"Don't you want back what you lost and more?" He knew offers would pour in as the corporate world she loved so much would want to appease their guilt. He saw no light in her eyes.

Carefully, Jesslyn mulled over what he said and she found that she didn't care. Everything that she wanted could be hers again, but it was too late. Five years away had made that kind of success obsolete. She had her own company. She did things her own way and she was successful. Maybe she didn't have the perks of the corporate execs, but she didn't have their worries about downsizing, making bad decisions. GiftBaskets was all she needed.

"It's like being sixteen and wanting desperately for the captain of the football team to ask you for a date," she said. "And have him ask you after you've fallen in love with someone else. Sometimes, it's just too late."

When she was a top executive, people wanted her job so they lied. When she had a little gift basket company, the same people wanted that so they could continue their activities. Working for someone else let them make her decisions. Now she controlled her life. And with her and Lena becoming more partners that just sisters, she had even more control. After the years of fighting to get back on top, she didn't want it. She was right where she wanted to be, careerwise at least.

"Carolann's dead. Didn't you tell me they always blame the dead person?"

Palladin crossed and sat down beside her. He'd said that when he accused Jesslyn of trying to lure Carolann into a shady lifestyle. He'd been wrong about both women. "It will clear your name."

"I don't need my name cleared. People will believe what they like. They can have it down in black and white and still not accept it. I don't want a corporate life, anyway. Maybe she was a blessing in disguise." What she really wanted to say was that, if Carolann and Mac hadn't trapped her in this chaotic little mystery, she never would have met Palladin. She considered *that* the silver lining in this cloud.

"You may not want it, but the papers are having a field day and it's going to come back to you. Now is the time to make up a plan. You'll be able to call your own shots."

"I call my own shots now."

She moved closer to him and he moved away. "I guess you don't need my protection anymore."

For the longest minute, she waited for him to look at her. When he didn't, she knew somewhere he was fighting demons. "I need to get back to my apartment, pay some bills, get my shop together. I don't even want to imagine what it's been like for Lena to run it."

"Good idea. The agents will be back tomorrow, and they'd like to debrief you before you go home."

"Fine. And then?"

"What?"

"Are you going to be in New York any time soon?" She was fishing for something to hold on to. Something that glimmered of hope for them.

"I don't . . . think so. I have some things to catch up on, also."

"After you catch up on . . . things, will you pay me a visit?"

He shook his head. "I don't think it can work for us. I don't know what I want right now."

"You need time to sort out your feelings about . . . Carolann . . . Mac . . . I understand . . ."

He let out a deep breath. "I don't see us as a long term couple. You're caught up in the mystery and I'm your rescuer. Why wouldn't you think you're in love with me?"

"And it's not love for you?"

"Sweetheart, I want you like hell on fire, if that's your definition of love. I'm just not sure what that word means anymore."

"You believed me when I told you I was innocent. Isn't that why you brought me here."

"No. I wanted you to be innocent, but I brought you here because if you were innocent, we could have a good time and then walk away. If you were guilty, I wanted to be the one to take you down. I always knew that mountain life isn't for you."

"I love your mountain."

"But one day you're going to look around and find nothing on this mountain worth what you can get in the city."

"You say that like you're someone who'll turn into a toad if you stay away from here too long."

"I'll always want to come back here. You won't."

She stood up and glared at him then turned toward the guest room. "You know darling, answer me something. How does it feel to know what everyone else wants or will do and not have enough sense to know what you want?"

By the time she finished her question she was inside the guest room and the house rattled with the force she used to close the door.

He scrubbed his hands over his face, calling himself every kind of idiot for letting her walk away. He wouldn't try to stop her when she left for good. He had nothing to offer her if she stayed.

It was a long time before he finally released a deep, weary breath and began to return his desk to some semblance of order. The worst part was that it hadn't helped. He was still as tightly wound as he'd been earlier.

Palladin knew she was wrong. He did know what he wanted—her. But he watched her sparkle each time they were in the city. She loved it. And he knew that love would starve if he kept her away too long. He also knew something she didn't. The adrenaline high from coming back from danger made you imagine you had it all. He didn't want to see her eyes when the rush faded. Where he found solitude she would find boredom. He'd seen it before—in Carolann, in Kaliq's late wife. Laura only wanted to escape from the small New Mexico town, and when Kaliq came through to do a story, she fell in love with his lifestyle more than with him. Even in Mac's ex. Barbara was a bored socialite who thought having an FBI man as a husband would be more exciting than a

CEO. Each woman had believed she could live with them, and as Mac said, they were cut from the same cloth. Dangerous-living men with adrenaline addicted wives.

Jesslyn had pulled the robe together and murmured something about needing to take a bath and Palladin was glad for the moment he needed to push his needs . . . wants . . . aside and do the right thing. She hadn't even looked back to see his reaction, and he was glad. He was fighting for control and it was a losing battle. He had to let her go, make her go. She'd fought too hard for success in the world of New York businesses. To stop now when the brass ring was in sight would always make them wonder if she could have done it. And there was the lie he told her about being over what Carolann had done. He wasn't and he didn't want help in healing.

Jesslyn filled the tub with hot water and bubblebath. She threw her robe on the towel rack after she removed a bath sheet. Then she climbed in hoping the steaming water would calm her nerves. She liked this deep, square-shaped tub, since it allowed her to sit down and let the water surround her body. Though he hadn't said it, Palladin was hurting and like a wounded bear wouldn't allow anyone to help.

Why was he so smart about so many other things and so dense when it came to their relationship? He'd made up his mind that she couldn't live in his world and he couldn't live in hers. She didn't even know how to defend against his decrees. He'd said she had to go home. She found the African Black soap and began to work up a lather as she applied it over her body.

"Maybe I should just tell him that home is where the heart is," she said out loud. And it sounded so corny she started to laugh. "A stitch in time saves nine. Maybe absence makes the heart grow fonder," she couldn't help herself. The old wives' tales seem to pop into her head. She was laughing so hard she didn't realize she wasn't alone.

Not until Palladin spoke, "I thought I'd try to comfort you, but I guess you've found a way to get over your anger."

She looked up and still couldn't stop the giggles. She saw the bottle of champagne.

"I thought we'd have a drink and at least part as friends." He said and shrugged his shoulders.

She stopped laughing. "Is that what you really want tonight?" Her eyes held his and demanded the truth.

"No. I want us to spend the night in the same room, like the other night. I want to make love to you one last time."

"Okay."

She remembered how he'd carried her to his room and she'd spent the night in his arms. He was giving her the chance to throw him out and to hurt him as much as his demand that she leave had hurt her. She just wasn't that kind of person. Why shouldn't their last night together be memorable. He'd probably need to think about it after she was gone. And in the back of her mind, she knew she really thought if the night in each other's arms was terrific then he wouldn't want her to leave.

"That's it? Just 'okay'." He couldn't believe she wasn't going to make it a little difficult. Make him pay for not being able to say what she wanted to hear. But she hadn't, or had she?

"What's the punch line?"

"I want to spend it in here."

"My bed's a lot bigger."

"You've decided that I have to go home, right?"

"If we're going to rehash that business in the living room . . ." He would never let her think by sleeping with him she could change his mind.

"Just answer the question!" She knew the answer but she wanted whatever happened between them to be on her terms.

"Yes. You have to go home." He stood up and stalked toward the door.

"Then I get to decide where we make love for the last time."

He turned and their eyes met. Palladin knew she was serious. It was here or nowhere. And for him that was just fine.

He came back and put the champagne bottle and the glasses on the platform surrounding the tub.

"Is that water still hot?"

As she realized what he planned, she lost her voice and just nodded.

Slowly, he began slipping out of his clothes. The absence of a shirt revealed a wide chest with black hair forming a large V. She thought she'd never really looked at his body before. Her mind had been racing ahead to the simple joining of their bodies. Pleasure. Need. Desire. But tonight, she wanted everything etched in her brain as a memory. She knew it would be the same for him. He'd never forget this time.

He tossed his shirt on top of her robe. "Enjoying the show?"

She let her eyes meander up his body to his face. "Absolutely."

The last time she'd been shy and turned away once he was completely naked. This time she was bold enough to relax and wait.

He kicked off his boots but had trouble pulling his jeans down. He stepped on the platform and over into the tub.

She heard herself make an audible gulp as he kicked his jeans away and she saw his erection. If he was this hard now, Jesslyn wondered if they'd make it to the bed.

They didn't. The first time.

Twenty-six

The next morning, she woke up alone. She'd expected it, and yet she'd fallen asleep hoping she was wrong—hoping she'd wake up with his arms around her as before. But she was wrong. The only thing to do was to go back to New York. She showered and dressed quickly. Most of her things had been packed the night before, so she only had to add her nightgown and toiletries to the suitcase and slip into the black slacks and matching turtleneck.

Joining Palladin for breakfast was the hardest part. She tried to keep the conversation pleasant but found herself chattering in a monologue, while Palladin made appropriate noises to show he was listening.

She stopped. "Why am I doing this?"

"I know . . ."

"I'm not talking to you." She took the dishes from the table and began loading the dishwasher.

"You don't have to do that . . ."

"More don'ts."

"I don't want to fight with you. I don't want you to leave."

"Let me ask you, Mister Rush, are there any 'do's' in your life?"

Palladin stepped toward her but the scowl on her face made him step back. "I *do* know it's best."

"I thought God was the only one who knew everything. Does He know you've taken over that department?" She slammed the door to the dishwasher closed and proceeded to set it. She waited for him to tell her it should be full before turning it on. Out of the corner of her eye she saw him step toward her again and change his mind again.

Jesslyn wondered if she had time to go into the exercise room and take her frustration out on that punching bag. She closed her eyes and began a slow enumeration of all the reasons why she should be mad at him. If she could stay angry until she was on her way back to New York, she wouldn't cry. She didn't want to cry because if reason couldn't convince him to let her stay, she damn sure wasn't going to use tears.

Palladin watched her closely. He'd never seen her like this. If he tried to tell her he understood, she'd lose it completely. She was very close to the edge now. He felt her anger rise. Here he was trying to do what was best for both of them, and she was acting like he didn't care . . . didn't love her. There was no way he would bring her here, then watch as she grew tired of the isolation or the travel time to get to work or even to move her business here or open a branch office. He had to force her to leave. It was best for her. She didn't think so now, but when she found someone who enjoyed the city, she would thank him. He quickly brushed that thought away. He didn't want to even think of her with someone else.

"After last night, I thought we could part as friends."

Her eyes grew cold as she stared up at him. "Is that

what last night was about? A way for you to clear your conscious with a charity . . ."

"How can you even think that! Can we just get to a point where we're civil before you leave?"

"Okay! Something we agree on because I don't want to fight. I just want to say it's better we quit now. I want to say it long enough and loud enough so I'll believe it." She walked out of the kitchen to the living room with Palladin right behind her. She picked up a small plant from the window and moved it to the end table.

"Damn it! Getting yourself all worked up is just making it harder . . . more difficult!"

His choice of words made his body react. He saw the slow smile spread across her face, and it told him she'd pushed him to the brink.

"Good for me. This may be the last chance I get. What I really want to do is . . ." She picked up the small plant she'd put on the end table and then looked at him.

"You throw one thing in this house and . . ."

"Excuse me." They both jumped.

The man in the doorway struggled to hide a smile as he said, "FBI, you didn't hear my knock but I could hear you and thought I'd better come in and . . . ease the tension."

"I'm Jesslyn Owens. He's Palladin Rush, the owner and 'expert on how everything should be done' over there who forgot to turn on his alarm again."

"I didn't forget. I left it off because I knew they were coming."

The men walked toward each other and shook hands.

"Rick Buckley, Mr. Rush."

"Palladin."

"Rick."

From Jesslyn's point of view, it was just another kind of male bonding. Rick reminded her of a younger Skip. The agent wore his blond hair cropped short, but his suit was more from the designer collection than from the off the rack department store. Politely, he explained why the debriefing was necessary. Mac was a long time civil servant and they needed to know when he went bad.

"If you prefer, Ms. Owens," agent Buckley said. "Mr. Rush can be with you."

Her eyes met Palladin's. "No. Mr. Rush's presence is not necessary." She saw his jaw twitch and knew she'd struck the right nerve.

"Use the den," Palladin said.

Jesslyn and the agent made themselves comfortable in the den and he began the questioning. Although she couldn't tell them much, she knew that neither Mac nor Carolann would betray their country. "He didn't seem concerned about money, just the idea of taking from one company and selling it to another. And how it would lead to him being assigned to head up the FBI."

"We don't believe he was in this alone," the agent said.

"I can't help you there. He never mentioned anyone else."

"We did find the body of Hank Reynolds. A professional job. Any views on that?"

"My . . . late partner knew him. I guess he just got in the way of ambitious men." She had the feeling they'd never know if it was Mac's order or Senator Gary's that ended Reynold's life.

The meeting was over after a few more minutes. The agent was satisfied that Jesslyn could shed no more light on the operation. In selling the information, Mac had crossed several state lines, so the FBI was looking into all the possibilities.

While Palladin and Agent Buckley talked, Jesslyn spent some time walking around a place she'd grown to love. She put on her coat and went outside.

Palladin had already arranged for the agent to take her back to New York. As soon as they finished, she'd have to leave.

How could he make love to her and not be in love with her? One moment, it seemed he was whispering all the right things and the next, he was helping her pack her bags. One moment, he seemed reluctant to end what they shared and the next, he couldn't get her away from him fast enough.

She was sitting on the steps when Kaliq arrived with the innkeeper in tow. "Jesslyn, you remember Trisha."

"Of course," she said and smiled. It had only been a few hours since the redhead had whisked him off.

"So how goes it?" Kaliq asked.

"As well as could be expected. All things considered, he's reached a decision."

Kaliq shook his head. "I'll talk to him."

"Don't," she said harder than she meant. "Please." She softened her request. Then to change the subject, "Have you been managing an inn long, Ms. Terrance?"

"A few years. I majored in hotel management."

"Have you always wanted to run a bed and breakfast?"

"No. I wanted a big hotel. I got hooked on that TV show 'Hotel' and thought it was the perfect way to have a fabulous suite and room service."

"I'm trying to convince her to come to Wyoming and manage my bed & breakfast," he said.

Trisha laughed and turned to Jesslyn, "Is it me, or did that sound more personal than job related?"

"Definitely personal."

Kaliq wheeled his chair up to the bottom step. "I am mortally wounded by your doubt. Where's Palladin?"

"Debriefing."

"And then it's your turn?"

Jesslyn stood up and walked down the stairs. She indicated her luggage by the car. "I've already had my turn."

The smile left Kaliq's face. "I can't believe he'll let you leave."

"Believe it. I certainly do." She was still able to let anger keep her from bursting into tears and start begging him to let her stay. If she gave him time, she was sure he'd come to his senses. But she also knew that it wouldn't be good to mourn forever. She'd build a life without him, if that was what he really wanted.

Trisha patted Jesslyn's arm. "Sometimes no matter how hard we want things to work, they don't."

"You're right."

Kaliq added. "Sometimes people don't try hard enough."

She would have argued with him, but at that moment, the door opened and Palladin and Agent Buckley appeared in the doorway. She knew her time on Palladin's mountain was over.

"I need a word with you, my man," Kaliq started.

"Later." Palladin's grim face said it all. He wasn't going to change his mind.

The agent nodded to Jesslyn and walked to the car. Kaliq and Trisha moved away to give the couple time to say good-bye. But Kaliq wanted to say something, and

Trisha pushed a protesting Kaliq away, insisting he give her a tour of Palladin's house.

Her bags were in the car. There was nothing left to do but say farewell and leave. Agent Buckley discreetly waited in the car and Jesslyn was glad that no one else was around when she had to say good-bye to Palladin.

"I don't know how to thank you for saving my life," Jesslyn began.

"You've thanked me several times," he reminded her. He glanced at the new bandage covering her right hand. "You returned the favor, remember?"

"Yes, I did . . ." She knew the FBI agent was waiting to take her to the helipad but she didn't want to go.

Palladin grimaced. "I hate good-byes."

She nodded. "So do I."

He leaned down and dropped a light, brief kiss on her lips. "Take care of yourself. Corporate headhunters are probably leaving messages on your phone, as we speak."

She managed a smile in return. "I don't think I want the corporate life any more. I'm happy with what I have."

He nodded his head in agreement, with a slight deepening of the corners of his mouth. "You seem to bounce back from trouble a little stronger."

She looked at him steadily. "Yes. I seem to win all my battles eventually. Well, most of them, anyway."

He kissed her again, longer and harder this time, as if he needed the memory. She allowed it because she knew that she did. Then he released her and stepped back. "Good-bye, Jesslyn."

Fighting tears, she said, "Good-bye, Palladin."

She didn't cry much when Egyptian Enchantment had destroyed her career. She didn't cry when Mac threatened her life. She knew she would spend nights crying over Palladin Rush—but not in front of him.

The FBI man was waiting to take her to the heliport and the short trip back to New York. She'd spoken with Lena the night before and couldn't hide the despondent tone as she gave her the arrival time.

Lena couldn't hold back her excitement. "Girl, everyone's been here. News people, TV people. Even a couple of guys from that tabloid TV thing."

"Don't go making promises about me giving interviews."

Her sister was on a roll and couldn't be stopped. "You better get in on this and collect some bucks. Maybe you can be the consultant on one of those made for TV movies and we can fly to Hollywood. Maybe Jeff would come along?"

She was sure he would. Since she'd been sequested at Palladin's, she realized she missed her sister's dating review.

"There isn't a Jeff anymore. This one is named Stephen," Lena said. "He owns that record store in the mall. He's bought a couple of gift baskets for his employees and stuff."

"Sounds like you got a new attitude along with a new man, big sister?"

"Well, I uh, don't know. But he's really nice." Then she changed the subject. "You know they arrested Frank?"

"I heard. All the time, he was the one who kept in touch with me, and I thought he was a friend. Now I know it was just to set me up. I hope he rots in prison."

Cold chills had swept over Jesslyn when Palladin had told her that Frank was the one driving the Jeep. He'd learned the skill while he lived abroad and never used it until he and Mac became desperate.

"My Jeep never left my property, but with a phony plate, they thought Carolann would tie me to it. She fooled them, though. She never believed that I would harm anyone by running them down."

Jesslyn was surprised when Skip made a halting invitation for Palladin and Jesslyn to come to his house for dinner. Perhaps it could work, if they didn't come over the same night. She wouldn't want him to risk this newly found respect he and Palladin had by trying to help them patch things up.

The sisters chatted a few minutes more and then just before they said good-bye, Lena asked, "Did it work out with Palladin?"

"No." A simple answer to a complex situation.

"Come on home. We'll talk."

Of course, that meant that Lena would talk and expect Jesslyn to listen and obey. All Palladin had to do was ask her to stay. Nothing dramatic. She wasn't asking him to marry her or anything that he didn't want.

As she slipped the receiver back into place, she turned to find Palladin standing there.

"Everything all right? Lena didn't ruin your business, did she?"

She didn't think he worried about her business when he forced Lena to take the helm, yet here he was, wanting Jesslyn out of his life, and it was suddenly a concern.

"Almost everything?"

"What's wrong?"

"Us."

"Don't."

"If you asked . . ." She leaned forward and put her hand on his arm.

He cut her off. "I can't."

He stepped away from her touch, as if he'd been burned. "It's better this way."

They both recognized his statement for the prevarication that it was, and yet he didn't move—not even a twitch of recognition. "You fought too hard to get back your career and I couldn't ask you to give it up."

"It's not the most important thing in my life now."

"You could run your business from here. But you're a big city lady. You like the things New York offers, and one day, you'd resent having to ask or tell me every time you wanted to go to the opera, see a movie, whatever."

"That's such a lie. You were *used* by your best friend and your wife. You can't get over that you weren't smart enough to catch on."

He didn't answer. And she could not win by staying. She could only hope to win by letting go and letting him heal alone. Their lifestyles had nothing to do with it. The *machismo* of the American male had everything to do with it.

She watched him for a sign, but he was distant—as if he'd pulled the door to his emotions closed and was letting his head make all the decisions. His heart had given up. But what bothered her the most was that he hadn't believed a word she'd said. Angrily, she struck back.

"You'd rather sit on this mountain and think about how everyone betrayed you, rather than make it the past," Jesslyn told him. "I thought you were stronger, smarter, more willing to share happiness and pain, but I was wrong. There is a big difference between solitude and loneliness. So don't try to fool yourself that you want solitude. You want to be some kind of misguided guardian angel, but you're just a coward. And I won't beg for crumbs from your table."

When he didn't respond, she turned and walked away. She didn't look back. He would get over it and put it in the past where it belonged, or he would allow it to eat away at him until he became a bitter man, all alone. Her heart ached for what might have been but she refused to plead any more. Nothing could be said for his choice. She walked to the car and climbed in beside the FBI man who had questioned her earlier.

Jesslyn wasn't sure if it was her imagination, but as she watched in the car's side view mirror, Palladin looked as if the shadows surrounded him. At the bottom of the hill, she asked the agent to stop the car. She got out and took one last look. The cold, March sun was shining off the snow. She remembered the first time she'd stood here and looked at the house. It seemed so different now.

Rick Buckley got out and came over to stand beside her. "Ms. Owens. I don't want to get out of line, but guys at the agency still talk about Mr. Rush."

"I'm sure he was a great agent." From the time he and Palladin shook hands, Jesslyn could tell the young agent was in awe of him. There was something about walking to your own drummer that appealed to everyone. But Agent Buckley, like Jesslyn, knew that everyone couldn't do it. Someone had to follow the rules.

"Yeah. But what they talk about the most is that he never leaves anything unfinished."

"You mean that fight we were having when you got here?"

"I mean whatever caused that fight."

She bit down on her lower lip and demanded her eyes not release any more tears.

"We'll see, Agent Buckley."

The cold, March sun bounced off the pure white snow-covered mountains and what had been a haven was now just a beautiful piece of architecture. She pulled her coat around her, got back in the car and was grateful that the agent said nothing as tears cascaded down her face. How had he chosen that hollow world over one with her?

Twenty-seven

Jesslyn didn't enjoy finding herself a minor celebrity when she returned to her business. Of course, by causing the downfall of a man determined to be president at any cost, meant spending much of her time avoiding the paparazzi. From all reports, the Senator meekly let them arrest him, and so far, had refused to offer any explanation. His family was in seclusion after making a vow to stand by him to the end. Jesslyn suspected that they would try to make it look as if Mac was the real culprit. It would be only fitting, since that was what he and Carolann had wanted to do to her.

Requests from talk shows that she didn't even watch poured in. Commercial offers came right behind them. She hated it. These were the same people who went into attack mode when Egyptian Enchantment fired her. Now they wanted to do theme shows around her. "Women who fought back from disaster." The offers were lucrative, but Jesslyn knew that it would also mean talking about her time with Palladin. And that time was too special. When she thought she was his ex-wife, he was protective but held her at bay. When she remembered everything, he was a warm, tender lover. When it was all over, he chose not to let her share his pain. Her only hope was that when he recovered, she'd still feel that they could be together. Jesslyn knew she would always love him but she never believed that being apart made you a stronger couple. She'd rather be alone than with someone who didn't love or trust her enough to tell her about his bad times as well as his good.

Jesslyn was almost grateful that a rock star and his wife had a knock down, drag out fight in one of the city's most elegant restaurants. It pulled the attention away from her, and by the time that died down, they were onto another scandal. She was still concerned, though, that there would be another frenzied attack once the trial began.

"Will you see him there?" Lena had asked.

"I don't know. He's confused for probably the first time in his life."

"Since you understand what's wrong, why don't you fix it."

"Because I'd end up always being the one to 'fix' things. I'd become his crutch."

Lena had forgiven Palladin for his harsh treatment of her and felt that if she could do it Jesslyn could but she left her sister alone—at least every now and then. When she saw a chance to compare Palladin favorably to anyone but the man in *her* life, she took it.

Other than a visit to her parents, Jesslyn jumped right back into running the business. She'd read once that exhaustion was a way of dealing with emotional pain. She'd be so tired when she got home that it was all she could do to shower and decide on what to wear the next day before climbing into bed and sleep dreamlessly until the alarm went off.

Palladin had taken over in his usual manner. He'd made a decision about both their lives and never consulted her. Letting disillusion from a failed affair short-circuit her career, however, would be disastrous. If she couldn't have him, she'd have success. And she'd find someone to escort her to all the things she liked. The ballet, the opera. Everything. She hoped it would make the papers. Then she'd send clippings to Palladin. She'd show him.

Blasting her tape deck with motivational tapes didn't keep her from thinking about what might have been. How was she going to get on with her life if she couldn't get him out of her mind? At times she could see his face when Mac told him about the abortion. All this time he'd blamed himself for the loss of a child, only to learn that Carolann's need to be the center of attention was responsible. Jesslyn hoped in the week after Mac's arrest that Palladin would feel that she was too important to lose. Instead, he insisted she get on with her life, acting more like a protector than a lover.

Two weeks after leaving Palladin's mountain, Jesslyn and Lena had flown out to see her parents in California before they sailed for Hawaii.

Her father was quite succinct about the failed relationship. "If a man throws away a chance to be my son-in-law, then he isn't worth your time. Find someone who is."

Although she tried to hide her pain, her mother picked up on it and Jesslyn gave an abbreviated version of her life in Pennsylvania.

"Sometimes, it's up to the woman to override decisions a man makes."

"Not this man, mama."

"Any man, honey. It's just knowing how."

They were overjoyed that Lena was settling down.

Both parents attributed the gray in their hair from worrying about the next scheme their oldest child would fall into.

When Jesslyn returned to New York a week later, she found herself leaving the answering machine on all day and curling up with a stack of paperbacks she'd been promising she was going to read and a few videotapes of movies she missed while working so hard with Gift-Baskets, Inc. for the past couple of years.

Everything came together after Mac's arrest. His link to Carolann brought a reinvestigation of the troubles Egyptian Enchantment Cosmetics had encountered while she worked for them. Although no proof rose to the surface, the general consensus was that Carolann had stolen the ad campaign, not Jesslyn. It was what Palladin had said: "They always place the blame on the dead."

Surprisingly, she'd had a couple of offers to come back to the corporate world. The headhunters were hungry to place her in prestigious positions with Fortune 500 companies.

And Jesslyn realized that getting back on top in the corporate world was not the most important thing for her. She still loved what she was doing. Being happy with your work was greater than a huge salary and perks. Besides, the financial plan that Palladin put together for her was working just fine.

Lucky I don't drink or use chocolate to stifle pain, Jesslyn said to herself. I'd be an alcoholic or weigh two hundred pounds, she mused. She called Ms. Cooperton to get her a cab. A stop at the store and a walk through the mall would be distracting enough.

* * *

"Hey, sis! What are you doing here?" Lena shrieked as she spotted Jesslyn in the doorway. "Checking up on me? The staff is taking care of everything."

Jesslyn laughed and strolled over to the little booth where Lena and Jeff were sitting. The "staff" consisting of two college students, Karen and Randy. Karen stayed in the shop doing administrative work while Randy made the deliveries. She'd hired them because they were bright and made no pretense that the fact Jesslyn had been involved in the biggest news story of their young lives had prompted them to apply for a job with her.

She'd come to hate lies. Since leaving a disheartened Palladin trying to deal with all the lies Mac and Carolann had perpetrated on him, she knew how devastating they could be. Yet if they hadn't lied, she never would have met him.

"Don't yell at me. I just felt like getting out and wound up here. Why shouldn't I watch my career-driven sister at work?" she inquired dryly as she slid into a chair across the table from them. On the side of the table was a decanter with the aroma of freshly-made coffee and another decanter with hot water, along with Styrofoam cups. In the middle of the table sat a large bowl that held a potpourri of herb tea, regular tea, single coffee packets both regular and decaffeinated.

"Glad you're here," Jeff said. "I've been trying to drag her away for lunch and she keeps saying no."

Jesslyn clutched her throat and stared at her sister. "Turning down a free meal? Do you have a fever?"

"Don't get cute," Lena responded. "I just don't feel like anything right now. And I still want to know why you're here."

"Where should I be?"

"How about on a mountain in Pennsylvania?"

"I haven't been invited." Jesslyn hoped the answer had enough bite to make her sister leave her alone. She got out of the apartment so she could find something else to think about. She should have known better.

"Sometimes you just have to push a little bit."

"And sometimes, you have to stop beating your head against a brick wall."

Out of the corner of her eye, Jesslyn could see Jeff growing increasingly nervous about the exchange. She dug through the bowl until she found cranberry-apple herb tea and began making herself a cup.

She took a sip and let it play across her tongue while trying to relax. This was not turning out like she planned. She wanted her sister to commiserate with her, not challenge her. Even though she knew Lena wanted her to be happy, she needed affection, not prodding. "I've been planning on a little trip," Jesslyn said. When Lena's eyebrow arched she shot her down. "No! I've been thinking more in the line of a seven day cruise to Bermuda."

"Why?"

"I need to get away and rethink some things."

"You need to straighten out that other little matter before you go traipsing off to foreign soil."

"You need to get off the soap box. I'm not going to call him."

Lena threw up her hands. "These are the Nineties. A woman can ask for what she wants, just like a man."

"Really?" Jesslyn said sweetly.

"Absolutely!"

"Good. This is what I'm asking, *leave me alone, about Palladin Rush."*

For a moment, her sister was taken aback. She'd always said what she wanted and Jesslyn had listened. She may not have used the suggestion but at least she'd listen. Now she'd become as stubborn about this as she was about getting back on her career horse after falling off a second time. She fell silent.

Jeff cleared his throat, obviously embarrassed at the sisters' exchange. Jesslyn knew her sister's diatribe halted only because they were in the office. But she was glad Jeff offered to call a restaurant and have them put together a lunch order and asked Lena to go with him. He could have had it delivered, but Jesslyn and Lena knew he was trying to separate them for a little while. Jeff could still be obnoxious at times, but he seemed more thoughtful these days.

They stepped out of the office, and Jeff made the same offer to Karen, who had been working so steadily all morning that she had to look at her watch to see that it was lunchtime before telling him her preference.

As she and Jeff walked away, Lena couldn't resist a parting shot. "I don't think you know your own power where Palladin's concerned."

Jesslyn, pleased with the effect, sat back and sipped her tea. Yet deep inside she knew her sister was right. Running away to Bermuda wasn't the answer. Deciding if she wanted to make the first move claimed priority.

After they left, Jesslyn found some orders that needed her approval. Her head was bent over the counter while she concentrated. Karen's trembling voice penetrated her brain and she looked up. Hoping, then sighing.

"Ms. . . . Ms. . . . Owens. I think you have a visitor?"

It was Kaliq. Even from a wheelchair, he was intimidating. On his usually bald head a navy beret rested in a slanted dip to the side revealing the large gold earring.

Jesslyn stepped from behind the counter and caught his hand.

"I thought you were in the air by now."

"Decided to make a stopover and see how you're doing."

Jesslyn signaled Karen to take over. The young girl rose from her desk and walked behind the counter where Jesslyn had been standing.

"Buzz me if you need help," she said to the girl and turned to Kaliq. "Come in the back and have a cup of tea."

They went into Jesslyn's office and she sat on the sofa and prepared tea for them. "Do you want anything to eat?"

"No. Got to watch my figure," Kaliq told her.

Her voice trembled, but she had to ask. "Have you spoken to Palladin recently?"

"Matter of fact. This morning."

"How's he doing?"

"He hasn't called you?" Kaliq's expression left no doubt that he was surprised at that.

Jesslyn shook her head. "I guess I'll see him at Mac's trial."

"Don't bet on it."

"Why not?" Her voice edged with fear.

"I think Mac's making a deal. He won't get out of serving some time, but a lesser sentence might be traded off for some other information."

"I see." Jesslyn busied herself with the tea again. She'd been hoping if he didn't call soon, the trial would bring them together. If he called her, it would mean he was ready to move on to a new life. If there was a trial and she could look into his eyes, she'd know if it could work or she should walk away completely.

"And how is the stunning Ms. Terrance?"

"She's chosen to stay in Pennsylvania."

"Too bad. Like someone else we know."

"Ah, but I'm going down to see her and give her another chance."

"Of course, you expect me to do the same?"

Kaliq leaned over and touched her hand. "The man had reasons to build walls. He thought it was to keep people around him safe. But he knows that it didn't work."

"I know you mean well," Jesslyn said. "But I can't create a life and leave a place just in case he decides that he wants me."

"Don't give up on him, Jess. Someday, he'll get over what happened."

Jesslyn stood behind Kaliq's chair and put her arms around his neck. "Like that line from a country song, 'Sometimes someday never comes.' But I'll give him, umm, six months."

"What a woman! I'll keep in touch."

The next day was Sunday and the shop was closed, so Jesslyn and Lena decided to have lunch at 44's.

"Now that I'm working in the shop more," Lena said. "Why don't you think about restructuring your workload?"

Jesslyn wanted to tell her that she'd already planned to do that when Palladin practically pushed her out of his doorway. Instead, she smiled and said, "Aren't you getting a little ambitious lately?"

"Guess so." She giggled. "Did you see the look on Dad's face when I told him I was staying in New York."

Jesslyn teased her sister. "Our parents are retired people. You can't give them shocks like that in this stage of their lives."

The buzzer from Ms. Cooperton meant their cab was waiting and they grabbed their coats and talked of business-related matters during the elevator ride.

When they reached the lobby, Lena asked. "When are you going to see him?"

Jesslyn knew exactly who her sister meant. She didn't pretend otherwise. "He's got too many problems right now. I don't think it's a good idea."

"Chicken."

"Why should I be the one to make the first move?"

"You love him."

"What makes you say that?" Jesslyn said. She knew that since she hadn't denied it, her sister would claim it as the truth.

Lena waited until the cab was on the way to the restaurant before she continued. "Sometimes men don't know what they want until they see it."

"If we're going to talk about Palladin Rush, you can tell the cab driver to pull over and you can have lunch alone."

Lena held up both hands in surrender. "The fact that you're pretty testy lately says I'm right *but* I won't push."

Of course, that declaration only lasted until they were seated in the restaurant and browsing over the menus.

"You said he was worth fighting for, so why are you sitting around here?"

"He doesn't want me. Are you satisfied?"

"I don't believe that. What did Kaliq want?"

"The same thing you do—me to call Palladin."

"And you're not going to listen to either of us?"

"No," Jesslyn lied. She was listening. She wished someone would push him to call her. Maybe Kaliq would talk to him before he left for Wyoming. Jesslyn found herself fighting to control her temper. She was so angry with Palladin for not believing in what they had. She was angry at her sister and Kaliq, who wouldn't leave it alone. But most of all she was angry at herself for not shoving her own pride aside and making the first move. If he said yes out of pity instead of love, she'd know. And she wouldn't be able to handle it. Of course, she wanted success, but not enough to pay for it with heartache. She wanted love, but not enough to become a pitiful beggar.

When she and Lena attended the first Breakfast Club meeting after returning from visiting their parents, Jesslyn had been the center of attention, for the first few minutes, anyway. Then, the women got started on creating business plans and it was back to old times—women helping women succeed.

Now they sat in 44's where Jesslyn and Carolann had lunched at the beginning of the great tumult in both their lives.

"Why don't you just call and say hello?" Lena suggested.

"I couldn't."

"Tell me the truth, did you two have a fight before you left? I thought he was crazy about you."

"It's like any crisis. You need each other to pull through it, and after it's over, you walk away." She tried to justify Palladin's decision more for herself than Lena.

"Doesn't cut it with me . . ."

"I don't want to discuss it."

That was the complete truth. She didn't want to discuss

it because she was afraid she would start crying or call him and curse him out. Neither was a terrific choice.

She relaxed when Lena began studying the menu.

Her sister didn't get it. Jesslyn couldn't beg Palladin to let her stay. If the man wasn't willing to try, she couldn't force her way into his life. After all, Jesslyn had helped him solve a case by showing him that his wife was a liar and a tramp and his best friend betrayed him. If that was what he saw when he looked at her, then they had no future.

Twenty-eight

Three weeks later, Palladin sat in his favorite chair and watched the sunrise. Once, this had been all he wanted. All he needed was to enjoy the changing of the seasons from this little area of his house. This had been his sanctuary, his mountain. But loneliness had replaced solitude. At every turn, he felt Jesslyn's presence.

The times he didn't think about her were in some ways worse. He thought about Carolann—and Mac. They knew him well enough to play on his guilt The fact that he held obligation, duty, above everything else. The one chink in his armor could only have been exploited by the people he trusted.

Jesslyn could have done the same thing. He'd lied to her, seduced her and then forced her to leave. But she didn't use coercion to hold him. The woman hit him with the truth. He felt used and he didn't want to talk with her about it. He couldn't share that with her. He'd rather be alone than be vulnerable.

She'd cast a spell on him the last time they were together. Making love in the guest room. He thought it was safe, that if they shared his bed he'd have memories to keep him from sleeping. Jesslyn knew what she was doing. She bewitched his days, until every time he turned he'd look at the guest room door and wish that she was still there. But if she had been there, she wouldn't have been in the guest room. His nights were as bewitched as his days. He'd lie in his bed and think about the one on the other side of the house and again wish she was there.

Sometimes he couldn't sleep because he missed the loving so much.

He'd spent more time cursing himself for being a fool to let her go. Acting as if New York was another country instead of two hours away. Hell! Some people commuted more than that every day.

It wasn't only that he missed her. He needed her. He was afraid he'd lost the one person who made him feel complete, the one person who took him on faith and never let go. He was the one who had chickened out. He was the one who was afraid to find a way for them to compromise on their lifestyles. And he wasn't waiting until the trial to see her. Mac's lawyers succeeded in getting a postponement, so there was no telling when the trial would begin. But could he convince her that he was free of the ghosts? Would she forgive him for turning away? There was only one piece of the puzzle he'd never told anyone. But he'd tell her and then they'd see if they could make it work.

For three weeks, Jesslyn had thrown herself into Gift-Baskets, Inc. Although she didn't want to think about Palladin, certain reminders crept into her daily activities. She drank café latte in the morning. She jogged. Even her sister couldn't believe that. She'd begun to believe that she'd been asking for too much. She should have just accepted his decision and gotten on with her life.

The telephone rang and Jesslyn picked it up and

looked at the number on her caller ID. Local. Not Pennsylvania. She cursed herself for hoping.

"GiftBaskets, Inc.," she said cheerfully.

It was a customer. She wrote up the order. As she looked at the pad, no excitement bubbled up when she noticed it was the thirty-fourth order of the day. Once, it had been an important goal for her.

The beginning lunchtime strollers announced it was a little after twelve. Lena had gone off to share a pizza with Jeff. He hadn't changed, but Jesslyn had learned one thing with Palladin. You can't force love out of a relationship anymore than you can force it in. If Lena was happy, that was what really mattered.

"I'd like to send a basket to someone," a voice said.

"Kaliq! I thought you were on a plane by now."

"Had to make a stop down here before heading for the airport." He wore a thick jacket and lightweight slacks. Jesslyn remembered he'd told her that while he had no sensation in his legs, the rest of him was just fine.

He maneuvered his wheelchair so that he was in the little alcove near the basket displays. Then turned to her. "What do you recommend for a man in love?"

She came from behind the counter and pulled up a chair next to him. "Depends. If it's for you, I'm sure I can whip up something special and sexy. If it's for a large size mountain owner, how does arsenic and dead roses sound?"

"Umm. The lady has a mean streak."

"Sometimes."

"I've got a plane to catch, so I don't have time to be nice about this. You two love each other. Don't let the past wash away your future."

"I tried . . ."

"Not hard enough. He suggested you leave and you took him up on it. You got close, something no woman has ever done before—not even Carolann. He wanted her. He went after her. But it was infatuation. Not love. Call him. Talk to him. Don't let him walk all over you. Stand your ground this time."

"We weren't on my ground. We were on his, *but* I'll think about calling him."

"And stop going after his soul." He crooked his little finger and she bent over as he whispered what she should go after. "I think you've already got it. But go for it, anyway."

"And are you taking the same advice with Trisha?"

"Well, she has a standing invitation to come see me, and that's up to the lady."

"Think she'll take it?"

Kaliq grinned. "She said to expect her in about a month. It'll take that long for her to put some things in order."

"Congratulations."

"I'll tell you something." he said. "When Palladin saw those pictures and realized you were in danger, he fell apart."

"Come on . . . No way."

"Trembling. He broke out in a cold sweat. Said he'd tear Mac's heart out if he hurt you."

"Really?"

"No. Actually, he said he'd tear off another part of his anatomy, but I can't repeat that to a lady."

They both laughed. Then he said, "Gotta go."

Jesslyn stood up and kissed the top of his head. "Take care of yourself and that pet falcon."

He handed her a card with his name and address. "Keep in touch."

"I will."

He wheeled away and left Jesslyn to think about what he said.

When she closed the shop she was thankful the feeding frenzy had died down and she no longer had reporters camped out in the mall.

As she reached her apartment house someone called to her.

"Jesslyn," said Eva Rothstein. "Hunter wants to show you his project."

Beaming, little Hunter held up a plastic bag containing water and several goldfish. "If I take care of them, I can have guppies next time."

"I'm sure you'll do a good job," Jesslyn told Hunter and then in a conspiratorial whisper, "Congratulations, Eva, you talked him out of the boa."

A glint of red caught her eye, and she turned to see a familiar Jeep parked across the street from her apartment. The special plate attached was only partially visible but enough so she knew that it said "Hellraiser."

Palladin stepped from the Jeep and started toward her. She knew that she could meet him half-way, but she'd made all the adjustments in this relationship she was going to. It was his turn. She stood quietly and watched him take long, sure strides toward her.

He walked over and stood in front of her. "For a moment, down there I thought you weren't going to wait."

"I thought about it for about thirty seconds."

"Are we going to have this conversation in the street?"

"I guess not."

He followed her into the building, nodding politely at the concierge. They were silent all the way.

Jesslyn unlocked the door, tossed her keys in the basket on the table and turned to Palladin. He noticed she was back to her old look with a white blouse that must have had twenty buttons up the front and a long gray skirt.

"If you've come to apologize . . ."

"I haven't."

Her eyes widened and her guard went up. "Then what are you doing here?"

"I came to beg for forgiveness."

Jesslyn's defense mechanisms dissipated. "I'm not sure I can handle a man on his knees . . ."

"I didn't say anything about getting down on my knees," he started.

She laughed. He was contrite, but not broken. Jesslyn didn't take her eyes off him as he closed the door and leaned against it. He took off his gloves, stuffed them into his coat pocket and hung the heavy black wool jacket in the hall closet.

She pointed to the living room, "Wait there, I'll make some coffee or something. I . . . I think I still have some of those international flavors you like."

"It should go with this."

She took the brightly wrapped package with its neon pink ribbon tentatively and unwrapped it slowly. Then giggled as she peeled back the box cover and revealed a large portion of a Mississippi Mudpie. The dessert she had rhapsodized over on their first date.

He stepped in front of her and dipped his head low and kissed her briefly but soundly. Then lifted his eyes to hers. "I had to taste you to make sure I wasn't dreaming." He kissed her again. "I got tired of being king of the mountain." He kissed her again, this time possessively, as he cupped her face in his hands. Then he ambled into the living room and sat on the love seat to wait.

Palladin stood up and took the tray when she finally joined him. He put it on the coffee table. Nothing was said for a few minutes as Palladin savored the deep mocha coffee while Jesslyn sipped peppermint tea. She opted for sitting on the sofa, keeping the coffee table between them.

He set his empty cup down and made no motion for a refill. Jesslyn set her unfinished drink next to his. It was time to make the dive or cancel the event—make the commitment or walk away.

"I owe you an explanation," he began. "I didn't shut you out because I didn't love you. I was just so hurt . . ."

"Because she told you she had a miscarriage and it was really an abortion."

"No. Because it wasn't the first time. It was the second."

Jesslyn gasped. How could anyone do that even once and she'd done it twice.

"I told you that right after we met she went to Hollywood and I went into the Service. Then we met again and got married. Quickly."

She nodded understandingly. "Because she was pregnant."

"Right. She was afraid of taking pills . . . She ran at the first sign of trouble . . ." His voice trailed off as he struggled to share the pain he was feeling. "A month later, she had what I thought was a miscarriage, but no one knew about that, not even Mac. When Kaliq was captured, she was pregnant again. She asked me not to go. I told her I had to. Then she told me I'd be sorry if I left her alone."

"You thought it was because she lost the baby."

"I thought that's why she wanted a divorce, and I've been trying to make it up to her since then."

He leaned back and looked closely at Jesslyn, "This won't be an easy relationship for us. I still like living on my mountain . . ." he warned as he reached across the coffee table and took her hand. "But I've got some plans to turn it into the corporate retreat it was supposed to be. You still love the big city. I'm willing to become part of the computer world and get a fax machine, satellite dish and anything else that makes you feel less isolated." He released her hand.

"Move to New York?"

"Why not? I can spend the weekend coaching my team, and we can use the cabin as a getaway place."

She was shocked into silence. She'd convinced Palladin to come off his mountain, at least some of the time.

They laughed but knew more had to be settled. Neither of them was starry-eyed about being lovers. This time they'd both wanted all the cards on the table. Face up. It would be the most honest alliance of their lives.

"I hear they're thinking of a commuter train between Pennsylvania and New York. The tri-state area is about to become a quad-state area. I'm not worried about my career."

He leaned forward. "What are you worried about?"

"The ghosts."

Palladin looked away for a few seconds but he never released her hand. "I can't explain what happened to me when Mac . . . said he'd had an affair with Carolann . . ."

"But I understood the betrayal. I told you that I'd give you time to sort things out, and you treated me as if I didn't have a brain. You always refuse any kind of help and I'm not sure we can pick up where we left off."

"I don't want to pick up what we left off. I want us to start over." He reached out and flinched when she backed away. "We can't forget what happened. I wanted the truth and I got it."

"But not the truth you wanted."

"No. But it was the truth I needed. *Now* I can walk away from the past."

"How can we start over when every time you look at me you'll remember that I cost you a friend and mentor."

"I'll also remember you were the one who risked everything. If you hadn't convinced me to keep it between the two of us, I would have told Mac."

"I know. I didn't want to be the one to destroy your friendship, but I remembered the car Carolann got out of that day, the car almost hit me."

"I thought it was Skip."

"I know."

"You were right about me being a coward. I had made such a mess that I was afraid of trying again. And I know that Mac would have killed both of us to keep his record clean."

"You want us to try to create a normal relationship."

"I don't believe in 'relationships'. I want you to marry me."

Jesslyn ran the gamut of complete joy about his proposal to abject fear that it might not work. "Darling, I . . ." She caught a twinkle in his eye and stopped talking.

He smiled. "Why do you always call me 'darling' when you're dragging your heels about something we both want."

"Wanting and having don't always work," she said and laughed. Maybe they should keep it as an affair.

"Ah, sweetheart, it's the times they work that count. The others are just lessons in life."

"Why do you always call me 'sweetheart' when you're trying to talk me into something I might not like."

"Because you're faster than I am in coming up with the worse case scenario." He brought her left hand to his lips and kissed her fingertips. "Before I make a complete fool of myself," he said. "I need to know where I stand. Did I make a trip for nothing?"

Jesslyn took a deep breath. "Why did you make the trip? Why didn't you just call?"

"Because if the answer's yes, I made the trip for nothing. I blew it. I'm going to go to a hotel room and get very drunk, sleep it off and go back to my mountain tomorrow."

"And . . . if the answer's no, you didn't make the trip for nothing?"

"I'm going to spend from now to daylight proving how much I love you."

"Then I guess we're in for a long night."

"It's all or nothing this time. We make a clean break or we get married."

"Okay. We . . . get married. Lena likes playing business owner and I think we should take her up on it until she changes her mind."

"And how do you feel about not running the whole thing by yourself?"

"Kaliq dropped by yesterday and I told him it was over. That I was tired of fighting for your soul."

"You don't have to fight for it any more. You own it."

She found herself staring down at black leather jogging shoes instead of boots.

"Do you remember how hard it is to get boots and jeans off?" he asked.

She felt a warm tingle cover her face and knew she was blushing. Laughter danced in his eyes.

"What did Kaliq say about my soul?"

"He said I was after the wrong part of you."

A slow grin spread across Palladin's face and Jesslyn grabbed a pillow from the chair and hit him. "Wipe that smirk off your face. He said to go after your *heart.* And I was planning a little trip to a certain mountain."

"I thought I was so resourceful. I liked the name *Glacier.* It made me feel invincible. But from the moment we met, you've chipped away at the ice wall and you've won.

"If we're going to be together, I need a couple of answers." He paused and she knew this was really hard for him. "When I married Carolann, I thought we wanted the same thing. That we'd settle down and have the 2.5 children like other people. She never told me that she didn't want children."

"You're asking if I want children?"

"I'm saying tell me now if you don't."

"And?"

"I'll accept whatever you want. But be honest."

Jesslyn got up and walked around before she sat down and faced him again. Her stoic face revealed nothing. "What did the lobby look like? Do you think I'd have bought this place if I didn't love children?"

He remembered their first date. The discussion in the elevator. And also Jesslyn knew the kids by name, grade and hobby.

"But what about Carolann and Mac? They'll always be in the back of your mind."

"Carolann and Mac are lies from my past. You are the truth of my present and future. And I love you."

Jesslyn released a breath she didn't know she had been holding. "About my career . . ."

Palladin held up his hand. "I'm the one who's mobile. You make the schedule that's best for you."

"But that's just it. I don't have to come to the shop every day. I like having a part-time career. Lena likes having a part-time career. We've already found our answers."

"Now if you can just as easily come up with an immediate solution to what I see as a *big* problem."

Fear flashed through her. "What?"

"What are we going to do about that blouse?"

He stood up and pulled her around the table and into his arms. She knew what he meant, in fact, the boutique owner warned her when she made the purchase that it could be one big regret no matter how beautiful the construction. Tiny mother-of-pearl buttons, hidden beneath lace. Lots of tiny buttons that were going to be a big problem now.

"Why did you pick today to wear this thing." That wasn't a question and she knew it.

"Well, obviously, I wasn't expecting company. But I'm sure we can figure something out."

"I'm sure we can."

He slipped his hand in hers and led her to the bedroom. Their children were going to be a little strange growing up in a log cabin and a neighborhood that housed one of the most elite prep schools in New York. They would have a stay-at-home father and a mother who made baskets for a living.

Palladin stretched out on the sleigh bed and Jesslyn marveled for a brief moment how comfortable his massive frame looked amid her frilly bed covers. His well-worn, straight leg jeans. Most men his size would seem ridiculous, but not this man.

Palladin sat up and pulled her down beside him and began unbuttoning her blouse. She'd loved the eighteen buttons down the front of it when she first purchased the suit. In fact, she'd loved them until this very moment. She just wanted him to rip them off instead of taking his time. She tried to unbutton the section at her waist but he tugged her hands away and gently placed them at her sides. The unspoken rule—don't help.

"This will teach you to wear this kind of Victorian version of the iron maiden," he said as he slowly released the next button and kissed each section he bared. "You're going to have to wait a long time for the kind of pleasure you know I can give you."

She sighed. At this rate they'd be here all night. Jesslyn unhooked her skirt and wriggled out of it. But he wouldn't allow her any other moves. Slowly he dragged his tongue across the top of her breasts, down to the still covered nipples which became hardened buds. He unsnapped the bra and repeated the motion on her bare skin. Sparks of pleasure shot up her spine. She wanted more. She wanted it now.

Deep, dark eyes staring into dark brown ones. He kissed her again, cherishing the feeling of being exactly where he wanted to be, doing exactly what he wanted to do. No way was she going to be the one punished by waiting until he worked his way down the blouse. Jesslyn shifted so her back was against the headboard.

"Remember when I got my memory back?"

"Uh huh," he murmured without really listening to her. "You tried to run and we ended up wrestling in the snow."

"I was chilled to the bone and you put me in the hot tub."

"And you made me that hot toddy . . ."

His breathing speeded up as his mind replayed that night of passion. "Uh huh," came his strained reply.

"And then you got into the tub with me."

No reply. She giggled softly as she fed him the same pictures that jumbled through her mind. She got the results she wanted. The glacier melted completely as she heard him utter a heated whisper, "I owe you a blouse." The next sound she heard were the buttons being torn from their moorings as the fire of his desire flamed.

And Jesslyn knew she'd won a battle with the demons that had separated them, a war with the problems of the past, the heart of the man she loved and the lesson that love's truth won over the sweetest lie.

Epilogue

"This is ridiculous," Palladin said. "Why don't you just eat a few crackers and let me drive."

"No. This is better for me."

"You're going to have a baby any minute, and you're driving yourself to the hospital."

He couldn't believe it had been eighteen months since they'd met. He was so sure she'd go stir crazy on his mountain and he wouldn't like the fast pace of New York. The wedding had taken place a month after he'd asked her to marry him. Neither wanted a lavish spectacle and being connected to the fall of a major presidential candidate had more negatives than positives.

Jesslyn had been shocked when he told her he was planning to revive the old plans for the log home. That it would become a conference center and lodge. He'd already started on getting the architects to build a couple of smaller cabins on the property.

"By the time our baby celebrates his first birthday the lodge with be in full service."

"His? How about *her* first birthday?"

"This one's a boy. Next time, we'll have a girl."

Jesslyn had sliced out a large portion of her life and had given it to him. She'd shocked him by coming to every practice for his little hockey team, even though he'd lost the first bet and the team didn't make the playoffs the next year. The month they'd spent in New York had proven that they could exist in each other's world. Once she thought that nothing could get him off that mountain, but she'd been mistaken. Love could do anything.

But he'd shocked her when he purchased a larger apartment in the same building—one with four bedrooms. She'd changed him from a loner to a man who wanted a family and other people around him. Still, he felt she made the greater change. Having a part-time career instead of taking the many offers that poured in. She told him she had the best of both worlds, but he knew that he was the one who'd been that blessed.

They'd settled into a comfortable pattern of dividing their time between two places. When they were ready to bring a child into their lives, they planned to spend the last stages in New York. Jesslyn, however, went into labor early and they were on their way to the same hospital Jesslyn had been taken to the night of the accident which seemed like years ago. None of his coaxing could make her change her mind about driving to the hospital, so he reluctantly played passenger. Luckily, he'd phoned Kaliq and Trisha and they were also on their way to meet them.

For a woman having her first child, she was amazingly serene. Palladin, on the other hand, waffled between being too nervous to sit still to staring out of the window as he prayed out loud that they would make it.

"What do you want, a boy or a girl?"

"I don't care."

"You like to coach, so a little boy would be nice."

"Great."

"What about names? We've been tossing around so many. Since you don't want him to be a junior, think fast."

"I have a whole bunch that I like."

"I plan to make this trip a few more times. Let's use them all. What do you want, a hockey team or a baseball team?"

He leaned over and kissed her cheek. She burst into laughter as he whispered, "Let's practice for a football team and settle for tennis doubles."

About The Author

Viveca Carlysle was born Marsha-Anne Tanksley in Detroit, Michigan. She grew up in New York City. Her love for reading is a gift from her mother, who started reading to her from the day they came home from the hospital. She is Vice-President of Romance Writers of America's NYC chapter. She belongs to Women Writers of Color. Currently she is a customer service supervisor with New York City Transit.